Christma

By

Melissa Klein, Rachel W. Jones, Linda Joyce, and Leah Noel Sims

Christmas in Jubilee

Contact Information: 4writersenterprises@gmail.com

Cover Art by EJR Digital Art
Edited by Stephanie L. Riva, CFA, Riva Reading℠

Published by:
Four Writers Enterprises, LLC
P.O. Box 190
Lebanon, GA 30146

Publishing History
ISBN: 978-1-7328559-1-5

Dedication

This book is dedicated to The Marine Toys for Tots Program.

The basic mission of The Marine Toys for Tots Program is to collect new unwrapped toys and distribute those toys to less fortunate children at Christmas.

https://www.toysfortots.org

Welcome to Jubilee, Georgia—where life is a celebration!

Jubilee is tucked away on Fancy Bluff Creek in coastal southern Georgia. The town's history reaches back to the days of English colonization by James Edward Oglethorpe, and of course, the town is also steeped in pirate history. Not far away, is Blackbeard's Island.

This small town is a place of hearty handshakes, welcoming smiles, and family ties. Folks have bonds centuries old…including some family feuds, too.

Here, the days flow with the rise and fall of the tides. Just as estuaries teem with life, life teems in Jubilee. With a constant calendar of festivals, holidays, and town-wide events, things are never dull.

Looking for the perfect escape where sweet tea is the beverage of choice, where sunsets are lavender, magenta, and gold? And if you're looking for love, friendship, and family recipes—Jubilee is the perfect place for you.

To find this southern town, pack your passport of imagination. Grab a map. Look for the southern branch of the creek flowing near Brunswick, Georgia. Follow the waterway west of I-95 to the big bend, and then dock your boat in Stiltsboro—the historic downtown area where the buildings sit on stilts and a wooden boardwalk connects shops, galleries, and restaurants.

Come on over to Jubilee! We're waiting to welcome you.

Table of Contents

Welcome to Jubilee—where life is a celebration!

The Best First Christmas

By Melissa Klein

Acknowledgments

I wish to acknowledge the help and support I receive from my family. You make every day worth celebrating.

The Best First Christmas

Chapter One

On the first Sunday in December, Reverend Angela Noel Duncan stood before the congregation of Jubilee Community Church, her black pumps covering places worn bare of varnish by her father's wingtips. "Please rise and sing "What a Friend We Have in Jesus," hymn number 328."

People hesitated. Gazes darted. Brows furrowed. But when the pianist played the introduction, the congregation joined in. Barely. Despite the church's name, and the theme of the song, the group sang with all the enthusiasm of the foghorn down by LaRoche's Point.

Angie had tried to hold the music program together after Reese McClellan's sudden departure. Unfortunately, she hadn't been the only one disillusioned by her ex-fiancé's deceptive ways. One-by-one, she lost the sopranos, the altos, the fifty-year-old organist, until she'd had to declare the Senior Choir on hiatus. Now it all fell to her: sermons, hymn choice, cleaning, lawn care.

From the back of the sanctuary, a male voice carried her way. As unfamiliar as it was pleasing, the baritone resonated at the spot beneath the gold cross her mother gave her as a confirmation present two decades ago. Angie glanced up from her hymnal, focusing on the newcomer who beautifully stumbled over the words of the time-honored hymn.

Beside the man stood a boy of about six years. Hair slicked back, eyes wide, mouth closed. The perfect addition to her favorite part of the church service.

Who was this father-and-son combo, and what brought them to her small church when they had so many houses of worship to choose from as they travelled down Church Street?

Following the weakest "amen" known to Christendom, Angie snagged the cloth-covered prop she'd stowed inside the pulpit and kicked off her shoes. "If the girls and boys will join me down front, we'll have our children's sermon." She lowered to the steps, tucking her robe around her ankles—a lesson hard-learned when a little boy peeked underneath her skirt a few months back.

Ellery and Mallory Jamison crawled past Mrs. Marshall and into the aisle, lifting a bit of heaviness Angie carried in her heart. "How does mom like her new job?" she whispered, giving Ellery a hug and adjusting one of the red bows that swung on the end of Mallory's braids. Angie's wasn't the only life upended by recent scandal. By necessity, their mother, Melanie Jamison, had returned to work.

After her husband ran off with Angie's fiancé.

"It's good." Ellery shrugged. "She brings home leftover muffins and cookies at the end of the day."

"Sounds yummy." Angie scanned the pews for stragglers. One of the many May kids was returning from the bathroom, and the youngest Bartell needed a few more words of warning from his mother. When the last of her usual audience settled in, Angie looked down the aisle. She smiled at the visitor's little boy.

He leaned into his father's arm.

I guess that's a no.

Angie turned to her group of a dozen or so of Jubilee, Georgia's most precious citizens. The reason she still left her bed when she most wanted to hide beneath the covers. "How many of you have ever gone a long time without food?"

One of the older boys' hands shot up. "Mama sent me to bed without dessert once. Longest night of my life."

The congregation tittered.

"I'm going to tell you about a time when a whole bunch of people had been listening to Jesus talk. They sat and listened for three whole days."

"Sounds like one of your father's sermons."

Angie's attention snapped to the Amen Corner. Jim Bledsoe—businessman, head deacon, jerk.

She cleared her throat. "In all that time, none of them had had anything to eat or drink."

"Didn't they die?" a little girl asked.

"No, but they sure were hungry, and Jesus asked his helpers if they had any food to give the people. But they did not."

"Why couldn't they order pizza?"

The little Bartell boy was always good for a couple of laughs, and while she waited for her audience to settle, she checked in with the visitors. The boy peeked over the armrest, watching as one might observe tropical fish in an aquarium.

"They were too far away from any town. Jesus asked his helpers to go to the people and collect any food that they might have. As it so happens, there was one boy whose mother had packed him a lunch of five loaves and two small fish. He gave away that food even though he didn't have to."

Angie pulled Melanie's masterpiece from beneath the cloth to "oohs and ahhs" from the adults. The culinary genius and The Bread Box's newest baker had created the requisite loaves and fish in an intricately woven basket—all from bread.

"Why did he do that, Pastor Angie? That's not enough to do anybody any good."

The Bartell kid eyed the bread. "You wouldn't catch me giving up my lunch."

Resting the basket in her lap, Angie cupped her hands close together. "Jesus took what little the boy had to offer." She spread her arms wide. "And turned it into something huge. There was enough food for everyone. There were even leftovers."

It killed Angie to destroy all Melanie's hard work, but therein also lay a lesson. She parceled out bites to each child, saving the cutest fish for the boy who was now leaning halfway into the aisle.

She caught each child's gaze, letting hers linger on the round, gray eyes of her farthest listener. "The reason I'm telling you this story is because I want you to remember little people can help do big jobs."

"Like unload the dishwasher?" Ellery asked.

"Absolutely." She winked. "Now it's time for me to talk to the big people."

While the little ones dispersed, Angie returned to the pulpit. She glanced at her notes. "We will continue our study of the Gospel of Matthew." Then faced her congregation. Her gaze locked with the newcomer's. Blond hair, gray eyes, nose as straight as a ship's mast.

A member of the Brown clan.

"Ho-ly Moses."

Jim Bledsoe jerked to attention.

Served him right for dozing during church, but hardly an appropriate outburst from a minister. And completely out of Biblical context. She coughed to cover her faux pas then took a moment to compose herself with a sip of water.

The first Sunday in Advent wasn't the only item of note on the calendar. Today had to be the first in the history of Jubilee a member of its most notorious family had crossed a church's threshold.

The walls hadn't fallen in.

The roof hadn't collapsed.

The stained glass hadn't shattered.

So why were her hands shaking and her knees quivering and her cross doing a tap dance against her breast?

Angie took another sip of water. "In this chapter, we find Jesus and his disciples..." She continued for several minutes, delving into the sermon matching the one she gave the children. Five verses and multiple points in her outline later, movement at the back of the room caught her attention.

The two visitors, members of the law-skirting, work-shirking Browns, were returning from what she hoped was only a trip to the restroom. She eyed the overflowing offering plates at the foot of the pulpit.

Guilt pierced her chest. The man had done nothing more than attend a worship service, and she'd judged him based solely on his family's reputation. Determined to make amends, she cut her sermon short, deleted the third verse of the final hymn, and gave the benediction from the church doors.

Mr. Brown and son would not leave without a

heartfelt welcome from her.

Unfortunately, Deacon Bledsoe got to her first. His bushy eyebrows narrowed. "Pastor Duncan, have you lost your calendar?"

She'd hoped—somehow, someway, by some miracle—she'd be allowed to skip the trappings and trimmings of Christmas. Ecclesiastical order dictated she heed the edicts of the church leaders. However, having grown up watching the machinations of this deacon, a spark of rebellion took hold. "I have several. An app on my phone, one on my desk, and the one you sent as a gift from your funeral home, so you'll have to be more specific."

The nostrils at the end of his beak flared. "The one that would clue you into the fact the season of Advent is upon us."

A pitchfork-toting devil perched on her shoulder and whispered arguments against following tradition. Theological, financial, and especially personal. All well-constructed and legitimate reasons for ignoring all things red and green, Bethlehem and baby, merry and bright.

A cancelled Christmas Eve wedding and missionary parents who would celebrate the holiday from South America had robbed Angie of the desire to celebrate the season.

She focused her hurt and pain, giving rein to her emotions. "I'll have you know, Mr. Bledsoe—" A tug on her robe cut off her words as clearly as the Lord had shut the mouths of Daniel's lions. She lowered her gaze to her pigtailed parishioner, the one in a white-crinoline dress. "What is it, sweetheart?" Now that she'd regained her good sense, Angie needed a moment to collect herself. "Did you have a question about the sermon?"

"No, ma'am. I want to put in a song request for next week."

Angie cupped the girl's cheek. "Anything, precious."

"I want us to sing, "Away in a Manger." It's my favorite."

Where the deacon's admonitions couldn't cut through Angie's pain, the girl's simple request could. Tears pricked the backs of her eyes. All the congregation wanted from her was five Christmas-themed sermons, a score of holiday hymns, and the same decorations they'd seen for the last decade. Surely, she could manage that much? It wasn't like they were asking her to live, breathe, and eat the season.

Deacon Bledsoe cleared his throat. "What's it to be, Pastor Duncan?"

Angie smiled at her audience, saving a genuine one for the little girl. "I'll have you know, I've planned a very special Advent sermon for next week, and I'll make certain your hymn request is first."

"Very good." He shook her hand, then stepped through the doorway to the vestibule. Just as Angie was beginning to think she could move on to less difficult topics with less difficult people, he turned to look over his shoulder. "My expectation is that next week's service will put the entire congregation in the holiday spirit."

Last year, she'd oozed holiday spirit from the day after Thanksgiving all the way through Epiphany. With a heart full of hope, messages of joy had flowed effortlessly. She'd also been happily engaged, and her parents had been able to come home for a visit. Now, producing the same would require carols playing nonstop, hours of prayer and meditation, and perhaps even a small miracle.

Chapter Two

Justin Brown stood with his nephew, Nick, in the corner of the sanctuary closest to the altar. Not because he wanted to admire the stained glass behind the pulpit. Not because he wanted the opportunity to play the beautiful baby grand. Not because he wanted to avoid speaking to anyone. So, not a problem there. He and Nick might as well have been invisible, which was the best he could hope for when any of his clan ventured into polite, law-abiding society.

Justin waited, wanting a word with the preacher. Who, by the way, was much prettier than a woman of the cloth ought to be. Finally, after he'd studied a depiction of the Nativity long enough to have it memorized, the crowd thinned. He tapped Nick on the shoulder. "You ready to go?"

"I guess." The six-year-old had silently taken in the church's wooden pews, chandeliers, and brassware with the same curiosity Justin had his first time inside a university lecture hall. A mixture of awe, fear, and hunger. He still seemed reluctant to leave.

"You behaved really well in church." He tousled the boy's blond hair. "I know it can be hard to sit still that long."

"It wasn't too bad. I liked watching the lady preacher. She's pretty."

"I'm glad you liked watching her, but I hope you were listening, too." With any luck she'd soon deliver a sermon about cleanliness being next to Godliness. Convincing the boy he needed a bath every night was getting old.

"I got some of it." His large gray eyes gazed up at Justin. "Most of the time I was thinking about my Christmas list."

His heart ached for his nephew. "Getting the gist is good enough for a first time. You'll do better as you get older."

Nick's mouth formed an O. "You mean we gotta do this again?"

"Every week."

The boy looked as though Justin had told him there was no Santa Claus. Except in Nick's case, the Jolly Man had never paid him a visit. No tree. No lights. No presents. And the concept of donkeys, wise men, and baby Jesus was as foreign as regular meals, bedtime stories, and kisses goodnight.

"Don't look so down. It's a good way to meet some nice kids." He nudged the boy forward. "Come on. Let's say hello to the preacher."

Beyond beginning a churchgoing routine for Nick and himself, Justin wanted specific help with providing his nephew the best first Christmas ever. He hadn't much experience to draw on. After all, the Browns weren't exactly family-holiday-celebrating people.

When it came their turn, he stuck out his hand. "Reverend Duncan, I'm Justin Brown and this is my nephew Nick."

He waited for her reaction.

Throughout the world, his last name was nearly as common as fleas on a dog and held no more significance than any other of English extraction. Not so in Jubilee. Brown equaled sloth, crime, and poverty as far back as the founding of the town.

She took the hand he offered, capturing it with both of hers. "Please, call me Pastor Angie. Reverend Duncan is my father. Welcome to Jubilee Community Church, Justin. I'm glad you and Nick joined us this morning."

From anyone else, he would have considered that statement at best a platitude, but more likely a bold-faced lie. Her wide smile made him believe she meant it. An anomaly he wanted to get used to.

"Thank you. My nephew and I plan to attend regularly." He'd been the first in his family to cross Fancy Bluff Creek. The body of water did more than divide Glynn County. It partitioned the wild from the civilized, the deceitful from the honest, and the lawbreakers from the law-abiders.

She bent down to speak to Nick. "That's great." She

pulled a napkin from the pocket of her robe and handed it to him. "I saved you one of the fish from the children's sermon. I hope you'll feel like sitting with me next time."

When Justin had contrived the church-going plan, it involved the help of a wiser, older gentleman. However, he was determined to raise Nick right. That involved getting help. Pleading if he had to. "I'm hoping you can help me with a particular situation." He nodded over Nick's head.

"Of course. I'd be happy to."

"It's rather involved and complicated. Could we meet somewhere?" Should he suggest her study or a public place? Either way could be problematic.

"Sounds urgent. Do we need to speak now?"

Justin couldn't recall the last time someone had been so quick to offer help. Usually, he figured things out on his own or paid for services he couldn't do himself. "Tomorrow will be fine."

"I'm free any time before noon tomorrow."

He settled on a public space, figuring it would put her most at ease. "How about The Bread Box?"

Pastor Angie's generous lips spread into the loveliest smile he'd ever seen. "That's my second favorite place in the world. What time works for you?"

Justin congratulated himself for making the correct suggestion. "After I get Nick on the bus, I have a gap until nine o'clock when I teach my freshman geography class.

Does seven thirty work?"

"I'm an early bird, so that's perfect."

He couldn't believe his luck. Breakfast with the pretty preacher. "It's a date." No, it wasn't a date. A woman like her would never be interested in a man with his background, despite how he conducted his life now. "I mean, I'll see you then."

Chapter Three

Angie returned to the parsonage following the service. In the galley kitchen her mother had painted a cheery yellow, she ate her go-to lunch of tomato soup and a grilled cheese sandwich. Taking after her father, Angie possessed more skill behind the pulpit than she did in front of the stove. She wasn't much of a decorator either. The two-bedroom cottage's furniture and décor dated back to her pre-teen years.

After washing up, she lay on the sofa for a quick nap before heading out to visit her shut-in parishioners. Unfortunately, the morning's conversations kept her mind whirling when she should have been observing the day of rest.

How in the world was she going to will forth the spirit of Advent?

Baby steps.

After her meeting with Justin Brown tomorrow, she'd decorate the sanctuary. Tackling a season-appropriate sermon would have to wait until later in the week.

Angie closed her eyes, only to have Justin's appear in her mind. So pensive and pleading. How could she help him? What she knew about kids wouldn't fill a communion cup. "Rest. You've got six visits this afternoon." She flipped on the TV, hoping the DIY show would help turn her mind off. No such luck. The small house being renovated made her wonder where Justin and Nick lived and how he came to have the boy in his care.

The thoughts churned as though on a hamster wheel and continued until Monday morning. Angie arrived at The Bread Box well before their agreed upon time, driven by the desire for one of Melanie's cranberry muffins, a cup of strong coffee, and relief from her curiosity.

Images of Justin's handsome face had inhabited her dreams. Dreams where he requested everything from teaching his nephew to ride a bike to taking Nick as her own. After that dream, she'd woken with a startle and hadn't been able to go back to sleep. As much as she liked her youngest parishioners, she wasn't sure being a mom was in her future. Especially since she'd sworn off men thanks to Reese's transgressions.

Coffee and muffin in hand, she settled in a booth in the farthest corner. Protecting Justin's privacy would be a challenge in the popular morning spot. Which begged the question… Had he wanted to avoid meeting her alone in her office? A considerate, but unnecessary gesture coming from a member of the Brown clan. Not that she was familiar with the folks who inhabited the marshlands and backwoods of Jubilee.

As the child of a minister, she'd been held to a higher standard than other teens, by her parents and the congregation. Her extracurricular activities during high school had been strictly limited to debate team and chorus. She'd certainly never had the occasion to join the more daring teens in town who crossed the creek to the Blackbeard's Hideaway, the honky-tonk run by Clevis Brown. In fact, Justin and Nick were the first members of the notorious family she'd spoken to since she'd been paired with Lucy Brown in freshman biology.

The bakery door opened. Justin entered, longish hair wet and slicked back, biceps and pecs giving his navy golf shirt a workout, thighs melted and poured into a pair of ironed khakis.

"Speak of the handsome devil," she muttered under her breath. No man had a right to look that good this early in the morning. Her pulse kicked up a notch. For a self-preserving split-second, she considered hiding beneath the table. She'd fallen for good looks and charm before, and had the shame, broken heart, and useless wedding dress to show for it.

He'd asked *Pastor* Angie for breakfast, not woman-Angie, so she straightened her clerical-collared shirt and waved to him.

Justin returned the gesture. Once he had his order, he headed over. "Morning, Pastor Angie." He slid in across from her. "Sorry if I kept you waiting. Nick couldn't find his homework."

She sipped her coffee, buying another moment to

settle her nerves. "I've just been here a couple of minutes."

"Good to hear." He bit into his bear claw and washed it down with coffee. "By nature, I'm a night owl, but I've had to adapt since taking the coaching position."

"You also mentioned teaching geography."

"Football coaching positions can be hard to come by, so I double majored in physical education and history at the University of Georgia."

That certainly didn't pair with her former lab partner. "Wow! I was there for my undergraduate degree. Two majors—that's quite a feat."

Justin wiped his fingers on a napkin, then wrapped them around the mug before him on the table. "Surprised anyone from my family made it out of high school, much less college?" His words were as cool as an autumn breeze, his countenance cold as winter.

"I apologize." Regret heated her cheeks. "That's not what I meant."

Justin's expression softened. "That's okay. For the most part, you'd be correct in your assumptions. However, I'm what you might call the black sheep of my family. The only one not to go into one of our many *enterprises*."

"Good for you." With her parents as positive role models, walking the straight and narrow hadn't been so much a conscious decision as a natural act. To make those choices against the flow must have taken extraordinary will. "I can only imagine how difficult it is to make that change."

"I'm an outsider no matter where I go. I don't fit in with my family, and most folks in town don't trust me any farther than they can throw me."

"Yet you came back. Why?"

"For Nick."

Her heart softened like butter left on the counter.

"My sister, Lucy, got into some trouble, and the courts took her boy away. I wasn't going to let my nephew become part of the foster care system, so I moved back and began the process of getting custody. He's been with me since August."

She couldn't have created a better example of self-sacrifice. "I don't know what to say."

He leaned forward. "Say you'll help me."

"Of course. Name it."

"I want you to help me teach Nick about Christmas."

She blinked. "Excuse me?" Had she heard right?

"The boy doesn't have a clue about the holiday. Religious or secular." He pointed at his chest. "I don't either for that matter."

"Nothing?" How could someone not know about Christmas? "No Santa, no reindeer, no Charlie Brown's Christmas tree?"

His brows lowered. "Charlie Brown? Wasn't he a cartoon?"

"Man, you are lost." And he'd come to the person

with the least holiday spirit in all of Jubilee. Even if she'd managed to get the sanctuary decorations down from the attic and peruse last year's Advent sermons, she still identified more with the green Grinch than Tiny Tim. It wasn't for a lack of wanting. She mourned for her loss of joy, of the hope that had once been so effortless. Tears threatened.

Justin didn't need a toy-buying tutorial, he needed a full-blown holiday master's class. Except, Reese McClellan had taken all her spirit with him when he'd left town.

"I can put you in contact with Mrs. Wallis." Her voice cracked. "She's the best cookie baker in town, knits stockings for all the children in the congregation, and keeps a tree up all year long."

"That's very kind of you, Pastor Angie. However, I was hoping to do more than make up for all the Christmases he's missed. To learn more than holiday traditions. The boy needs something…deeper, more meaningful. That's why I came to your church. Why I want you to help."

Her stomach roiled at the thoughts. Of telling him of Christ's birth. Of showing the pleasure of giving to others. Of sharing sentimental treasures. All the things she'd done with her parents. All the things she'd hoped to do with Reese and their future children. "I'm sorry. I can't. I just can't do it. There's simply no way I can manage."

Shock registered on Justin's face. Then disappointment. "I see." He rose. "I'm sorry to have taken up your time." He left the bakery on a pair of long-legged strides.

Angie buried her face in her hands. "You only thought eating that half-gallon of peppermint ice cream was rock bottom." An image of Justin struggling to instill values in his nephew had her throat tightening. "This is a new low for you."

Justin had been rejected by the very person who ought to welcome him. Her father never let a personal struggle get in the way of caring for his flock. And neither would she. Angie bolted from the booth and raced out the door.

Justin was just shutting the door to his truck when she caught up to him. "I'll do it."

He lowered the window. "What's that?"

Goodness, gracious, and glory! This was going to be like spinning straw into gold.

"Give me your address. I'll begin with the Christmas story from the Bible."

Justin's grin almost made it worth the uphill slog she was about to face. Almost. Her lesson would require she rip one of the bandages off her wounds, to delve into precious and painful memories as she shared the news of great joy. "Would Thursday evening work?"

"Perfectly. I'll see you at seven o'clock."

Angie returned inside the bakery. "Better get cracking on the wreaths and candles." Perhaps they'd act like an inoculation against the pain when she pulled out her family's decorations.

Melanie leaned across the counter. "What was that all about?"

Angie let out a breath. "Just following up with a potential new member." She trotted over to the booth where she and Justin had been sitting and grabbed her purse.

"Yeah. Right. What's next, my ex going to start paying child support?"

"I'm sorry for what you're going through." She reached across the counter to give Melanie a hug. Their two men had skipped town together, taking the church's savings and leaving broken hearts. "You will let me know if you need help with bills or the kids' Christmas presents."

"Don't mind me. I've just got a case of the grumps." Melanie brushed tears from her face. "Anyway, just watch yourself with those Brown folks. From what I hear computers, TVs, and cars aren't the only things they've been known to steal.

Chapter Four

After supper Thursday, Justin and Nick sat across from each other at the round white table, attending to homework. He made a point of them eating all their meals there as well. No screens either, a habit that had been harder for him to break than his nephew. "You done with your math homework?"

Justin stowed the geography quizzes he'd been grading in his backpack, then eyed the kitchen. Countertops were as clean as he could get the faded laminate. Wooden floor swept free of crumbs. Stainless appliances gleaming.

The first grader attacked his paper with the eraser. "Almost." He scribbled a number, then moved on to the next addition problem. "Two more rows to go."

"Take your time." Justin patted his nephew's shoulder. "It's accuracy, not speed, that counts here." The doorbell rang, sending him toward the door. "She's here. You can put that away for now."

"Why is the preacher lady coming again?"

The last thing Justin wanted was for Nick to think his lack of Christmas experiences was his fault or to cause the boy embarrassment. He endured enough of that at school.

"Pastor Angie is coming by to give us Advent

lessons.'

"More school? I thought you said I was smart."

"You are, but neither of us knows much about religious things." They didn't know much about normal family life either, but he was working on that. "She's going to teach us about baby Jesus and why we celebrate Christmas."

"Do you think she'll have a snack with her? That bread from the other day was good."

Justin couldn't contain a chuckle. One day, food might not be the boy's first priority. Today was not that day. "Let's open the door and find out."

He did and was caught off guard by the pastor's appearance. On the two previous meetings, she'd worn her dark hair in a twist at her nape. Tonight, the locks flowed below her shoulders in waves that accentuated her fair complexion and forest-green eyes.

"Hi." She cocked her head. "Did I get my days mixed up?"

"No, not at all. Please come in." He stepped back to give her space to enter. "Can I offer you some coffee?"

Pastor Angie shucked out of her pea coat to reveal a bright red sweater. "No, thank you. As much as I rely on it in the morning, it's a little too late for me to indulge now." She studied his small living room. "I think your home and the parsonage are built from the same plans. Only difference is yours could be in a magazine."

"It ought to. Ordered everything you see straight out of a catalog just as it was pictured." He pointed to the beige sofa in front of a large picture window. "Please, have a seat." Justin sat across from her in one of two recliners.

She held up an oversized bag. "I brought props. Is it okay if I set it out on the coffee table?"

In his usual, quiet, way, Nick had eased into the room. He took a step closer. "Is it more bread?"

Anxiety tightened Justin's middle. "I promise; the boy gets three squares a day."

She laughed. "I'm sure he does." Her gentle smile eased the sense of judgment he carried around with him. "Sorry, Nick, you can't eat what I brought, but you can keep it afterward."

When Pastor Angie pulled the first wooden piece from the bag, Justin's breath caught. She set the six-inch camel on the table and reached for another. "They're made of olive wood." One after another, she extracted beautifully carved animals, shepherds, wise men, and angels. "I saved my favorites for last." Mary and Joseph were adorned with a light coat of paint, and the baby Jesus had a gilded halo.

Nick, who'd stepped closer with each revelation, examined the pieces. "Cool. There's so many of them."

"I'm glad you like them." She brought out a large barn-like structure. "My parents brought them back for me from a trip to the Holy Land."

Justin stiffened in his seat. "We can't accept this." Wouldn't accept charity, even if it was one of the most beautiful works of art he'd ever seen. "It's too nice." His days of relying on the largess of others were over. "And expensive."

"It's also durable." She picked up one of the sheep, rubbing it between her thumb and forefinger. "I played with this when I was Nick's age, and I thought he'd enjoy it as well." She pointed to the boy, who'd arranged all the animals in one corner of the table and the humans in another. "I think I guessed correctly."

Justin drew in a breath. "I don't know…"

"It will benefit me as much as it does your nephew."

He failed to see how giving away a childhood treasure could be of help. He cut his gaze to Nick. Yeah, like prying those pieces from the six-year-old's hand would be possible. "It's a gift we graciously accept." He nudged Nick. "Don't we, buddy?"

Nick's eyes shone "Yes, ma'am. Thank you."

Pastor Angie slapped her thighs. "Now that's settled, on with the lesson. The story I'm going to tell you comes from the second chapter of the Gospel of Luke."

Justin had a general idea of the Christmas story. Family goes to Bethlehem. Baby is born in a barn. Angels sing. Wise men bring weird baby gifts. However, the way she told it—her inflections in speech, dramatic pauses, and her use of the Nativity set—made the story come to life.

"The shepherds returned, praising God for all that they had seen," she said.

"What happens to Mary and Joseph and Jesus after that?" Nick asked.

Her ready smile broadened. "That's for our next lesson."

"Cool." Nick jumped to his feet. "What will you bring me then?"

"Hold your horses, big man. You can't expect her to bring you a present every time you see her."

"Oh, okay." His chin dropped.

"How about we meet at my house next time?" She stood, taking her coat and purse. "An important part of celebrating Jesus' birth is giving and helping others." She leaned down to Nick. "And I could use some help with my cookie baking."

"Can we, Uncle Justin?" He danced from foot to foot.

"Sure thing, kiddo." This was exactly what he'd had in mind when he walked into church last week, and he couldn't imagine a more kind and enthusiastic teacher. Why had she been so reluctant to help? He narrowed his focus on the pastor, catching a falter in her smile. Instinct insisted it had something to do with her willingness to part with a childhood treasure.

"Does Saturday morning work with your schedule?" she asked pulling on her coat.

Her hair was caught beneath the collar, and he longed to ease it free. To see if it was as soft as it looked. Instead, he shoved his hands in his pockets. "It does."

Pastor Angie once more bent to Nick's level. "I have a riddle for you before I go. What job did the wise men have?"

He shrugged. "I don't know. Being rich?" The boy hadn't had much to find funny in his short six years, and he thought in concrete, practical terms.

"Nope. They were firemen."

Nick blinked. "I don't get it."

"Because they came from afar."

Angie laughed at her joke, and Justin would have joined her if it weren't for Nick's puzzled look. "I'll explain it to you later." He opened the door for her, wishing he could find a way to delay her leaving. "Thanks for the lesson and the Nativity. If I can pry the pieces out of Nick's hands, I'll set them up on the mantel."

"It was my great pleasure to share them with you. See you Saturday."

"Nick and I are looking forward to it." He nudged his nephew. "Aren't we, buddy?" For entirely different reasons, though.

"Will some of the cookies have frosting?"

A broad smile lit up her face. "Of course. What's the good of Christmas cookies without loads of frosting?"

Chapter Five

In her small kitchen, Angie stacked sugar and flour canisters and sticks of butter, along with a set of copper cookie cutters and tubes of icing. The lesson with Justin and Nick came mid-holiday baking marathon, and her kitchen table and counters were piled high with peanut butter fudge, peppermint bark, and her mother's signature shortbread cookies. Still left to tackle were the mini fruitcakes and butterscotch haystacks.

Having admitted defeat on her ignore-Christmas stance, she'd resumed her family's holiday tradition of giving baked goods as gifts. Too bad the outward act hadn't created inward change. Not even the scent of cinnamon and cloves stirred joy for the season.

What if Reese had taken that from her as well as the contents of the church's savings account?

From somewhere in the tower of brightly-colored tins her phone chimed with her mother's ring tone, and Angie scrambled to answer the rare call. "Hi, Mom." Emotions that had been simmering from the moment she first pulled out her mother's recipe book bubbled over. "How's it going?" she managed to choke out.

"Your father and I are well. Although some of the villagers have the flu."

Worry added to her loneliness. Her parents served in the northern Peruvian city of Piura, which had only a couple small hospitals. "I'm glad you two have managed to stay well. Please let me know if there's anything you need from home. I'll get it off to you."

"We have everything we need, sweetheart." Janie Duncan was the consummate minister's wife. Efficient, caring, and content with bare necessities. "Speaking of packages, I mailed your Christmas and birthday presents. They should arrive just in time."

"That's great." Not only would she spend Christ's birthday alone, but her own the following day as well.

"It's not much. Just some things I found in the market. I hope you like it."

"I'm sure I will."

"Your father wants to talk shop with you now, so I'll say goodbye. Love you, dear."

Tears tightened her throat. "You too, Mom." She drew in a deep breath and prayed for the strength to speak to her father without breaking down.

"Angela, how are things in Jubilee? Congregation still growing I hope." His sunny, upbeat voice hit her full force. Like being tackled by golden retriever.

However much she welcomed this unexpected call, she had to wonder about the reason behind it. Did one of her parents' friends report her lack of adherence to the church calendar? It wouldn't be the first time she'd been tattled on. Shortly after replacing her father, Angie had invited a musical group to play during a Sunday evening service. An older member of the congregation took exception to the bass guitarist's long beard, resulting in a call of concern from her father before Angie could get out of the church parking lot.

"The Mattsons have moved back from Savannah, and we had a new family visit this past week." She left out Justin and Nick's family name to avoid questions. "Also, you should know Miss Marlene Mae had an accident and is in the hospital."

"I'm sorry to hear. Chelsea has a lot on her shoulders. Keep an eye out for her as well as her mother."

"I have been, and I plan to check in again the first of the week."

"And Melanie Jamison and the children? How's she doing after…"

Her father had taken the scandal personally. He'd been the one to hire Reese as music director. "I asked if we could include the kids on the giving tree, but she said her parents were playing Santa this year."

"Sounds like you have everything well in hand. Efficient as ever. It's reassuring to know the church is thriving under your care."

"Thank you for your words of encouragement, Daddy." But more than anything, she longed for him to ask after *her* wellbeing. Was she thriving? Did the broken engagement weigh on her heart? Where she would spend Christmas Day? The thought probably never crossed his mind. The man chugged along Sunday after Sunday, year after year. Never showing signs of strain or a crisis in *his* faith.

"Angela, keep up the good work. Talk to you again soon." With that, he ended the call. Most likely rushing off to tend to some parishioner's physical or spiritual needs.

Her father's steadfastness acted as both a goal to attain and condemnation for her shortcomings. Heaviness weighed on her chest, making it difficult to breathe. "Am I even in the right profession?" What if she should have gone into accounting instead of following her father into the ministry?

Chapter Six

Justin and Nick walked the three blocks over from Oak Street to the parsonage. For the first time, the early December morning held enough chill to make sweatshirts a necessity. Unfortunately, they'd discovered too late Nick had outgrown the one he'd arrived with back in August.

Why hadn't he thought to look ahead at Nick's winter clothes?

A good inch of arm showed below the cuff and the waistband didn't meet the top of the jeans. After their cookie baking lesson with Pastor Angie, Justin would hightail it to Walmart for bigger clothes. Despite the wardrobe issues, at least he could see physical evidence he was doing an adequate job parenting his nephew. Another inch and a few more pounds, and Nick would be where he needed to be on the growth chart.

Arriving at Pastor Angie's front door, Justin looked his nephew over. He gave the boy's unruly cowlick a quick swipe. "Remember your manners, but don't forget to have fun."

Wide gray eyes looked up at him. "Yes, sir. Can I ring the doorbell now?"

"Have at it."

The pastor must have been standing close by because

Nick's finger had barely touched the button when she opened her door. "Welcome." She motioned them in. "The cold air feels good this morning, doesn't it?"

"It does."

Justin looked down to see Nick struggling to get the green sweatshirt over his head. "Here, let me help you with that." He gave the hem of the shirt a hard tug, nearly ripping the boy's ears off in the process. In the end, though, they managed to free Nick from the shirt.

After that, Justin had a moment to notice the home's interior. A small, rectangular living room lay just beyond the front door. Through a large opening was a dining room, with the kitchen beyond that. The two bedrooms and one bath had to be down the narrow hall. "You're right; our places are exactly the same."

Pastor Angie nodded. "This whole neighborhood was built post-World War II by the most unimaginative contractor on the planet. To my knowledge there are only three different floor plans." She leaned down to Nick. "You ready to bake cookies in my cookie-cutter house?"

He nodded. "Can I eat some too?"

"Of course. You'll be our taste tester."

Nick and Justin followed Pastor Angie into the dining room where the piles of plastic-wrapped treats covered the table. "It looks like some elves have already been hard at work."

"It's a tradition my mom and I have." She slipped an

apron with a picture of Mrs. Santa Claus on the front over her head. "Some will be presents for my friends, others I give to my elderly parishioners and those without families."

Nick's eyes widened. "You're giving this away?"

"Most of it. I'll save some for me to enjoy."

Her living room might have been devoid of Christmas decorations, but the dining room and kitchen looked like holiday central. Smelled like it, too. The warm scent of butter, chocolate, and peppermint hung in the air. "I agree with Nick. This is a lot of work. Wouldn't it just be easier to buy gifts?"

"It might be. However, baking brings me a lot of joy." She pulled a folding stepstool out of the crevice between the fridge and the wall, opened it in front of the sink, and motioned Nick to climb up.

While his nephew washed up, Justin studied Pastor Angie. He looked past the bright red sweater, jingle-bell earrings, and the wide smile that might crack any minute. "Are you sure about that? You don't look very joyful to me."

She froze midway through drying Nick's hands. "I'm still working on catching the holiday spirit. The past year has left me feeling a bit down." Yet, she kept her voice light and cheerful.

"That's odd, a preacher who doesn't want to celebrate Christmas?" Justin asked.

Nick stared up at her. "Are you like the Grinch?"

Pastor Angie tousled the boy's hair, freeing his cowlick from the confines of the hair gel Justin had used that morning. "Trying not to be."

"What happened?" More than simply a need for spiritual guidance drew him to her. This woman had a way about her that made him want to know more. Not just more. Maybe everything.

Tears pooled in her eyes.

"Shoot, sorry. That's none of my business. Forget I asked."

"You might as well hear it from me." She dabbed the corners of her eyes with her sleeve, then moved Nick and the stepstool over to a work area she'd already set up. "If you sit still long enough, somebody's sure to tell you their version of the biggest scandal to our church in two decades." She drew in a breath and let it out slowly. "I was supposed to get married Christmas Eve." She lowered her voice to avoid Nick hearing. "However, my fiancé ran off with another member of the congregation."

"That would knock anyone for a loop."

"To top it off, today should have been my bridal shower."

No wonder she'd been reluctant to help. "And here I am asking you to dive head first into Happy Holiday Land." Part of him wanted to scoop up his nephew and beat a hasty retreat, another wanted to take her in his arms.

He reined in both impulses. This whole scheme was for Nick's benefit.

"I really did enjoy meeting with you and Nick this week." A genuine smile lit up her face. "Sharing the Good News is the best part of the job." She opened a cookbook, then bent down to Nick's level. "Ready to get started?"

He nodded like a bobblehead doll. "Yes, ma'am."

"Good. Today you, Uncle Justin, and I are making sugar cookies. When we're done, if we don't eat too many, you should have enough give to your classmates."

In addition to reading the Christmas story from the Bible, Justin had also read Clement Moore's *'Twas The Night Before Christmas.* "Got to save a couple for Santa as well."

"Him, too." She handed Nick two sticks of butter and pointed to a large stand mixer. "Let's do this thing."

For the next hour, the pastor took Nick through the process of making dough, rolling it out, deciding which figures to use, and baking the shapes. She explained what she wanted him to do, then stepped back and let the boy try on his own.

Justin mostly observed, but he couldn't help commenting on her competency. "Do you know it took me two weeks to figure out how much Nick could do on his own? Those first few days, I did everything except chew his food for him."

Nick snickered. "Uncle Justin didn't even know I

could tie my own shoes."

"We've had a steep learning curve, haven't we, buddy?"

Pastor Angie smiled. "I admire you for stepping up when Nick needed you. Changing your whole life for the sake of someone who can't do a thing for you says a lot about your character."

A flash of heat ran through him. Plenty of ladies had complimented his singing, looks, and a few other talents…None had quite the effect as Pastor Angie's words of encouragement. "Thanks. Just doing my best." He toed the tile floor. Were his ears on fire?

"I'm just telling it like I see it." She looked around the kitchen and dining room. "And I see a whole lot of cookies."

"Nick, what do you tell Pastor Angie?"

He did more than use his words, the boy wrapped his too-thin arms around the lady. "This was the funnest thing ever."

She cleared her throat. "I had a good time too. Perhaps, if you and your uncle want to, you can go with me to the Senior Center to drop off some of my tins."

"Name the date and time," Justin said. He'd asked for these sessions to benefit Nick, but the boy wasn't the only one enjoying time spent with the lady minister.

Her phone rang before she could respond. "Excuse me just a moment. We'll make arrangements as soon as I see who this is."

Chapter Seven

Angie checked the screen and groaned internally. Her day had been going so wonderfully. "Good afternoon, Deacon Bledsoe. How are you doing on this fine day?"

"I'll get right to the point. Mrs. Palmer has fallen and broken her leg."

"Oh, no, that's horrible. When did this happen?"

"Earlier today. I was told she was trying to hang the star on the tree when the ladder collapsed. She's over at Jubilee General. They'll do surgery in the morning, and she'll be completely off her feet for the next eight weeks."

"There's still a little while before visiting hours are over." She did a mental inventory of her freezer. "Do you know if Don and the boys need a meal brought to them?" The church had a meal ministry, but they often included her in the rotation.

"I think they're fine for now. The biggest problem is she won't be able to manage the live Nativity on the twenty-second."

"That's a shame. She's been in charge since I was in the Cherub Choir. It just won't seem like Christmas without the pageant."

As long as there'd been a Jubilee Community Church, there'd been an outdoor production of the Nativity.

Families from all over the area made it part of their holiday traditions. Even people who'd moved away returned specifically to attend.

"That's why you need to assume responsibility for its direction."

"I couldn't. I can't. Isn't there someone else you can ask?" Her pulse raced, palms became moist, mouth tasted like she'd been sucking on cotton.

"Are you refusing?" His booming, deep voice rose in pitch and volume.

"No, Mr. Bledsoe." Refusal would result in more than a phone call from her father. But surely the man had to understand the limits of her abilities. "I'm admitting that I'm out of my depth. My theatrical experience is limited to a seventh-grade play."

"No time like the present to learn a new skill. Rehearsals have been underway since August, so I'm sure you can manage."

"If you say so. I'll collect the script and music from Mrs. Palmer tomorrow."

"Excellent. Good to hear. Perhaps you'll prove equal to your father after all."

"All I can do is give it my best."

"Speaking of efforts, I'm anticipating a stellar sermon in the morning."

Actually, he'd be hearing the one she delivered two years ago, but she wasn't about to tell him that. She'd decorated the church, inside and out, and had another creation from The Bread Box to share in her children's sermon. "I certainly hope you'll receive a blessing from it."

"We shall see," he said. "Goodbye."

A long sigh escaped her lungs. Why couldn't she get a pass this year? This really was more than she could manage.

"Problem?"

Justin's concerned expression reminded her she wasn't alone. It also made her feel as though he wouldn't judge if she wasn't Patty Perfect every minute of the day. "Only the kind that might result in me looking for a new job if things don't go well. I'm now in charge of our church's annual Christmas pageant. Other than participating as a child, I know nothing about the inner workings."

"Do you know how far along the former director was? Do the actors know their lines? I overheard you mention a choir. I assume there will be singing."

"Those are all perfectly logical questions, and I don't have the answer to a one of them."

"I don't have any acting experience, but I can read music, and I'm good at bossing people around. Consider Nick and me at your disposal."

"You'll help?"

"You've been helping me. Seems like turnabout is

fair play."

Angie leapt on her rescuer, throwing her arms around his neck and hugging him. "Praise the Lord. It looks like my December is finally turning a corner."

Chapter Eight

As promised, Justin and Nick returned to Jubilee Community Church following the Sunday morning service. Inside the small brick building, adults and kids milled about the vestibule and sanctuary waiting for practice to start. He'd timed their arrival as close to start time as possible to avoid the inevitable awkwardness. "Hang out here with me, buddy." He tugged the boy to his side. "Pastor Angie must be running late, but when she gets here she'll tell you where you need to go."

Nick nodded, more interested in the decorations filling the church than the chilly reception they were getting from church members. He pointed to the large tree in the corner, breaking free to study it closer. "Why does it have pink and blue paper angels on it? And there's writing on both sides."

"They're the names of boys and girls who need things, and the people here can pick one of them to buy for."

Nick planted his fists on his hips. "You told me Santa brought the presents."

Great. Now what?

Panic tightened his gut. He'd been hitting the Santa-sees-you-when-you're-sleeping line hard and heavy. Laid it on thick. They'd written a letter, bought a stocking, even figured out a plate and cup to put the cookies and milk on. "He will."

"Last year I got two sweatshirts and a pack of underwear from a lady at my old school."

Justin remembered all too well being called to the front office to receive his and Lucy's charity Christmas presents. A few small toys, but mostly socks and underwear. Once he even got a set of Spiderman sheets. Never the gaming system he dreamed of. Not that he'd resented the practical gifts. Without the community's largess, there would've been nothing.

Nick's little face scrunched up. "You told me only good kids got presents from Santa."

He patted the boy's head. "You've been excellent. At home and school. You've got nothing to worry about, buddy."

"I must have been really bad when I lived with Mama." His shoulders hunched, and he looked at the floor. "Because Santa never did come to see me."

Justin's stomach turned. Bile rose in his throat. "Oh, buddy, no. I'm sure you were as good as you knew how to be."

Pastor Angie joined their conversation, having entered the vestibule from a flight of stairs leading to a basement level. She bent to Nick's level. "I overheard what you and Uncle Justin were talking about, and you know what?"

Still not looking up, Nick shook his head.

"I bet Santa Claus is very upset he's missed you in the past. You not getting presents was a grown-up mistake that had nothing to do with you." She nodded in Justin's direction. "I feel certain your uncle has registered your name and address with the North Pole."

"Oh, definitely." Never in the history of parental drowning had anyone latched onto a lifeline the way he did. "Way back in August when I registered you for school." He hated lies, but better to cling to a fib than tell the boy his mother misspent every dime Justin ever gave her.

Nick's face lit up. "Plus, I put my address on the letter we wrote."

"Aren't you clever." Pastor Angie shot them both a smile, then pointed to a woman Justin recalled from a PTA meeting. "Miss Melanie will take you and the other kiddos downstairs to practice your songs for the Nativity play. Do you need me to go with you, or can you follow along with the others?"

"I can do it." Nick turned to Justin. "I know, listen, follow directions, and think before I do."

The mantra was finally sinking in. "Good job. Please wait with the lady until I come to get you."

With his nephew out of hearing, Justin let out a breath. "Thanks for bailing me out. I couldn't buy a parenting clue if someone gave me a thousand bucks."

"Not that I'm an expert, but from what I hear, most moms and dads are learning as they go as well."

"I'm glad to hear that. I keep wondering if the other parents got a manual that I missed out on."

Justin sensed the gazes of the adults and wondered why she was delaying the start of practice. Only to a point. He enjoyed her company. Needed her encouragement. Staring into those dark-green eyes of hers was no hardship either. "Maybe I shouldn't have started that whole Santa thing. I just wanted him to have the same experiences the other kids do."

"You would have been fine either way. He brought presents to all my cousins, but my parents chose not to include him in our celebrations. We all turned out fairly normal." She touched his arm. "You can't fix what happened to Nick in the past. You can only make things right now."

Electricity zinged from the point of contact. "Were you a cheerleader in high school?" Too late, Justin slapped his hand over his mouth. Nick wasn't the only one who needed to work on his impulsivity.

She laughed, not in judgment of his bonehead query. More a self-deprecating chuckle. "No, definitely wasn't part of that crowd, and definitely not a preacher's kid activity."

"You should have been." She was every bit as pretty

as the girls who'd stood on the sidelines while he played quarterback, and she had far more depth of character. "You're very good at encouraging others."

Her cheeks turned a lovely shade of pink, proving his point about her attractiveness. "Thank you for your kind words. They are very much appreciated. I could also use a bit of help."

"Sure. That's what I'm here to do. I can manage outdoor lighting, sound, in a pinch I can even do some kid wrangling."

"I just got word Mr. Young has dropped out, so we're a down a wise man." Her enticing smile could convince him to perform nearly any task. "The robes are comfortable and stylish."

"Are there any speaking lines?"

"Speaking…no."

He narrowed his gaze. "What aren't you telling me?"

"Deacon Bledsoe, Mr. Thompson, and Mr. Young were singing, "We Three Kings.""

He shrugged. "Easy enough. Back in college, I was in a band for a hot second."

"Were you perhaps the front man?"

"Let me guess, there's a solo involved."

She spread her thumb and forefinger about an inch apart. "Just a small one."

"Fine. I'll do it, but you have to do something for me as well."

Her gaze widened. "Short of committing a felony, I'm in."

Justine released the urge that had been beating at the door of his lips since she walked into the church. "Have dinner with me this Friday night, Pastor Angie."

She hesitated, making him wish, not for the first time that afternoon, he was better at thinking before he spoke.

Just as he was about to withdraw the invitation, she spoke. "I accept your invitation under one condition."

Of course, she wouldn't want to socialize in a town where everyone knew her. Or more important, knew his family. "We could drive up to Savannah if you like."

"That's not it. I want you to call me just plain Angie."

He could have led the Jubilee Jaguars to a playoff win and not been as pleased. The prettiest, kindest woman he'd ever met wanted to eat dinner with him, in public. "Okay, just plain Angie. Be prepared to be wined and dined at Jubilee's finest restaurant."

Chapter Nine

Angie swiped the savagely hot flatiron through a section of her wavy hair and hoped for a silky-smooth result. While she was making unrealistic wishes, she wanted the pterodactyls in her tummy to settle and her mind to stop playing date-disaster-what-if. She'd never been this nervous with Reese. Then again, he'd never looked at her with the same intensity Justin did.

Should have been a clue right there that everything wasn't on the up-and-up when it came to attraction.

So not a problem with Justin Brown. Decidedly un-pastoral thoughts had flickered through her mind on more than one occasion. "Being a minister doesn't make me numb," she told her half-made-up reflection. "I'm allowed an urge or two, I just can't act on them."

The melodic chime of her doorbell startled her out of the pep talk. Angie grabbed her phone from the bathroom counter and checked the time. "He's fifteen minutes early." She still needed to change into the plumb-colored dress she planned to wear. Opening the door, she expected to see tall, blond, and brooding. Instead, short, round, and USPS thrust two boxes toward her.

"Delivery for you, Pastor Duncan," her long-time mail carrier said. "Must be Christmas presents from your folks." He thumped the larger box. "This one here's all the way from Peru."

"Thank you." Melancholy surged, and for a split second, she feared she'd embarrass herself by bursting into tears. "I bet you're right. Mom said she'd mailed me a package."

Tommy Thompson waggled his bushy eyebrows. "You be sure to wait until Christmas morning to open them."

"I will. It'll give me something to look forward to."

Tommy's broad smile faltered. "I know you must miss your folks."

"I do." There were the tears, again. Good thing she hadn't put on mascara yet. "But I imagine I'll get a phone call from them sometime that morning."

The man turned to go. "You tell them, I said hello."

"Will do."

"You enjoy those presents."

"I—" She couldn't get the fib past her lips. The three of them had a present opening tradition that would prove impossible to continue alone. And a traditional Christmas morning breakfast. Followed by a volunteer-at-the-soup-kitchen tradition.

Traditions!

The tins on the table.

"Hold on just a second. I have something for you." After scurrying off, she handed over her small gift. "A token of my appreciation and well wishes to you and your family."

"Thank you kindly." His smile returned. "Missy and I will surely enjoy them."

After she'd closed the door, Angie checked the label on the larger of the two boxes and saw her mother's tidy handwriting. She broke open the tape and lifted the lid to find several small tissue paper-wrapped bundles. The red and green ones she placed on the mantel, setting the smallest one off to the side. "I'll open this one after church on Christmas Eve." The rest she'd save until after her from-scratch sweet rolls on Christmas Day. The one wrapped in purple paper she'd open on her birthday.

With that taken care of, she turned her attention to the smaller package. "Great Aunt Bess?" Why would her mother's maiden aunt be sending a present? The octogenarian had stopped sending birthday cards once Angie reached adulthood. She tore into the cardboard to find another box. Wrapped in silver paper. With white doves, hearts, and bells.

"Nooo."

Her engagement to Reese had been announced proudly in the local paper and through family channels. The breakup had been equally communicated. Or so she thought. Somehow Aunt Bess hadn't gotten the message. "Yuck. I'm going to have to explain the breakup all over again." She set the package on the coffee table and stood.

"But not today." She'd have to hurry now in order to be ready when Justin arrived. The doorbell rang just as she lifted the flatiron to her head. "Great." At least she'd had the good sense to change clothes.

This time when she opened her door, Justin stood on the other side. His smile morphed into confusion. "Did I get the time wrong?"

"No." She put her hand to the unfinished side of her hair. "I'm running late."

"That's okay. You look great the way you are," he said, although he'd clearly taken pains with his own grooming. He'd recently shaved; a smudge of shaving cream still clung to his jaw. His haircut looked no more than a day or two old, as well. The charcoal gray suit was a change from his usual khakis and golf shirt uniform, so was the red and green tie. "Our reservation at The Carriage House isn't until seven thirty. Take whatever time you need." When he took a seat on her sofa, his trouser legs rode up to reveal matching socks.

Maybe I should change into something more festive.

Between the sadness brought on by her parents' gifts and the wayward wedding present, the last thing Angie wanted to do was celebrate. In fact *bah-humbug* would leap from her lips if she wasn't careful.

She didn't want Justin to think she wasn't looking forward to their date, however. He and Nick were the bright star in her dark season. "I'm ordinarily a punctual person." She pointed to great-aunt Bess' gift. "But, I got sidetracked with that."

He regarded the package the same way one might a large spider, a wad of gum on the sidewalk, or some other object to be avoided. "Is that what I think it is?"

"Unfortunately." Not so many months ago, Angie would have relished opening the gift. Would have enjoyed adding it to her trousseau. Would have written the most sincere thank you note.

Woulda, Woulda, Woulda.

"What are you going to do with it?"

"Return it, of course. With the same sanitized explanation my mother gave the rest of our family."

Justin stood, taking both her hands in his. "Listen, I can tell this has knocked you for a loop. If you'd rather not go out, we can reschedule."

Her hands warmed in his grasp. Her heart, too, for that matter. She met his gaze, finding kindness and understanding in the stormy gray color. "Absolutely not. I'm not going to let a little thing like that throw me."

"We can stay in and order pizza if you'd rather not deal with people."

That suggestion had bad idea written all over it. As much as she found comfort in his empathetic character, and held strictly to her beliefs about intimacy, there was a limit to her self-control. "No, no, The Carriage House sounds like a great idea." She tugged her hands free, lest the attraction get the better of her. "Let me get my coat, and I'll be ready to go."

Chapter Ten

Seated across the table from Angie, Justin didn't know how he'd gotten so lucky. He also didn't know if he should mention she had on two different earrings and that she'd forgotten to put makeup on her left eye. Check that. Even he wasn't that dumb when it came to women. Besides, she didn't need mascara and eyeshadow to make herself attractive. He'd never met anyone with a bigger heart. A heart that was hurting, he learned tonight when he saw the would-be wedding present and the holiday gifts on the mantel.

She shifted the leaves of her salad around the plate without eating more than a bite or two. "What's Nick up to tonight?"

"He's visiting the Jamisons." He kept his voice as nonchalant as he could manage considering how frustrated he was over the situation that led up to Ms. Jamison's generous hospitality.

"I didn't know he and Ellery were buddies. Aren't there a few years' difference in their ages?"

"There are. Ellery is in fourth grade, but Nick and Mallory are in the same class. She's the one who invited him over."

"Oh, how sweet."

"They all are, actually. Very kind."

"Unlike some others?"

"You don't want to hear my issues. I'm sure you get tired of people unburdening themselves on you all the time."

"I don't mind at all. It's what friends are for. Besides, I've been pretty free with my woes."

"Silas Bartell, one of the boys in class, had a sleepover birthday party tonight, and he invited all the boys in the class."

"Except Nick."

"Right."

"It's the same stuff I dealt with as a kid. People make assumptions. I didn't know whether to cry or put my fist through a wall. My nephew's one of the best behaved kids in the class. Tries to be friends with everyone. But some folks won't give him a chance because of who his family is. Sometimes I just want to pack up the car and drive out of here."

Angie took his hand. "I am sorry. If it's any consolation, I know the family. They're not as nice as they'd like everyone to think they are."

"Nick has made some friends. When Mallory heard what happened, she asked to have Nick over."

"That's pretty astute for a six-year-old. I don't know many adults who are so empathetic."

"There're a couple others at school who are beginning

to warm up, and the staff at the high school are great. But that might have something to do with my winning season."

"What about the church?" She leaned in, her expression growing more serious. "How have the members of my flock been?"

"You can be proud of them for the most part. Mrs. Marshall had Nick and me over for dinner the other night, and the Palmers asked us to sit with them last Sunday."

"I saw that. Most everyone's open-minded, as well as open hearted."

Their steaks and baked potatoes arrived, and after Angie offered a quick blessing, they spent the next several minutes enjoying their meal and some innocent town gossip. "I also heard the state's going to build a bypass that will connect Highway 541 to I-95," she said.

"That'll take all the tourist traffic away from Jubilee, won't it?"

"I'm afraid so. I can't imagine how bad that will be for our businesses."

"Devastating, I imagine." Justin sensed someone's gaze on him. He set his fork and knife on his plate and scanned the room.

Great! Mr. and Mrs. Bledsoe were eating dinner with another couple he'd seen at church but hadn't met. Just what Angie needed—the man who seemed to be looking for a reason to find fault with her. The urge to bark, "Mind your own business," tempted him. They stared openly as if they'd never seen two people on a date before.

"What?" She wiped her mouth with her napkin.

"Undertaker at six o'clock."

Angie spread her lips into a huge smile. "My favorite person in all the world."

The man chose that moment to come over to their table. "Pastor Angie, what a surprise." His gaze widened as he took in her half-done appearance. "I didn't know you entertained all the church's newcomers with a dinner out."

She pressed her lips together and breathed through her nose. "You know very well that I don't."

"How's the Nativity pageant coming?"

"Quite nicely, thanks to Mrs. Palmer's groundwork." Her voice oozed with practiced patience. "The only change I've made is to arrange to have a real donkey for the Virgin Mary to ride into Bethlehem."

"Are you sure that's wise? What of the expense?"

"Don't you worry about a thing, Deacon Bledsoe. Everything is well managed and in budget." She waved at the people he'd left behind. "Now, I'm sure you're as anxious to get back to your guests as I am to return to my date."

Date! She claimed me in public.

Justin had half expected her to make up some reason for them being together. It wouldn't be the first time someone had done so. He spent the rest of the meal feeling ten feet tall and as proper a Jubilee citizen as Deacon

Bledsoe—minus the whole snobby, undertaker thing.

The buoyant mood continued all the way to her front door. The door he had no intentions of crossing again tonight. Dating a minister called for a different set of rules. Rules he wasn't entirely sure about.

She unlocked the door, then turned back around to face him. "I had a wonderful time tonight."

"Me too. Can I see you again? I mean, besides Sundays." His heart beat against his chest.

"I would like that very much."

"While you're being agreeable, would it be okay to ask for a kiss?"

Her eyes danced. "Certainly, feel free to ask."

A chuckle bubbled up. "Angie, may I kiss you goodnight?"

She tilted her chin in invitation. "I thought you'd never ask."

Justin cupped her cheek and touched his mouth to hers.

Lips, soft and sweet, moved against his. Well before he was ready, she pulled away. She touched her lips and smiled. "Good night."

After she'd closed the door, Justin stood dumbstruck on the other side. "I've just had my last first kiss."

Chapter Eleven

Angie arrived at the church on the afternoon of the live Nativity with a two-page to-do list and a big grin on her face. She'd left Justin and Nick back at the parsonage putting the finishing touches on the wise man's costume. According to the six-year-old, the Magi needed to add more bling to the box of myrrh he'd present to the Christ Child.

Nick wasn't the only one excited about the pageant. A bit late in the season, but joy flowed freely though her like she hadn't experienced since childhood. Success tonight would push into jubilation territory. Although, she was still riding high from the kiss she and Justin had shared. Not much could top that, and it certainly helped keep her mind from absent parents and the stray wedding present. This holiday wasn't like she'd planned, wasn't perfect, but it had potential to change her future.

Inside the utility closet, she collected the sound system and a book light to clamp onto her clipboard, then she ran by her office for extra script copies. "Please, let Mr. Thornton finally remember his lines."

A dozen other last-minute mishaps skittered around in her brain, but she left them up to the only One who could control them at this point and headed to the open field to the left of the parking lot. The church was setting aside funds to eventually expand its facilities onto the two-acre meadow, but for now, it was used for picnics, Easter egg hunts, and softball games.

Facing the parking lot, the Bethlehem set was made by a retired shop teacher from cedar trees off his land. The pitched, shingle roof of the innkeeper's home and barn looked nearly identical to the crèche she'd given Nick. The town's feed store owner had placed the long-used manger inside, along with several bales of straw.

Angie ticked those items off the list, then moved on to the rest of the pre-rehearsal tasks. Soon, Melanie arrived already wearing her blue and white robes, as did Joseph and most of the other cast. Finally, arriving in her truck and trailer was Tabby, the owner of the donkey that would convey the Virgin Mary to Bethlehem.

With Joseph leading Alexander, and Tabby standing close by, Mary and donkey practiced until all involved appeared at ease. The rest of dress rehearsal went off with just one hitch. Sam the Shepherd was missing. Angie called his cell several times, leaving ever more urgent messages. A return text stating that the whole family had come down with food poisoning had her scrambling for a replacement. Thank God, Tabby was game to don a robe and say a few key lines.

By sunset, the audience filled the meadow and sidewalk along Church Street, sitting on blankets and lawn chairs in a semi-circle around the set. Clouds blocked the stars but also kept the evening from being too chilly. At the appointed hour, Angie cued the narrator, who began with reading from the Gospel of Luke. A spotlight followed Mary, Joseph, and Alexander as they lumbered across the meadow on their way to Bethlehem.

The children began singing, "O Little Town of Bethlehem" only to have their voices nearly drowned out by the audience's "ahhs." Angie willed the audience quiet. The church budget didn't allow for wireless microphones, so only the narrator's voice was amplified. The audience calmed, allowing the children's clear voices to fill the night sky. The pageant couldn't have progressed more perfectly, and Angie began envisioning the addition of better lighting and wireless mikes next year. Perhaps even more animals. Mary sitting serenely on the lowly donkey's back added to the play's authenticity.

The choir moved to the second verse as the Holy Family approached the innkeeper. Angie held her breath. Could Mr. Thornton repeat his rehearsal perfection? He opened his mouth, shooting a wild look toward her spot at stage right. "I have no room," she stage whispered.

Well, there's our glitch.

"I have no—"

A crack cut him off. Sparks streaked across the sky. The audience erupted in shouts.

As did Alexander.

The donkey's fearful bray rose above all others, including the poor cherubs who were valiantly continuing in song. Another rocket popped, and red embers rained down on them. The four-legged cast member broke free from Joseph, unseated Mary, and bucked his way toward the little choir. Actors and audience alike scrambled out of the way, tumbled over each other, and fumbled for the animal's halter.

Angie raced across the meadow, where she confiscated the narrator's microphone. "Please remain calm." She caught a glimpse of Tabby racing after her pet. "The donkey's safely out of the way." But what of the ones setting off the fireworks? "Lights," she called. "Shift to the audience so they can reseat themselves." And perhaps identify the mischief makers before they had the chance to do more harm.

Now that everyone could see, the audience began to settle. Chairs were righted. Families regrouped. And the Cherub Choir returned to the place at stage left—albeit with crooked halos, bent wings, and grass-stained robes.

The glint of gold and purple robes among the jeans and sweaters caught her attention. Justin had two boys by their collars and was dragging the middle-schoolers toward the sheriff. "If everyone will please indulge us for ten minutes, we'll regroup then continue with the play." Though they might do so with only two wise men. She could easily speculate what had transpired, but the reason behind the stunt escaped her. All that would have to wait. She called for the actors to assemble behind the set, and after seeing the only injury was to Melanie Jamison's pride, she led them in a quick prayer and resumed the play.

Unfortunately, the star-spangled interruption took the spark out of the actors. The Angel of the Lord jumbled his lines, stating, "I bring you news of all people which will be of great joy and good." The children's rendition of "Go Tell It on the Mountain" started off flat and stayed that way. Angie could feel Deacon Bledsoe's condemnation clear across the pasture. The phrase, "This is how we've always done things," rang in her ears.

Justin and the other wise men proved to be the highlight of the evening. He returned just in time to offer his gift to the baby Jesus and to join in the best version of "We Three Kings" she'd ever heard. The fact she was falling for the magi singing the baritone part might have had something to do with the opinion, but she would challenge anyone to deny they made a great trio.

Finally, the play reached its conclusion. All assembled sang "Silent Night," and Angie could put her directing days behind her. "I'm sticking to my core skills in the future," she muttered as the crowd dispersed. "Regardless of what happens to Mrs. Palmer. She can direct from a wheelchair if she has to."

Justin's approach did put a smile on her face. "Great job with the solo."

He squeezed her hand. "Thank you for the compliment, and before you ask, no, I won't do it again for the Christmas Eve service."

She chuckled. "Am I that transparent?"

"Absolutely. That's okay though. It's one of the many things I enjoy about you."

Her heart did a happy dance, and she looked around the meadow to see if it were possible for her to sneak a quick kiss. Feeling daring, she leaned in.

"Care to explain what happened?" Deacon Bledsoe had managed to enter their private conversation without her noticing.

She straightened and Justin dropped her hand. It wasn't that there was anything wrong with a pastor and parishioner dating, it just wasn't something she wanted to discuss with the man who stood before them—narrowed, beady eyes and glaring at her like the root of all evil lay in her lap.

"I don't know."

"That's part of the problem, Reverend Duncan." The use of her official title was the equivalent of her mother calling her Angela Noel. "You're disengaged from the majority of your flock. Your focus is on a favored few."

Justin cleared his throat. "Angie didn't know these boys at all, and was just as surprised as the rest of us."

"But you're in the know, I assume."

"A couple boys thought our production needed a star

to make it more authentic, so they set off some fireworks.

The town's undertaker sneered. "Relations of yours, I assume."

Angie absolutely did not believe in violence, but she was willing to make an exception at the moment. Instead, she shoved her hands in her pockets and prayed for restraint. "That's uncalled for."

"The sheriff and I spoke with their parents," Justin said. "They apologized to Ms. Jamison and will be offering their grass-cutting services to the church for the next year."

"Plus, they made this year's live Nativity memorable." Angie wanted to put a positive spin on the boys' shenanigans, in part, to spare Justin more judgment.

Deacon Bledsoe huffed. "Not for the right reasons. Reverend, I can't help but think if your time and attention were better channeled, this embarrassing mess could have been avoided."

Her mouth gaped. A low rumble escaped Justin's lips. He took a step closer to Deacon Bledsoe. The last thing she needed was for him to jump to her defense. She touched his arm. "I assure you my attention is placed where it should be." Righteous anger surged through her. "And one more thing, don't bother calling my father. I'm in the pulpit now, not him.

The man snorted. "Not for long, if I have my way about it." He stormed off, leaving her head spinning.

Why is he blaming me?

Justin took her hands. "I'm so sorry."

"This wasn't your fault any more than it was mine. Can't even blame Alexander. Two young men bear the responsibility."

"But they're my kin."

"Still not your fault. At least now I've got someone to mow the churchyard."

"I don't see how you can be so easygoing. Bledsoe threatened your job."

The crowd had thinned to a few stragglers. "You let me handle him.," She sounded more confident than she felt. "Why don't you take Nick home? I'll see you in the morning, and after the service, we can discuss the Christmas dinner menu."

"Yeah, sure. We can talk tomorrow."

Chapter Twelve

For Justin, Sunday morning began before dawn and with not-so-gentle pokes of Nick's finger into his side. "Is it morning yet? Can I wear my blue jacket to church? I already tore another loop off my Christmas calendar. Do you know there's only two more days until Santa gets here?"

He tried ignoring the insistent prodding and string of excited jabber. The hours following the Nativity play hadn't been ones of rest. Guilt, like molten lead, mixed with grief and certainty at the center of his chest to form a decision. One he dreaded acting on as much as he loathed the result of his inaction.

"Is it time for church yet?"

"Not for a couple more hours." Facing Mr. Bledsoe at church was only slightly better than running into the man in his professional capacity as the town's undertaker. Although when it came down to it, Justin wasn't exactly looking forward to interacting with the others who considered his attendance suspicious. More than anything, he dreaded the hour spent watching Angie as she led her flock through the worship service. Her melodic voice, the earnest way she spoke to the children, the occasional smile she sent his direction. All lovely, and the last time he'd enjoy them.

"Why aren't you talking to me, Uncle Justin? Did you get drunk last night?"

"No, buddy, I didn't." Not that the thought hadn't crossed his mind, but when Nick had come in the house, the booze went out. He sat up, stretched, and tried to think if there were enough eggs in the fridge for an omelet. "What would you like for breakfast?" At this hour, he had time to create a tummy-filling feast for the boy.

"I already made cereal, and I didn't spill any milk." He tugged on Justin's arm. "Hurry and get up. I want to talk to my friends at church. Did you know that donkey almost ran over Ellery? He called it an A-S-S."

"Really?" Justin ran his fingers through his hair and wondered if that was something he needed to tell Ellery's mother. Probably not. It was, after all, a legitimate name for the animal. Besides, he was still too new at the parenting thing to offer critique of anyone else's child. "You're going to have to wait a couple hours, buddy. Why don't you go in the living room and watch cartoons while I take a shower."

By midmorning, Justin had run out of delaying tactics. Early or not, Nick insisted they leave for church. The two set out on foot with the sun providing enough warmth and walking the half mile would hopefully tire the boy enough that he could sit reasonably still for the service. The hour sped along in a blur of standing and kneeling, songs and prayer, sadness and heartbreak. *Heartbreaks*, three to be exact, since his decision affected Nick as well.

As usual, Justin hung back after the close of the service while Angie spoke to her parishioners. Unlike their first visit, Nick ran off to the playground with a couple kids. Justin studied the stained glass depicting the Holy Family's entry into Bethlehem and wondered if last night had gone according to plan, would his life's trajectory have continued along the same path?

Probably not. If his cousin's kids hadn't acted up, someone else in his family would. Or Mr. Bledsoe would have found another reason to label him unsuitable for Angie. Or he could simply screw things up all on his own. He was certainly capable of that.

"Where's Nick?"

Justin turned to face Angie, who'd shucked out of her robe and had her purse in her hand. He couldn't help thinking how nice the blue topaz earrings he bought her as a birthday present would look with that dress, and the purple sweater Christmas present was sure to accent her ivory skin and her dark-green eyes. He drew in a breath and prayed for the courage to do the right thing. "I sent him outside for a while so we could talk."

Her smile faltered. "What's on your mind?"

Justin gestured to the front row pew, then pulled out the piano bench to sit across from her. "I'm not sure how to begin."

"I find it's best to speak the truth, simply and from the heart." With her back erect and her expression calm, she might have been speaking to a member of her flock. The tremble of her hands clasped in her lap told otherwise and let him know she had a clue where their conversation was headed.

"When Nick and I came here that first Sunday, I never considered you'd be so kind to us. Certainly never imagined I'd have feelings for you. But you were, and I did."

"Did?"

"I mean, I do." He swallowed hard. "However, I don't think it's in our best interest for us to continue to see each other. Hopefully by the New Year, everyone here will have forgotten all about the time members of the notorious Brown clan invaded their church."

She leaned forward. "Is this about the Bartells leaving Nick out? I assure you they're in the minority."

They weren't, and the fact Angie didn't pick up on the opinions of her parishioners was all the more reason why he needed to break things off. Before her congregation turned against her.

"It's more than that. If Nick and I stay in Jubilee, and I'm not a hundred percent sure we will, folks like the Bartells are something we'll have to put up with. However, I'm not willing to drag you down with us. Mr. Bledsoe threatened your job last night. All because of your association with me." He almost took her hand. The need to touch her clawed at him. Instead, he crossed his arms. "I care too much about you to do that."

Angie crossed her arms. "Can I get a word in edgewise?"

He clamped his lips closed.

"Believe me, I've given the church far more to wag their chins about in the last year than dating you."

"I've made up my mind, and I ask that you respect my decision."

She blinked. "Of course."

"I appreciate it." He stood. If he stayed any longer his resolve would become as solid as the waters in Fancy Bluff Creek. "I also appreciate everything you did for Nick. Your religious instruction added a great deal of meaning to his Christmas."

"Just doing—" Her voice broke. "Just doing my job."

Justin rushed down the aisle with the sound of her crying nipping at his heels. He found Nick on the swings and called him over. "If we hurry, we can get over to the mall to see Santa before the line gets too long."

"Again? Cool." The boy raced over, then stopped, his face scrunched up in confusion. "I thought we were going over to Pastor Angie's for lunch."

"Change of plans."

"But she's still coming over Christmas morning to

watch me open my presents? And Christmas Eve, I'm going to get to sing with the choir and hold a candle, aren't I?"

"I'm sorry, no." Justin brushed his hand over the boy's ever-present cowlick. Tears filled his eyes and matched the ones spilling down Nick's cheeks. "It'll be just the two of us, but I promise to make it as special as I know how to." His words rang hollow. No additional presents under the tree could replace the person who'd taught them the very best meaning of Christmas.

Chapter Thirteen

Christmas morning Angie woke as the sun began to lighten the sky. She pulled on jeans and a bright red sweatshirt, then headed to the living room for her shoes and car keys. The crew running the Christmas dinner at the homeless shelter could always use an extra pair of hands, and getting elbow deep in sweet potatoes, dressing, and turkey had the twofold benefit of continuing at least one family tradition and keeping her mind off Justin and Nick.

As she reached for the coat she'd left on an armchair, her gaze caught on the reindeer-wrapped packages piled next to the ones from her parents. She grabbed the guys' gifts and hurried to her car. "No reason Nick shouldn't have his train set even if Justin doesn't want me."

At the Brown household, she set the gifts on the stoop, prayed a blessing over the two men who'd come to mean so much to her and then backed away.

She'd almost made it to her car when a voice called to her. "Hold up."

Angie drew in a breath before turning around. Why hadn't she counted on them being up so early? "Sorry if I woke you."

Justin stepped onto the porch and pulled the door closed. "Are you kidding?" He tapped his chest. "Santa just finished assembling Nick's gifts when he woke up." He did look like he'd pulled an all-nighter, but with a glow of satisfaction added to his red-rimmed eyes.

She gestured to the boxes now in Justin's arms and tried to keep her voice even. As if she'd simply been passing by. "Those are just a couple of things I picked up for you two."

"Would you like to come inside?" He took a step in her direction. "I've got coffee."

Her heart pounded. "Thank you, no." She couldn't get the words out fast enough. "Got to go."

Except, Nick flung open the door, raced past his uncle, and cut off her quick escape. "Pastor Angie." He latched onto her and began tugging her inside. "Come see what Santa brought me." The boy presented each item in his horde for her examination. "I got books, Hot Wheels, and a bike. Three presents, just like baby Jesus, right Uncle Justin?"

Justin shrugged. "It seemed appropriate."

Emotion washed over her. "What a lovely tradition."

Nick pointed to the gifts Justin brought in. "Is one of them for me?"

"You bet. And something for your uncle." While Nick ripped into his box, she whispered to Justin. "You don't have to open it if you don't want."

"Why wouldn't I accept a gift from you? I like you a lot, Angie. I just don't think the two of us would work together."

She wanted to disagree with him. Justin and Nick were everything she wanted, and sitting there with them felt as right and good as any experience she'd had since her parents left for Peru. The self-doubt perched on her shoulder whispered, "But what do you know about men? You fell for Reese didn't you?"

Justin nudged her. "Did you hear what I said?"

She shook herself loose from those negative thoughts. "No, sorry. I was a million miles away."

"Some place not very nice. You looked as though you were about to cry."

"I'm fine." She waved away his concern. "What was the question again?"

"Was Mr. Bledsoe pleased with your Christmas Eve service?"

"I suppose he was. I really only hear from him when he's displeased."

"So he's not going to fire you?"

"Much to Mr. Bledsoe's chagrin, he doesn't possess the authority, and after speaking with my father, I recall the deacon giving him as much grief as he gives me."

"That's good to hear. Not the part where he harassed your father, but that he can't act on his threats. I was afraid…"

"You don't need to worry. In my position, people are always going to feel it's their right to express their opinions about me. It's my job to stay true to my beliefs regardless of the costs." She met his gaze. "For the record, I believe you are a good person, and with time, others will see that as well. Now, I've said far more than I intended." She stood. "It's time for me to go. I'm due at the soup kitchen soon."

Justin joined her at the door. "Nick come tell Pastor Angie thank you."

The boy placed the piece of track on the floor and walked over. Staring at his feet, he muttered, "Thank you for the train set."

"You don't seem happy for a kid on Christmas morning." She longed to gather Nick into her arms, but instead she cupped his cheek. "Did Santa not bring you everything you wanted?"

"Not really."

Justin took a knee. "I'm sorry, buddy. I did…I mean Santa did the best he could."

"Why don't you tell Uncle Justin what you wanted, and maybe he can get it for your birthday."

Nick leaned in and whispered.

Justin flinched. "What?"

The boy jabbed a finger at her. "I want Pastor Angie to come live with us. I asked Santa. I even prayed to baby Jesus."

Angie kneeled. "Oh, buddy. It doesn't work that way. I thought you meant a video game or LEGOs."

A broad smile replaced Justin's grin. "See, buddy"—he winked at Nick—"in order for Angie to do that, she and I would have to get married. We're not there yet." He stood, turned to her, and took both her hands in his. "Maybe down the road when she and I have gotten to know each other better."

Her pulse hammered in her ears. "What are you saying?"

"I was wrong to let a few people's opinions keep me from the woman I love. I was an idiot for believing you couldn't handle problems that come your way. I am a Class A Scrooge for ruining our Christmas."

With Justin's words, her grief fell away. All she'd lost had been returned to her twofold. Joy resonated from her soul. "I agree with the first two, and you're forgiven. But you haven't ruined Christmas."

"I haven't?"

"Not at all." She wrapped her arm around Nick to join them in a circle. "In fact, this is the best first Christmas this family has ever had."

THE END

Melissa's Recipe

Angie's Chocolate-Dipped Shortbread Cookies

2 cups butter, softened
1 cup white sugar
2 teaspoons pure vanilla extract
4 cups all-purpose flour
6 ounces semi-sweet chocolate, finely chopped

Preheat oven to 350 degrees

In a large mixing bowl, cream together butter and sugar. Stir in vanilla. Add flour, mixing well. Sprinkle the counter with powdered sugar and roll dough into 2 logs. Wrap each in plastic wrap and chill in freezer for 30 minutes.

Once the dough becomes firm, slice off 3/8 inch rounds and place onto a parchment lined cookie sheet. Bake 16-18 minutes until the edges are just golden. Allow to cool in pan before transferring to a rack.

Place 3 ounces of chopped chocolate in a glass bowl and microwave for thirty seconds at a time, stirring between each interval until it has just barely melted. Remove from oven and add remaining chocolate. Stir until smooth.

Dip 1/2 of completely cooled cookie into chocolate then place on cooling rack. Place in airtight container.

Melissa Klein

Melissa Klein writes contemporary fiction set in the South. Whether facing the demands of caring for a child with special needs or the struggles of a soldier returning home, her characters take on the challenges life throws at them with perseverance, courage, and humor.

While she won Georgia Romance Writers Unpublished Maggie award and Rose City Romance Writers Golden Rose award, she still hopes to win the lottery. If she does, she'll buy a huge farm in north Georgia and convince her children to live next door. Until that time, she lives in Atlanta with her husband, who puts up with frozen dinners when the words are flowing.

Melissa's website:
http://www.melissakleinromance.com/

Home for Christmas

By Rachel W. Jones

Acknowledgments

It's an honor to belong to this group of talented authors. I'm excited to share this journey with Linda, Leah, and Melissa—the creation of a town, its citizens, and traditions; to craft stories of friendship and hardship, heartache and love.

Our writer voices have combined to produce a volume of stories that intersect in our small Southern town. May you enjoy your visit to Jubilee. Our hope is you will want to return each time we publish a new holiday anthology in this series.

Melissa, Linda, and Leah give weekly encouragement to my writing endeavor. They are my cheerleaders when life turns rocky. I couldn't ask for better critique partners or friends.

Randy, my husband of forty years, continues to offer his love and support. He gives his time, effort, and resources to assist me as I pursue my passion for breathing life into characters and creating their stories. He is my real-life Prince Charming.

Home for Christmas

Chapter One

One hot coffee.
One *hot* stranger.
One hot mess.

It was an ugly, unavoidable caffeine collision. And she had caused it.

Liz Marshall jumped back, managing to steer clear of the steaming liquid. Her hands sprang to her cheeks. "Oh! I'm sorry."

The stranger dropped his cup on a nearby table and pulled the coffee-soaked shirt away from his skin. "Crap, that's hot."

She held out her hands, wanting to be helpful but not knowing what to do. Would he welcome the touch of the woman who had just doused his crisp, white shirt with coffee?

A barista stepped from behind the counter and tossed a towel in his direction. "Dude, use this."

The customer caught it and muttered, "Thanks." He pulled his shirttail from his pants and wiped his stomach.

Mesmerized by the flat six-pack displayed before her,

Liz was unaware the barista had moved in her direction until he spoke. "Don't worry, Liz. It was an accident."

"Of course it was an accident." Her shrill voice accented the words. Liz chewed her bottom lip.

After dabbing at his ruined shirt, the guy looked up. "What was so important that you did a one-eighty right into me?"

"I remembered something I needed to tell my friend." Liz wasn't about to reveal she'd just come up with the perfect pet name for Courtney's new boyfriend. "Is there anything I can do?"

"Do you happen to have a clean shirt with you?"

Liz shook her head. "Again, I'm sorry. I have to go." She sprinted out of the coffee shop, keeping a quick pace for a block until there was plenty of distance between the location of this morning's blunder and herself. Slowing to a walk, Liz ignored the twenty-eight-degree New York state temperature.

Her impulsiveness always had consequences. She dove into interior design school without realizing she'd have to forfeit time from singing. On a whim, she entered a contest at Parsons School of Design and won. Not just the monetary prize, but also a job interview. She accepted the position at Lang Renovations, but had not considered how much she'd miss her folks or her hometown of Jubilee, Georgia.

Consequences.

She blew into the cold air. Water vapor danced like foggy mist in front of her. At least this morning's stunt wouldn't affect her life.

I've had better starts to a Monday. Guess my day can only improve.

A chill ran up her spine as she hurried inside the office building. After hanging her coat in a locker, Liz stopped by the lounge for a second cup of coffee. The cheery Christmas music didn't work its magic this morning.

A coworker followed her to the coffeepot. "Where's that smile that can brighten even a cold Monday morning?"

The melodic drawl of the only other Southern transplant Liz knew didn't soothe as usual. "Georgette, the most awful thing happened at the coffee shop."

"What was that, darlin'?" She poured a liberal splash of creamer in her cup.

"I turned and fell into this gorgeous man. I caused him to spill hot coffee down the front of his shirt." Liz plopped in a chair at the nearest table.

"Nice." Georgette joined her at the table and leaned in. "Did you get his name?"

Liz glared. "No, I didn't. I apologized and ran away." She placed her hand on her cheek and sighed. "But he's a hunk."

"Sounds like you *did* fall. Fat chance you'll see him again."

"I might. Maybe he's new in town—and the coffee shop will be the place he stops each morning for his caffeine boost."

"I'm sure he's looking for other options as we speak."

The lounge door opened. "Come on, you two. The boss has called a meeting."

The owner and CEO of Lang Renovations, Inc. entered the room and got right to the point of the meeting. "I want to inform you of a change in management. My wife has been patient for many years as we worked to build this company. The time has come for me to focus my time and energy on Nina. Effective immediately, my nephew will be assuming the interim role of CEO."

Murmurs of surprise filled the air. A chill did a repeat performance up Liz's spine.

"Please work with him as you have with me. This company is a success because of your dedication and loyalty."

The door at the front of the room opened. A man entered. He wore khakis. And a soiled white shirt.

Liz gasped.

The CEO continued. "Everyone, meet Mitchell Lang. Your new boss."

****

Mitchell surveyed the eyes directed at him. "Good morning." His gaze wandered across the faces. Unconquered butterscotch curls halted his perusal. Bewildered green eyes made his I'm-your-boss-now words stick in his throat.

Coffee girl.

His fingers slid down his shirt. He cleared his throat to allow the words to pass. "I know this is sudden. There will be no dramatic changes to the workflow, so continue with your day as usual. We'll have a formal meeting tomorrow morning. Ten o'clock sharp."

The employees filed out of the conference room. He nodded at those who bothered to meet his gaze.

Mitchell felt his uncle's hand on his shoulder. "There are a few things we need to discuss, Mitch. Have a seat."

"I thought last week's meetings covered everything."

"This is a new development. Do you want some coffee?"

Mitchell glanced at his shirt. "No thanks. I've had my fill for the day."

His uncle chuckled. "You might want to consider leaving a change of clothes in your office. You never know when you might need them."

"Good advice. So, a new development?"

"Mr. Ramsden has decided he wants his renovations completed by December twenty-sixth instead of the original finish date of the thirtieth."

"It's doable, but only if everyone works through the holiday."

When his uncle didn't reply, Mitchell's eyes widened. "You want me to cancel Christmas?"

"I'm merely delivering a message. However you choose to deal with it is your decision. There's one caveat. If you do not adjust the timeline for Frederic Ramsden, he will not sign the contract for the renovation of his summer cottage on Lake George."

"Don't worry. I've got this."

Uncle Walter laughed. "I'm not worried. I'm retired."

Par for the course. Mitchell was well versed in meeting the unexpected head-on. But he'd never been a Scrooge.

Chapter Two

Liz hurried into the pet rescue shelter and left the sting of cold air behind.

Greetings of "I'll Be Home for Christmas" settled in her ears. In the small break area for volunteers, twinkling lights, garland, and poinsettias claimed her attention, flooding her mind with memories of past Jubilee holidays with her parents. Shopping, ice skating, cookie baking.

Her smile disappeared when reality broke into her reverie. This year could never be like the Christmases she'd known for the past twenty-eight years. This holiday would be the hardest she'd ever face.

This first Christmas without her father.

That momentary pain caused Liz to clutch her stomach. An uncontrolled whimper escaped her throat.

Courtney popped into the room. "Thanks again for swapping your nights this week."

"Works out great for me. I need to do some cuddling. Any new residents that need TLC?"

"We have one newbie. A red long-haired miniature dachshund. Her owner died yesterday. A friend of the woman said she'd take Tallulah, but she's in an assisted living situation. No pets allowed."

"Aw, that's sad. Tallulah may need this more than

me." Liz opened a cabinet and pulled out a clean scrub jacket. After snapping it over her clothes, she deposited some doggie treats in the pocket. "Lead the way."

"I do love connecting humans with canines. A little time with this sweetie, and your rough morning will be a distant memory."

"I doubt that. My rough start got worse. The man I sloshed with coffee is now my boss."

Courtney halted her steps and faced Liz. "What?"

"Mr. Lang decided it was time to retire. We figured he'd bring his son into the business, but instead, he gave the job to his nephew. Temporarily."

"And he just happened to stop for coffee on the way to meet his employees. I hope he's not the grudge-holding type."

"He seems okay… but he only said a few words. We have an official meeting tomorrow morning."

They walked into the small socializing room that held four cages, two rocking chairs, an area rug opposite the cages, and a shallow toy box. Plus one canine. Short on legs but long on ears.

"Liz, this is Tallulah. I'm going to leave her in our visitation room a day or two so she won't be overwhelmed. I'll pick a buddy to stay with her tonight. Hopefully, if I find the right companion, it will be soothing."

Liz unlatched the cage and coaxed the timid animal to

the door with a treat. She reached for the floppy-eared, sad-eyed dog. Holding her close, they settled in a rocking chair. She stroked the dog's fur while murmuring soft words meant to comfort. The dachshund's only response was a low sigh.

Wish I could take you home right now.

Courtney occupied the chair beside them. She reached over and scratched Tallulah gently on the head, then echoed the dog's sigh.

Liz studied her friend. "How is the budget shaping up for next year?"

"Could be worse, so I'm not worried—yet." Courtney put her hand on Liz's arm. "I want to tell you again how grateful we are for your donation."

Liz smiled. "I can't think of a better way to spend my holiday bonus. I love volunteering here. So I'll do whatever I can to help keep the doors of Man's Best Friend open. I should receive my bonus check around the fifteenth. You'll have the money before I fly home for Christmas."

Courtney stood and took the dog from Liz. "That's it for now, girl. We have to get dinner ready for you and the other dogs." She placed her in the cage and secured the door. A muffled ring came from her pocket.

Liz stood. "I'll get dinner going while you take care of that."

Courtney nodded as she answered the phone and

stepped away.

Liz began prepping dishes of dog food. Her mind drifted to Jubilee. To her mother, cousin Violet, and Aunt Marge. She could hardly wait to see them. Mr. Lang always gave his employees the business day before Christmas Eve off. The way the calendar fell this year, she'd work Thursday, the twentieth, then take the 5:29 p.m. flight to Georgia. She'd be home in time to attend the live Nativity at Jubilee Community Church on Saturday.

After loading the dishes of food on a utility cart, Liz proceeded to the common area. Seven of the twelve cages had occupants. It wouldn't surprise her to return after the New Year to find a full house. The holidays not only impacted humans but canines as well. Last January, two dogs had been brought to the shelter. Christmas purchases that hadn't worked out. Those fellas had been better off waiting here for someone searching for just the right pet than living where owners had bought them as a gift without thinking it through.

Liz had always wanted a dog, but her father's off-the-chart allergies had ended that dream. After settling in White Plains, New York, she had found a stray outside her apartment one morning.

The temptation to keep the dog while trying to locate the owner had been strong. But the apartment lease didn't allow for pets, and she'd always been a rule follower. Liz surrendered the stray to the rescue shelter. Surrendered her heart and found bliss as a shelter volunteer.

Liz pulled the utility cart through the door of the doggie dormitory, and the greetings began. The different timbre of barks harmonized, each requesting her undivided attention. She looked above the cages and smiled at her artwork on three adjacent walls. She had dubbed the mural Doggie Heaven, had enjoyed depicting thirty breeds of four-legged friends running, chasing, jumping.

The barking crescendoed as she opened the first cage. She scooped up the brown Pekingese mix. "Hello Arnie. Are you ready for dinner?" The dog licked her cheek. Laughing, she lowered him to the epoxy floor, pushed a bowl inside the cage, and locked the door, then moved on until dinner was served and the cart was empty.

She found Courtney taking inventory in the storage room when she finished her task.

"Dinner detail accomplished," she informed her.

"Great. Thanks for coming by. Curt will be back soon to close up tonight."

"I can stay longer if you need me."

"No, thanks. Go home and have a bubble bath with a glass of wine. Relax and get a good night's sleep so you're ready to meet the new boss in the morning. My only piece of advice is to skip the coffee shop. Just in case he's there."

"Good idea. I'll get my caffeine in the break room tomorrow."

After bundling up, Liz stepped outside into the cold night. She missed the star-filled sky of Jubilee and many other things about the town where she'd grown up. This trip home would be bittersweet, but still, she wanted it.

Too bad a bubble bath and a glass of wine couldn't fix everything in life.

****

A festive wreath on the door of the steakhouse reminded Mitchell the holiday season was in full swing. He pulled on the handle and stepped inside. The expected Country and Western music had been replaced with Sleeping at Last crooning the lyrics to "Have Yourself a Merry Little Christmas." Not a bad sound, but he was neutral when it came to the whole holiday thing. He didn't mind that others celebrated, but there was no Christmas tree or holiday cookies or caroling in his corner of the world.

Arriving a bit early, and knowing Eric always showed up a few minutes late, he placed his name on the waitlist and ordered a brew on tap from the bartender. Mitchell claimed a barstool with the door in his view. Pine garland decorated the length of the bar. Twinkling white mini lights highlighted the red holly berries popping through the greenery.

He had spent the last several years during the December holiday season flying a cargo plane stuffed with packages for delivery. He liked helping his friend, and at

35,000 feet in the air, it distanced him from all the folderol. At least that's how he viewed Christmas, unlike the majority of inhabitants on Earth. This dinner was all about catching up and Eric requesting his help with getting the deliveries made, to keep his customers happy.

Too bad I can't do it this year.

The ten-year difference in their ages had never been a problem. Though their relationship began as teacher to student, they'd progressed easily to friends by the time Mitchell had gained his pilot license. Uncle Walter had been a good role model, his cousin, Derrick, a friend. But the person he most wanted to emulate was Eric.

He loved him like an older brother. This man who had taught him how to embrace and navigate the endless blue highway. This man who had never asked Mitchell why he did his best to avoid holidays. This man who accepted his need not to talk about it.

Mitchell took a draw of his beer as he watched the door. Eric crossed the threshold and began a search of the space. When his gaze reached him, Mitchell threw his hand up in greeting and moved toward his friend.

"Your timing is improving. I figured I'd be on my second beer by the time you showed up."

"Mitch, how's life treating you?"

"I can't complain. I started a new job today. How's Dottie and the kiddos?"

"The kids are good, and Dottie is… *great*. You'd be

so lucky to wind up with someone like her."

Not on my list of priorities.

"Maybe someday."

"It won't happen if you don't look."

They followed the hostess to a table. The surrounding signs of Christmas were hard to ignore. Poinsettias, wreaths, lights, a ten-foot tree. Mitchell brought his focus back to his friend as Eric ordered a beer.

"I've got new pictures of the kids." Eric scrolled through his photos and held out the phone.

Mitchell accepted it and found himself studying the image of a lanky, dark-haired boy in a red and white jersey. "Zach is playing football?"

"You realize he is twelve and started middle school this year. Slide to the right. There's Amelia in her costume from her first ballet recital last spring."

"Wow. When did she start dancing? The last time I saw her, she was carrying a stuffed animal in her arms."

Eric reached for his phone and smiled. "Can't stop them from growing up. And you...a new job? You told me last year how much you like freelancing. Like being the boss of your life. Like taking a few weeks in December and working for me. I guess this means you won't be on my roster of seasonal help this year."

"Sorry, no. The job is temporary, but it will probably last for six months. My uncle decided rather suddenly to retire. It's been the expectation that my cousin, Derrick, would fill the position, but he has an obligation to his job in Germany. It may take until summer to tie things up and move back home.

On a Monday evening, it wasn't long before steak dinners were placed on the table. The sizzle of prime beef on a hot plate made Mitchell's mouth water. They dug in. A lull in conversation accented Mariah Carey singing "All I Want for Christmas Is You" while they started the meal.

Mitchell didn't want to leave Eric shorthanded. He had to make Eric understand the choice he'd made. "I need to do this for Uncle Walter and Aunt Nina. They were so good to me when my mom died. They get more of the credit for raising me than my father."

"Does your job make you happy?"

"It pleases me that I help companies realize their potential. Help them reach their goals."

"Does it bring you joy?"

Mitchell wrinkled his forehead in response.

Eric propped his elbows on the table and clasped his hands. "I like my shipping business, but it's my family that brings me joy. It's important the things you spend most of your time doing bring you joy. Joy is man's reason to exist."

An image of coffee girl with her hands on her cheeks after their morning collision flashed in his mind. His chest tightened.

"Why all the concern about my happiness? My joy?"

"I watched while I taught you. I saw a closed-off young man become bright-eyed and engaging when he was flying. Like you had entered a new dimension. You became a new person."

A flush of adrenaline tingled through Mitchell's body. "That's what you saw?" Surprise drove his vocal pitch upward.

"I want to give you the opportunity to be that person, bright-eyed and happy."

"To be honest, I'd rather be flying than playing interim CEO. Sorry it won't work out this year."

Eric pulled his napkin from his lap and wiped his mouth. "I understand. I've got other news. I've changed the name of my company."

"Why? What's the new name?"

"I needed to incorporate my new service into the title. Swales Airline Cargo and Charter Service, Inc."

"Adding charter service. Smart move. What sweet ride do you have for your passengers?"

"I purchased a midsize Learjet five months ago, and business has been booming. So I've decided to open two more locations. One in the Southeast and one in the Midwest. Got feelers out for a couple of people to head up the new locations."

Wow. Wish I had the nerve to leap into new territory.

"Congrats, man. Do you fly much with the charter service?"

"I hired a full-time pilot, but I cover some of the jobs myself. I promised Dottie the plane would be on the ground for the holidays. I'm not sacrificing family time for any amount of money."

"Smart man. I know what Dottie's like when you piss her off."

Eric laughed. "After fourteen years of marriage, I've learned it's to my advantage to keep my wife happy. About the charter service—I want to offer you a position to head up one of the locations. The wheels are in motion, so I'd need you on board by March to help with finding a location and set-up."

His heart pounded, then froze. "I made a promise to Uncle Walter."

"I don't want an answer tonight."

Eric's words brought relief, restarted his heartbeat. "Okay. Thanks for the offer. It means a lot. And you, stick to your holiday policy. Enjoy your family."

Later, as he walked to his car, the adrenaline high faded. Warmth invaded his chest as a childhood image of his mother surfaced. They snuggled on the sofa, a holiday storybook in her lap while they watched the blinking lights on the Christmas tree. The feeling fled as quickly as it had come. Unannounced, but not unwanted.

His mind shuffled to his immediate future. Stiffening hair on the back of his neck signaled a state of unrest. Tomorrow he would share the updated plans for the

Ramsden job with his new employees—and the interruption of their holiday plans.

Chapter Three

I need coffee.

Liz walked into the empty break room and beelined it for the coffee pot. She preferred confidence to the mental distress accompanying her this morning.

Meeting the new boss, a reason for caution.

She drew in a deep breath of the brew and smiled. "Ahh."

He had said no dramatic changes.

Her shoulders relaxed.

"Mitchell Lang." The name rolled easily off her tongue, though she had not meant to speak it out loud. A good-looking man with unruly dark brown hair. Usually, that would drive her crazy, wanting to tame the disobedient locks. But on him, it looked natural. And those intense green eyes.

The door to the break room opened, and the gaze of those bright eyes took her by surprise.

"Good morning. We haven't formally met. I'm Mitchell Lang."

She sat her cup on the counter and extended her hand. "Hello, Mr. Lang. I'm Elizabeth…Liz Marshall. It's nice to meet you." She reached for the coffee pot. "Would you like some—"

He held his hands in front of his chest, palms outward. "No, thank you. I've had my morning coffee."

"Well, I have a few things to do before the meeting. I'll see you there."

Liz escaped to her cubicle and sat in front of her computer. Stomach fluttering, heartbeat racing.

The man is pure eye candy.

It took a few minutes to push the effects of her new boss aside, but there was plenty to be done before she left for Jubilee. She had been home a few times since her father's death eight months ago. Short trips. But this holiday vacation promised lunches and shopping with her friends, Tabby and Chelsea, and her cousin Violet. Not to mention precious time with her mom.

At five minutes to ten, Liz rose and followed several coworkers into the conference room. Right on the dot of ten o'clock, Mitchell entered and faced the group of thirteen employees.

"Good morning. I see everyone is present. I will begin by telling you this is a temporary position for me. I will head up the company until my cousin returns from Germany. He will assume the role of CEO at that time. Yesterday, I said there would be no dramatic changes. That is not the case today. The timeline for the Ramsden project has been adjusted. It is now slated for completion by December twenty-sixth, instead of the thirtieth."

A cacophony of murmurs from the crowd stopped

Mitchell's words.

Someone called out, "There's no way that can happen."

Mitchell motioned for silence. "It is possible, and I've agreed to Mr. Ramsden's request. I know December twentieth was to be your last workday and you would be returning on the twenty-sixth. As of now, your last day will be Christmas Eve, *if* we have finished."

Someone asked, "What happens if we're not done?"

"We'll work Christmas Day. Please adjust your calendars accordingly."

"I might just take my bonus and resign. And I might not be the only one," someone in the back called out.

"Please be aware"—Mitchell adjusted his cuffs— "should you decide to resign due to this inconvenience, you will not receive your bonus check. I will be available after two o'clock if anyone has comments or questions."

Mitchell walked away. Noise erupted.

Liz's breath hitched. Disappointment consumed her.

It looks like the only way I'll be home for Christmas is in my dreams.

****

Liz settled on the sofa, gas logs glowing. She situated a throw over her legs, hoping to add a cozy element to her rattled evening. The Weather Channel predicted six to eight inches for Christmas Day. She had not given the upstate New York holiday precipitation any thought. Her location on the twenty-fifth was supposed to be Jubilee, with little chance of even a dusting of the white stuff. Plans to trade sturdy snow boots for fashion boots were not going to happen. And now she'd have to deal with all the inconveniences that blinding, crunchy, penetrating snow brought with it.

"Dishes are done. Laundry is going. But did I need to mop the whole floor because I spilled some orange juice?"

She sighed loud enough to rattle the blinds over the window, but not loud enough for anyone who mattered to hear.

"I waited a day to see if Mr. CEO would reverse his decision. I can't put it off any longer, even to have a conversation with myself about snow. I have to tell Mom."

Liz picked up her cell phone and pressed her mother's name. It rang twice.

"Hello, my sweet girl. How are you?"

"Good, Mom. You okay?"

"My evening has picked up, now that I'm talking to you. And in eight days, you'll be here! I was thinking since it's imperative that I work next Friday, it will be a good time for you to visit your friends. On Saturday, you and I could do some shopping before the live Nativity. Oh, and I can't wait for you to hear Reverend Angela preach on Sunday morning. It took a while for me to get used to seeing her instead of her father behind the pulpit. However, her lessons are excellent."

Liz's chest tightened. Pain pricked the back of her throat.

Just blurt it out.

"Mom, wait. I would love to do all those things, but I can't do them if I'm in New York."

"Whaaat?"

"We have to work through the twenty-fourth and maybe Christmas Day, too."

"Lizzie, no. Why?"

"It boils down to a rich client wanting his way. I can understand why Mitchell, our new boss, agreed to his request. Anyway, I think Mitchell is doing the best he can with the circumstances as they are. It's dismal that it happened in December instead of say, September. No one would be this upset about Labor Day plans."

"But it's Christmas."

Liz heard the strain in her mother's voice. "I didn't want to make this call, but now you have time to change your plans. I don't want you to be alone."

"I have the same worries for you. What will you do for Christmas?"

Liz pushed the blanket aside and stood. "Probably spend part of the day with Courtney and Curt and my furry friends. There's a new miniature dachshund. Tallulah is the sweetest thing."

"I'm glad you have your volunteer work with the dogs. I suppose they'll need some love and attention on

Christmas, too."

"One of my coworkers always has a Christmas Eve party." She wasn't sure Georgette would have a gathering this year since they were scheduled to work. But it would make her mother feel better thinking she had someplace to be.

"I will pray that some turn of events will allow you to come home. I miss you."

"Good idea. Miss you and love you, Mom."

"We'll talk in a few days. Love you, Lizzie. Goodnight."

Liz sat and placed her phone on the sofa table. "You had to do it. Had to do it. She needed to know." She pulled the blanket up to her neck. Nausea rippled in her stomach. A tear slipped from the corner of her eye.

"I miss you, Dad."

Chapter Four

Mitchell lifted the leather messenger bag from his shoulder and set it on the desk while he wrestled his vibrating phone from the pocket of his jeans. "Somebody's starting my Thursday early." He raised an eyebrow at the name on the caller ID.

"Derrick. This is a surprise."

"Hope I'm not interrupting your morning workout."

"Finished an hour ago. I'm at the office. What's up?"

"We need to talk. Dad called yesterday. He told me about the mess Mr. Ramsden has stirred up with his inappropriate request to finish his renovation early."

Mitchell paced in front of the desk. "Things are not too cheery around here. But what's a boss to do?"

"That's why I'm calling. To help you make some decisions."

"So really, you're calling to tell me your viewpoint."

"Look. The customer isn't always right. You've got thirteen loyal employees who've had their family holiday time shot to hell because of one man."

"I know that, but I can't let Uncle Walter down. I can't screw up his business the first week I'm in charge."

"Isn't that what you're doing?"

Mitchell rubbed his temple. "Okay, Cousin. How

would you handle this?"

"I'd tell Ramsden to take his business elsewhere. Lang Renovations has a stellar reputation, and not because of one customer. He may be our biggest account, but we don't have to bow down to him. Losing this client will not have as much impact as you think. Losing good employees could."

"I agreed to stand in for you, but I'm not about to lose our largest account on my watch."

"I'm just asking you to think about it. Our employees would thank you for restoring their holiday time."

"Any chance you might get home a few months earlier than you mentioned?"

"Mitchell Lang, running away from a challenge? Thought I'd never see the day."

"Running toward a challenge. I have a chance to do some flying on a regular basis."

"And you want me to come home early…because…?"

"I have a job opportunity to fly more than I do now, but I need to be available by March."

"Sorry, I don't think I can pull it off."

Mitchell returned to his chair, shoulders slumping.

Dream over.

"You and Gina have a good holiday. See you in June." Mitchell deposited his cell phone on his desk and pushed his fingers through his hair.

He grabbed his coffee mug and headed to the lounge. The chatter ceased when he entered the room. Ignoring the chilling atmosphere, he filled his cup with hot liquid. Turning, he noticed one table piled with containers and plates covered with plastic and foil. "What's going on? Potluck day?"

Georgette stepped forward. "A cookie swap."

"I don't understand."

"Everyone has brought three dozen homemade cookies to exchange."

"Not everyone," a random voice called out.

"You can't expect Mr. Lang to participate when he didn't know about it," reasoned Georgette.

Mitchell sipped his coffee. "So how does this work?" His gaze landed on Liz. "Ms. Marshall?"

"We all brought in three dozen homemade cookies. Everyone's name is written on three separate strips of paper and placed in the hat. When it's my turn, I'll pull three names and take a dozen cookies from each person whose name I've drawn. I came to work with my fruitcake cookies, and I'll leave with an assortment baked by others."

"I hope I draw your name," Georgette said. "Your cookies are fabulous."

Mitchell focused on the containers. A fuzzy snapshot of a five-year-old holding up sticky fingers covered with red and green sprinkles appeared in his mind.

Mom and I made the best sugar cookies.

He gave a slight shake of his head, trying to dislodge the image. "I'm gathering data to make a decision. I need each of you to stop by my office at some point today. It will take about five minutes."

Silence.

"All right, people. Do your thing here, but do it fast. There's plenty of work to be done."

Mitchell returned to his office. He sat and stared out the window while he finished his coffee. The sky was heavy with low-hanging clouds, not a speck of blue in sight. A snow sky. He closed his eyes, and a faceless snowman appeared. His mother stood beside the stacked boulders of snow, her hands full of items to create a face. He'd had magical holidays when his mother had been alive. His father had been a different man before her death. And when she died, he lost him, too.

A light tap on the door pulled him to the present.

"Mr. Lang, is this a good time?"

He stood. "Liz, come in and leave the door ajar. By the way, my uncle is Mr. Lang. Call me Mitchell."

"All right, Mitchell. What information do you need from me?" She sat in the chair situated in front of his desk.

He reclaimed his seat. "I was surprised that no one came to speak with me after my announcement on Tuesday. So, I decided to ask a few questions. Thank you for getting the ball rolling."

"You're welcome. Probably the reason you had no response to your offer was Georgette advised everyone to let the news sink in and for some to take a cooling-off period before discussing anything with you."

"I see." Mitchell pick up a pen, rolled it between his hands. "So, these short meetings will accomplish two things. I'll learn a few things about everyone. And since some time has passed, those with something to say will get their chance. "

Liz crossed her legs. Placed her hands on her knee. "What exactly did you want to learn about me?"

Green eyes searched his face.

Everything.

It took an effort to pull his gaze away. He focused on the folder in front of him. "Specifically, I want to know what plans I've derailed since announcing we'll be working on the holiday."

"How will that help you get to know me?"

"If you had a ski trip planned, I'd know you like to ski. Maybe you're missing dinner with your eighty-year-old great-aunt whom you've spent the last ten Christmases with so she wouldn't be alone. I'd see that you are loyal, maybe lack a sense of adventure, but have a kind heart."

"I had plans to fly home and spend Christmas with my mother."

"Where's home?"

"A small town you've probably never heard of.

Jubilee, Georgia."

"What are your plans now for the twenty-fifth?"

Her fingers curled into her palms. "I had this conversation with my mother last night. I volunteer at the Man's Best Friend rescue center. I'll offer to help my friends with the feedings so they can have some time away from the kennel."

"You like dogs. Nice. I'm sorry you canceled your plans with your mother."

"I *didn't* have a choice."

"Would you have considered resigning because of the change?"

"I was upset enough, but I've offered my bonus to the dog shelter. My dad taught me always to follow through, keep my promises."

"So, you were going home to visit your mother. Your dad doesn't live in Jubilee?'

Liz rubbed the back of her neck. "Not anymore. Do you have other questions?"

"Not right now. Thank you."

In the evening, Mitchell sat at his desk perusing the notes he had taken during the day. He leaned back in his chair and sighed. Twenty Christmases without his mother. He had learned to live without the anticipation of special days. To live without the holiday activities. To live without the family gatherings. Eventually, all holidays lost their uniqueness. Another sunrise and sunset, with nothing special about the time in between.

He picked up the piece of paper—a list of each employees' family sacrifice. And for what? To maintain the account of an old man who didn't care about holidays or family time.

He had never seen himself as someone like Mr. Ramsden. Cold. Distant. Selfish.

Maybe that's how most of his employees sized him up. Not Georgette. Not Liz. Maybe Eric was right—he had a spot to fill in his life. But was Derrick right, too? Should he renege on the completion date and give his employees the time off they deserved?

The time he deserved?

Chapter Five

Mitchell strode down the hall with a determined stride on his way to a meeting. His mind kept circling back to his conversation with Eric. Telling him he'd be lucky to find someone like Dottie… and it wouldn't happen without some action from Mitchell.

He stopped outside Liz's cubicle. A cinnamony scent circulated in her section of office space. A quick flash of his mother stirring the same aromatic concoction on the stove at Christmastime zipped through his brain. An image of her homemade apple pie. He smiled at the memory.

"Good morning, Liz."

She looked up. Troubled eyes met his gaze. Troubled eyes alluding to something awry in her life. Troubled eyes suggesting she could use a friend.

She straightened. "Mitchell. Can I help you?"

I want to spend time with you. Eric would be proud.

"Do you have your bimonthly budget report ready?"

"We usually give those to Janice on the fifteenth and the thirtieth of the month."

"Great. I'd like to see it, too. Can you bring a copy by my office?"

She shuffled some papers on her desk. "I can give you one now."

"I'm on my way out. Bring it by at two o'clock."

"Will do."

That afternoon, Mitchell motioned Liz into his office when she tapped on the open door. He continued his phone conversation while she chose the chair she had occupied yesterday.

He studied her heart-shaped face. She smiled. An obligatory smile, unlike the usual bubbly beams that jolted his heart. He ended the call. Reserved, she pushed the report toward him. He missed her usual cheerfulness. "I've been thinking about how we met."

"Ahh. Dousing a stranger with hot coffee. Phenomenal."

"A surefire way to get someone's attention."

"Unless it was an accident." Liz's eyes widened. "You *do* know it was an accident?"

Mitchell propped his elbow on the desk, rested his chin in his hand. "Yes, I know it was an accident. Therefore, we need a do-over. Let me take you to dinner."

Liz pursed her lips. After a pause, she asked, "Tonight?"

His hand fell away. Mitchell receded into his chair. He had wanted to hear 'yes' with a capital Y. With heartfelt yearning. Why hadn't he considered that a beautiful woman like Liz might be in a relationship? Or maybe she was stinging from crushed holiday plans. "You're busy."

"Previous commitment. The same place I spend all my Friday evenings."

Boyfriend.

"Some other time, maybe." He tried without success to keep the disappointment from coloring his words.

Liz stood. "Do you like dogs?"

"That's a strange, out-of-the-blue question."

"But your answer does not have to be in the form of a question."

Mitchell smiled. "A Jeopardy fan." He had managed to rekindle the glow on her face. "I don't have anything against them. Just that one big dog that pushed me to the ground when I was four and made me think he was going to eat me."

"Oh. I was going to ask if you'd like to go with me to Man's Best Friend. Maybe it's not such a good idea."

Something that happened twenty-seven years ago isn't keeping me from spending time with you. Even if I have to share you with some dogs.

"It's a great idea. Can't think of a better way to spend my evening." He squinted his eyes. "You don't have any huge dogs there?"

"You never know. But since I like you, I'll make sure the big ones stay in their cages."

"I'll be ready."

****

Liz stepped into the dog shelter with Mitchell

following behind.

"Hi, Curt." The indoor warmth prompted her to remove and pocket her gloves. "I didn't expect to see you. Curt, this is Mitchell Lang. He's helping me tonight. Mitchell, this is Curt Talbot. He and his sister, Courtney opened Man's Best Friend about three years ago."

The men exchanged a handshake. A barking-dogs rendition of "Jingle Bells" played in the background. Mitchell grinned. "I like your choice of music."

"It's great, but I can only play it when Courtney's not around."

"Where is she?" Liz asked.

"Primping for a date. I'm doing my brotherly part to support her social life. I took her shift tonight."

"I knew it; chivalry is not dead. My mother will be pleased to hear this."

Curt laughed. "Now I impress older women when I'd rather dazzle daughters."

Liz laughed. "How many furbabies do we have tonight?"

"We're up to eleven."

"Please tell me that number includes Tallulah."

"Yep, she's still here."

She touched Mitchell's arm. "You've got to meet her. Follow me to the lounge, and then we'll take her to the exercise area.

Once Liz had the dog engaged in a game of fetch, she

looked up at Mitchell. He smiled and moved to stand beside her. When the dachshund returned with the tennis ball, Mitchell squatted, took it from her mouth, and threw it.

He straightened. "This is a nice facility. How often do you volunteer?"

"Tuesday and Friday nights. I love coming here."

Tallulah returned, and Liz picked her up for a cuddle. "Too bad my Mom doesn't live here. You'd be a good dog for her."

Liz focused on Mitchell. "Spending time with these sweet dogs helps melt away tension. Tunes out the sadness for a while." She sat the animal on the floor and tossed the ball.

"That probably goes both ways. The dogs are no doubt happy when you're here."

Curt approached with a collie. "Let's swap out and give Scotty some time in open space."

Liz took the dog's leash. Curt retrieved Tallulah. "When you're finished with Scotty, I'll have dinner ready to go."

"Sounds good." She watched for signs of distress from Mitchell, but he knelt by the dog. Talking in a soothing tone, he rubbed the animal's back. She unhooked the leash. He tossed the ball, and the collie barked and dashed after it.

"Well, Mitchell. I'd say this do-over thing is working

okay for you. Not so much for me."

He stood and frowned. "I don't understand."

"You've learned several things about me yesterday, but the only thing I've discovered about you is you're more comfortable around my furry friends than I thought you'd be. And after that sad story about a dog knocking you down."

"Let's fix it. Go to dinner with me."

Warmth spread throughout her body. A disloyal emotion. Mitchell Lang had ruined her Christmas plans.

The collie dropped the ball at Mitchell's feet and began barking. He tossed it, then turned and faced Liz.

"Today I learned you're from Georgia, you were going to spend Christmas with your mother, and you've pledged your bonus to this amazing animal shelter. Go to dinner with me, and we'll even the score. I'll tell you two things about me."

Maybe I meant what I said to Mom. He's doing the best he can for the business. Perhaps it warrants getting to know him better.

"Two things for the three you know about me? How is that even?"

"I told you my dog story. Dinner?"

Unable to resist his charm, Liz nodded and smiled.

After finishing the volunteer duties, they walked briskly for three blocks to Romano's Italian Bistro, a restaurant Liz had never experienced. When Mitchell suggested Italian fare, she recalled one other restaurant nearby. A romantic ambiance enhanced by low lighting, excellent wine, beautiful music. An opportunity for quiet, even intimate conversation. Definitely not a first-date place. Would Romano's provide the same atmosphere?

Her concerns fell away when they entered the cheerful space. Red and white checkered tablecloths dressed up with white daisies in black coffee cups shouted casual. Distressed wood chairs appeared worn with longevity. The aroma of homemade Italian recipes made the little out-of-the-way eatery a knockout choice.

They settled in with wine to wait for their food.

Beep.

Liz caught a momentary flash of unease rush across Mitchell's face. "Go ahead, check your message. I'm going to the Ladies' Room."

She returned to find two steaming plates of food that rivaled the looks of her mother's home cooking. "Everything all right?"

"All good. Let's eat."

Liz watched Mitchell expertly twirl spaghetti around his fork. The main reason she'd ordered her eggplant parmesan without the side of pasta—unruly spaghetti and no patience to deal with it in front of this man who caused an explosion of goose bumps each time she encountered him.

She took a bite of her entrée, savoring the flavors.

After waking this morning to the sad memory of canceling her airplane ticket, she'd had no hope of ending her evening this pleasantly. With Mitchell, who made her heart race whenever she settled her gaze on his magnificent, green eyes. Green like a field in Ireland.

Liz wiped her mouth and returned her napkin to her lap. "Thank you for insisting on dinner after feeding the canines. I didn't have time to shop last weekend, so my choices tonight would have been a frozen dinner or an apple with peanut butter crackers."

"I'm glad you said yes. I don't care to eat alone in public. Shopping"—he gave a quick headshake—"not my thing, so carry out is usually the way I play it."

"I guess single life can't always be one hundred percent appealing."

"I'm not sure there's anything out there that's perfect. A friend recently told me to look for things that bring joy. I enjoyed helping with the dogs."

"One day I found that stray dog, and I discovered a void in my life I hadn't been willing to acknowledge. Because of my apartment regulations, I did the next best thing to fill the void. Careful, Mitchell. You might get hooked, and then you'd have to become a volunteer, too. Or adopt a small dog."

Mitchell laughed. "I think my mom was more traumatized than me. I've had no problems interacting with dogs."

"That's great. Now let's get down to business. The reason I agreed to dinner."

"What two things do you want to know?"

"What kind of work did you do before winding up temporary CEO of the company? Will they take you back?"

He laid his fork aside. "I'm a business coach. I freelance, so stepping in to help family wasn't as difficult as being employed by someone."

Liz smiled sheepishly.

"You have one question left. Make it a good one."

She had never experienced such a pull to a man. Enticing. Magnetic. And she wanted to connect.

"What are you doing for Christmas?"

Chapter Six

Mitchell gave up on sleep a full hour before the alarm sounded at five o'clock. The tension in his stomach was a signal to finally settle the internal dispute that had plagued his weekend.

His mental struggle had started Friday night with Liz's Christmas question at dinner. He'd said, "Christmas is just another day." That refrain had played in his head intermittently long after their evening ended. Now he wasn't sure that was true. Everywhere he looked, the holiday season caught his attention. Memories surfaced. Thoughts of spending the twenty-fifth day of the month alone caused an emptiness he could no longer ignore. What was happening to him?

He spent the weekend grappling with how he had forced his indifference toward Christmas upon his employees in the form of work. Work that would keep them from their family festivities. It wasn't right. Then the business side of his struggle kicked in. If he revoked his decision, the company would miss lucrative work.

He sat on the side of the bed, pushed a hand through rumpled hair. The recent memories of his mother prodded him to remember the past. Town celebrations, presents under the Christmas tree, gathering with his family. His employees would miss sharing the holiday season with their loved ones unless he agreed with Derrick and reversed his decision about the Ramsden project.

A fresh image of Liz surfaced. Dressed in red standing by a Christmas tree. Laughing. Blissful. Content.

His conflict ended.

A spark of energy pushed him upright. He stepped into the shower. This morning he would inform everyone that Lang Renovations, Inc. would close for the holidays. He would prefer to deliver this kind of news in person, but his schedule wouldn't permit it today. And he wanted to announce it ASAP.

"Email it is, and Merry Christmas to all."

****

With her hands wrapped around her favorite cup, Liz settled in the office chair and sipped her peppermint tea. Thoughts of Mitchell brought sadness.

He doesn't celebrate Christmas.

Georgette stepped into the cubicle. "Bless that young man's heart."

"Who?"

"Mitchell. Haven't you seen his email? Quick, pull it up." Georgette shifted foot-to-foot while Liz read silently.

"Is this legit?"

The smile on Georgette's face fell away. "Oh, I don't know why it wouldn't be."

"Neither do I." Liz jumped up and hugged her friend.

"I'm going home! I'm as excited as a kid on Christmas morning. Don't know if I'll be able to concentrate today."

"Your mother will be delighted. It's going to be a merry Christmas after all. But time off means I'd better get to work."

"See you later."

Liz sat. What had made him change his mind? She wanted to discover things about Mitchell Lang. The positives were adding up. He liked dogs, and he *wasn't* a Scrooge.

She hurried to his office and found darkness. She winced and stood by the door until Mitchell's assistant ended her phone conversation.

"Need something, Liz?"

"I wanted to see Mitchell. Will he be in soon?"

"He has several meetings off-site. If he returns, it will be later in the afternoon."

Disappointment at the news caught her off guard, caused her chest to tighten. Not only was he hot, but Mitchell had also shown his compassionate side more than once. Falling for him was not a good idea. He told everyone from day one this was only temporary, and he'd be moving on.

Falling for him would be a *huge* mistake.

****

Mitchell hurried to the door when Liz passed by his office. Yesterday, he had missed seeing her and her reaction to his email. He called her name. She turned in his direction. He was gut-punched by her red eyes and cheeks.

She swiped at her right eye. "Did you need something, Mitchell?"

"Yes, step inside."

She hesitated then walked into his office, choosing to stand as if holding an enemy at bay.

"I can't *not* notice that you're upset. I'd like to help if possible."

She crossed her arms. "There's nothing you or anyone can do. I canceled my plane ticket to Georgia when you altered our holiday schedule. Now the airlines are booked, probably overbooked. So, I guess I'm spending Christmas in New York."

Before he could reply, she exited the office. A sudden coldness hit at his core. How could he fix this? He circled back to his desk and picked up the phone.

"When you have a minute, would you stop by my office?"

He rubbed his eyes as if the action would erase what had just happened. A knock on the door claimed his attention. "Come in, Georgette."

She stepped inside.

Mitchell pushed the door to an almost-closed position. "Have you seen Liz today?"

"Yes. She's having a rough time."

"It's physically evident. When I asked Liz if I could

help, she said there was nothing anyone can do. Then she hurried away."

"She wants to go home for Christmas."

"Can't she drive to Georgia? Of course, that would take longer, but she'd make it home for Christmas."

"It's complicated, Mitchell. Liz will have to tell why. If you don't need me for anything else, I have plenty of work." She turned at the door. "For both your sakes, talk to her. Today."

Mitchell decided the office was not the place for this conversation. That evening, he stood at Liz's apartment door. Was he crossing the line coming to her home? The memory of Georgette's words pushed him to knock.

After a few minutes of silence and then another knock, the door opened. "What are you doing here?"

Mitchell's heartbeat raced when he was confronted by sharp words, red eyes, a splotchy face. He had to fix this. Holding out his hand, Mitchell said, "Please don't shut me out. I know you're angry with me, but I may have found a way to make this up to you."

Avoiding eye contact, Liz gave a deep, weighted sigh. She stepped back, opened the door wider.

Restlessness took control as Mitchell crossed the threshold. His confidence wavered when he realized he didn't know her situation. What had made him decide he could offer a solution to her troubles?

Liz pointed to the sofa, giving a silent invitation to sit

as she chose a lounge chair. "I want to apologize for what I said earlier. My personal life is a mess, my own doing. I should have waited a few days before canceling my ticket."

"Why? I changed your plans. You had no idea—*I* had no idea I would reverse my decision. It's on me."

"It doesn't matter. The result is the same regardless of who's at fault. I have no way to get home for Christmas."

"Do you own a car?"

"Yes, but I won't drive home."

"Can I ask why?"

Liz's eyes became bright, threatening tears. "In March, my father died in a car accident. In atrocious weather. He didn't want his coworker to make a necessary trip to Virginia for family business alone, so he rode with him. They both died. When I couldn't find a plane ticket, I told my mom I'd drive home. But it upset her. The anguish she would experience waiting hours for me to arrive safely—I won't put her through it."

I need to hug her.

He leaned in. "I'm sorry about your father. Maybe I can help."

"Are you offering to drive me?"

"Better. I'm offering to fly you to Georgia."

"How?" She squeezed her eyes shut for a moment. "What?"

"All you need to know is I'm a pilot with

connections."

"No. You have to give me more than that if you expect me to fly away with you in some small plane. Which I'm not too crazy about doing."

"Flying in a small plane or flying with me?"

"I don't do well in confined spaces."

Mitchell stood. "You're in luck. I know where I might be able to borrow a midsize jet."

"That's got to be a substantial connection. But what if I can't get a flight back by the twenty-seventh?"

"Do you have ingredients for hot chocolate?"

Liz's eyebrows squished together. "Um, hot chocolate?"

He nodded.

"Sorry, the best I can do is instant cocoa."

"Here's the deal—I'll work on borrowing a jet if you'll make the drinks."

"You'd do that for me?"

He placed a hand on her shoulder. "That's what friends do."

She gave a tight smile. "I'll be in the kitchen."

He pulled his phone from his pocket. His fingers shook while he punched Eric's name on his contact list.

"I need a huge favor." Mitchell took precious seconds to close his eyes and take a calming breath. "First let me say this. Liz may not be Dottie, but I'd do anything for her."

"That's something worth hearing," Eric said.

"I need your Learjet to fly Liz home for Christmas—and probably back a few days later."

"Done."

"Don't you want details? I only have a couple of minutes to talk."

"Call me later, and we'll work out the specifics. Merry Christmas, Mitchell."

Staring at his phone, he pushed out a relief-filled breath. "Okay."

Waiting for Liz, he gazed around the room. Christmas was present but not overwhelming. Swags of fresh evergreen garland dressed the front of the mantel, anchored by large red bows on each end. A tree in the corner boasted bright lights and colorful ornaments. Gas logs glowed. A throw placed just-so over the arm of the sofa brightened by throw pillows with prints of wreaths, bells, and trees.

Liz returned with two cups of cocoa. She placed them on the table and looked at Mitchell with inquisitive eyes."

He slid his phone into his pocket. "Mission accomplished. I borrowed a Learjet.

Liz rushed forward and threw her arms around his neck. "Thank you, thank you, thank you."

His arms reached around her waist. The unexpected embrace felt natural, made him wish for mistletoe. He leaned her away but continued to hold her arms. "Not a problem. I don't have plans."

Liz sought his eyes. "Then you can spend Christmas in Jubilee."

Chapter Seven

On December twenty-first, Liz rolled her suitcase to the front door of her apartment. She slid the matching satchel off her shoulder. The last ten days had sped by with a whirlwind of emotions. Attraction. Anger. Anticipation.

The suggestion that Mitchell remain in Jubilee for Christmas had poured from her mouth before she could stop herself. Once his agreement sank in, she called The Sandpiper, Jubilee's finest B&B. She was grateful they found a spot for Mitchell. Without him, she wouldn't have a chance of getting home for the holidays. And she'd miss out on a prime opportunity to see him in a non-work environment.

She checked and rechecked her hair and makeup, the doorbell finally putting a stop to her primping. She wiped sweaty palms on her jeans before opening the door to her knight. Rather than shining armor, an unbuttoned jacket revealed a red and white plaid shirt, his neck encircled with a green scarf. Blue jeans hugged all the right places and completed the package causing her mouth to go dry.

With great effort, she managed, "Hi."

"Morning." Mitchell stepped inside and proceeded to the sofa.

"What are you doing?"

"Waiting."

She frowned. "Waiting?"

"Aren't you going to make one more run through the apartment checking your curling iron, locks, the gas stove?"

"My curling iron is in my suitcase. I completed my checklist before you got here. I'm all set."

He gave a hearty laugh.

"What?"

"I knew you'd have one; you're so organized at the office."

"You have something against checklists?"

"Not at all. Makes my life easier. I built in time for a run-through, but since you're ready, we have time to talk."

"I'll talk all day long about anything, let's just do it while we're flying to Georgia."

Mitchell stood. "Whatever you say." He picked up her luggage and stepped into the hall, allowing her time to lock the door.

****

Within the hour, they settled in the jet and were airborne. Mitchell gained altitude to rise above the most congested area of the sky. Finally cruising at 41,000 feet, he glanced in Liz's direction.

Dazed, mouth open, hand to heart.

Crap. She's going to flip out.

He tried for his best soothing tone. "You okay?"

"The sky, it's all around me. It's incredible!"

Relief washed through him. He'd never dealt with a panicked passenger and didn't want to figure it out today. "A bit different from staring out a little window back there. So, you like your seat assignment?"

She turned toward him, a big smile on her face. "Best one on the plane. How long have you been a pilot?"

"I got my license eight, no, nine years ago. I was twenty-two. Do you fly much?"

"Once in my childhood, more since I moved to New York."

"You didn't like flying when you were a kid, and now you do?"

"I flew for the first time when I was fourteen. My family took a trip to Ireland. Mom's lifelong dream. I did fine on the flight. My father did not like to fly, but he loved my mother. So, he put her wish before his anxiety. Our extended family is within reasonable driving distance, so there was never any reason to fly. Ireland being the exception."

"It sounds like your father had a big heart." Not like his dad's that had shrunk when Mitchell had needed him most.

"He did. And I'm not putting him on a pedestal when I say that. He showed me by his actions and his reaction to life."

Silence followed while Mitchell gave his attention to the instrument panel. He settled back in his seat for the next leg of the flight.

Pulling her phone from her purse, Liz slid her finger across the screen. She held up her phone. "My dad and me at my graduation from Parsons School of Design."

"You have his eyes. That's a good picture."

"Thanks. Why aren't you spending Christmas with your family?"

Mitchell drew in a deep breath. He wasn't naïve. He'd known the questions about family would come, and there wasn't a good or bad time to talk about it.

"I haven't celebrated Christmas for over a decade."

"I kinda thought so by your declaration that Christmas is just another day. Don't you want to spend time with your family?"

"My mother died when I was thirteen. After that, my dad worked all the time. We don't spend time together now."

She touched his arm. " I'm sorry, Mitchell."

She was invading territory he didn't want to visit. "Tell me about Jubilee. If I'm going to spend the next few days there, I want to know what to expect."

Her eyes sparkled with excitement. "Jubilee is the best place to be at Christmastime. Sadly, we missed the parade. It's always on the second Saturday of December. And the cookie-baking contest is over. And the tree lighting in the town square has been done." The sparkle fizzled.

He took her hand and squeezed. "That just gives you more time to visit with family and friends."

"There's that and the live Nativity at Jubilee Community Church tomorrow night."

"That's the spirit."

"Don't worry. I'll save time for you, too, Mitchell Lang."

****

Forty minutes from the regional airport, the driver dropped Mitchell at the Sandpiper B&B, then Liz at her home on Butler Street. She unpacked and wandered through the quiet house. In the family room, she paused in front of the built-in bookcases that flanked the sides of the original brick fireplace. The left side housed volumes of books. Fictional, biographical, self-help, travel. Her parents had planned to see the world during retirement. A tear caught at the corner of one eye.

That won't happen now.

She shifted to the right side with pictures and other family mementos displayed on the shelves. A visual of her family tree.

The encased American flag that had rested on her grandfather's casket during his funeral service. The last picture of her mom and dad together. She touched the frame gingerly. Pictures she wasn't aware she'd missed until now.

Moving into the kitchen, she found the note on the menu board stating they'd have takeout for supper. She sat at the table and sent a text to her friend, Chelsea: *Made it home. Can't wait to see you at the live Nativity.*

Liz checked the time. "At least three hours until I see Mom." Since setting foot in Jubilee, Liz had experienced an overwhelming urge to see her mother. Unable to wait, she took Uber to PM Monogram Service, her mother's business.

The building stood in the historic area of Jubilee. A two-story brick structure that began as a department store in the 1940s, it occupied the space where Jubilee's first saloon had stood in the late 1800s. Liz loved the history of their town. Even if she had remained here, she'd never learn of all its past, as far back to its humble beginning as an English settlement.

She opened the door quietly and put a finger to her lips when her mother's assistant opened her mouth to speak. "Is my mother on a conference call?"

The young woman shook her head.

"Tell her you have a customer with a complaint who wants to speak with the owner."

Liz moved closer as her mother stepped from her office. Her heart filled with love.

"I'm sorry—" Her mother looked around, then rushed to Liz and folded her in a hug. She pulled back to look at her then hugged her again. "I'm so glad you're home, Lizzy!"

"Me, too, Mom."

"Sharon, make us all a cup of tea, please."

"None for me," Liz said.

Her mother smiled. "Such a nice surprise. I was expecting a disgruntled customer, but I got you instead."

"Thanks to my boss. I'll tell you all about it tonight. And no takeout for dinner, I'm cooking."

"When am I going to meet the young man who granted my Christmas wish?"

"I don't know, Mom. Mitchell's staying at the B&B. He said he was going to enjoy the downtime. I don't think we should disturb him."

Mom settled her hands on her hips. "Elizabeth. Anne. Marshall. Invite him to supper. It's the least we can do."

I wouldn't mind seeing Mitchell again.

Liz slapped her hands together. "I've got to go. See you tonight."

"Since you're preparing dinner, I'll bring dessert."

"Sounds good." She kissed her mom on the cheek and hurried out the door.

At six o'clock, Liz pulled a corn casserole from the oven. She stirred ingredients of her signature dish in a large saucepan, pleased that she would be introducing Mitchell to the wonders of Southern comfort food. Mom walked into the kitchen carrying a handled brown bag.

"It smells heavenly, Liz. Did you get in touch with Mitchell?"

"Yes, he'll be here for dinner."

Because she couldn't keep the smile from her face, she turned her back to her mother and placed the lid on the large saucepan. Being back in Jubilee gave Liz joy. Spending the evening in Mitchell's presence, euphoria. "What's for dessert?"

"I called The Bread Box bakery after you left this afternoon, and by the end of my day, a peach cobbler was delivered to my office."

"Perfect."

When the doorbell rang, her mom pushed her out of the kitchen. Liz smoothed her hair before turning the doorknob. Mitchell stood before her. The collar of a red button-down shirt peeked above the V-neck of a gray sweater. Black denim jeans completed the non-boss look. His face wore the universal sign of happiness accompanied by a light layer of facial hair that screamed sexy, in contrast to his usual clean-cut look. Green eyes twinkled a holly-jolly message.

Liz's heartbeat galloped. "Please, come in."

"Thanks. Let's get one thing clear. I don't expect you to spend your time in Jubilee cooking meals for me."

Mom joined them in the family room. "Nonsense. We eat, too."

"Mitchell, meet my mother, Peggy Marshall. Mom,

this is Mitchell Lang."

"We're happy to share our supper with you. Come in, and we'll get started. I'm famished."

He held out a poinsettia plant in a white wicker basket. "For you, Mrs. Marshall. A thank you for the invitation. And for you, Liz, I thought you might like to store pictures of your trip home."

She accepted the album covered with vintage fabric of a snowy scene. A beautiful church decorated with evergreen wreaths on its doors surrounded by trees dressed in snow. A sparkly red ribbon with a pearl center completed the holiday look. Liz opened it. "Oh, it's a journal, too. How thoughtful. Thank you, Mitchell."

"Yes, thank you, Mitchell." Mom set the plant on the sofa table. "I'm going to check on dinner." She hurried away.

Liz stared at the potted plant and sighed. "Ohhh."

"Something's wrong." His forehead wrinkled. "Is your mother allergic to poinsettias?"

Liz walked to the fireplace. She turned the key on the side of the hearth, lowering the flame of the gas logs. Facing Mitchell, she said, "My dad always brought her a poinsettia for Christmas."

"Great. I've upset your mom. Maybe I should go."

"No, please stay. She'll feel even worse if you leave."

Mom returned, picked up her hostess gift, and carried it to the dining room. Liz motioned for Mitchell to follow, and she watched Mom place the gift in the middle of the table.

"Lizzy, I've put everything in serving dishes. Would you help me?"

"My hands are empty. Let me help, too," Mitchell said.

Minutes later, they settled around a table filled with fried green tomatoes, chicken and dumplings, corn casserole, and a pitcher of sweet tea. Liz and Mitchell sat across from each other. Mom sat between them at the head of the table.

"I've heard about Southern cooking. It smells great."

"Never been south of the Mason-Dixon line? Here, try the tomatoes, one of my favorite dishes."

"Thanks, Mrs. Marshall." He took the serving plate from her. "D.C. is the farthest south I've been. Most of my travels have been west."

"I'm glad bringing me home is expanding your horizons geographically."

"Mmm. Liz, these dumplings are the best I've tasted in the longest time. Mitchell, what do you think?"

"Delicious. I don't experience home cooking too often."

"We're all one-person dwellers, right? I know I don't cook as often as I used to." Mom set her fork aside. She touched one of the red poinsettia's petals.

"About the plant. I wouldn't have brought it if I'd

known it would make you sad."

Mom smiled, her eyes glistening. "Not sad at all. Maybe this is my husband's way of making sure I got my poinsettia this year."

Liz fought back tears. Unable to talk, she squeezed her mother's hand.

"Now, Mitchell, as long as you're expanding your experiences, we need to make sure you see the sights of Christmas in Jubilee. I'm sure Liz can come up with a perfect itinerary for you."

"Muth-er. I'm sure Mitchell can Google 'Jubilee' and find some things he'd like to do."

"Maybe so, but I would think, as a thank you for bringing you home, you'd be willing to show him around our lovely town. I know he could go with you to the live Nativity tomorrow night."

"I thought we were going together."

"We were, but Reverend Angela needed some last minute help." She raised her shoulders, her palms outstretched. "What was I supposed to do?"

Liz rolled her eyes at Mom. "Fine." Throwing a smile covered in Southern sweetness at Mitchell, she asked, "Would you like to go with me to the live Nativity tomorrow night?" She watched him struggle to hold back his laughter.

"Sure, that could be interesting. We can work out the details tomorrow."

"Who's ready for dessert? I brought home the best peach cobbler in the state of Georgia."

"Best in the state? I can't pass on that," Mitchell said.

When Mom left the room, Liz placed her hands on the table and leaned in. "I'm sorry about that. You don't have to go."

"Sure I do. After bringing a poinsettia that reminded both of you of your loss, I'm going to do whatever she asks me to do."

Mom returned with a serving tray. "Here we are. Mitchell, I hope you like yours with a scoop of vanilla ice cream. Did I miss anything?"

"No, Mom. You're up to speed."

But you could stop pushing.

Chapter Eight

On Saturday at dusk, Mitchell left his room at the Sandpiper B&B to wait for Liz. Spending time with her came with a price tag of sitting outdoors and watching a play with a religious focus. But, he was willing to pay the price. He hadn't been in a church since his mother's funeral. He wasn't against religion, just hadn't made it a part of his adult life.

He had spent the earlier part of the day without direction, watching polite Southerners move at a pace as slow as the disgusting molasses he'd seen other diners pour on their pancakes that morning. It made the time until he'd see Liz seem twice as long, but also gave him time to ponder his situation. Specifically, missing out on the opportunity Eric had extended to him, something he wanted. The upside, and he always tried to find the positive in a given situation, was he'd remain in the same city with Liz until Derrick returned. Maybe after he left Lang Renovations, they would continue to see each other. Socially instead of professionally.

He spotted Liz walking up the sidewalk, a blanket in her arms, he stepped out onto the porch. "I'm ready for this Jubilee tradition. How about you?"

"I'm here, aren't I?"

He reached the bottom of the stairs and took the blanket from her. "Why the frown?"

"I don't need my mother playing social secretary for me."

"So you're irritated because you didn't ask me first?"

Liz crossed her arms. "I'm an adult. If I want to ask you out, I'll…ask you out."

And I'm glad you did.

They walked two blocks in silence. Arriving at the meadow by the church, they worked together to spread the blanket on the ground among the crowd. The noise level, appropriate for such a large gathering, came to an abrupt halt when the narrator began reading the Gospel of Luke. A spotlight appeared in the night following Mary, settled on the back of a donkey, and Joseph. The children's choir began singing "O Little Town of Bethlehem."

"Kudos to whoever found an animal that knows how to follow a script."

"Tabby does a great job with her four-legged menagerie."

The children continued to sing while the Holy Family approached their destination. As the innkeeper began to speak, a crack cut off his words. Streaks of sparks lit up the sky. Shouts exploded from the spectators. The donkey brayed, forgot the script, and ran headlong into the audience.

People scurried, some lawn chairs overturned. More popping sounds cut through the confusion.

One kid shouted, "Hey, that's not in our script!"

Mitchell turned to help steady a Jubilee senior in her chair.

"Dang!"

When he heard Liz's ladylike expletive, he refocused and watched as she rubbed her ankle. "What happened?"

"I didn't scramble fast enough, got kicked. At least it wasn't the donkey that got me."

"Here, let me." He took her left ankle between his hands and gently massaged. His gaze connected with hers. His massage was intended to be platonic, but it felt like more.

Reverend Angela's voice sounded through the microphone. "Please remain calm. The donkey's safely out of the way. Lights, shift to the audience so they can reseat themselves. If everyone will please indulge us for ten minutes, we'll regroup, then continue with the play."

"Thanks, it feels better now," Liz said.

Mitchell released her ankle and they settled to watch the remainder of the production.

When the last song ended, the crowd gathered their things. Heaviness pressed inside his body. Disappointment ensued that their night together was ending soon. Mitchell and Liz folded the blanket. They had walked a block when Liz began limping.

"You're not good. How far away is your car?"

"Two more blocks. I can make it."

When they arrived, Liz settled into the driver's seat while Mitchell walked around the car and slid into the passenger side. He had hoped to arrange more time together, but that might not be possible if her ankle was injured. The ride to the B&B was short and quiet.

Liz shifted the gear to park. "I'm glad you got to experience a little of Jubilee tonight."

"Sorry about your ankle."

She smiled. "I'm glad I came, even though I was kicked."

Mitchell exited the car. "Take care of yourself. Night." He waited until she drove away before turning toward the stairs.

A yawn overtook him. Hours spent lackadaisically made for a long day when he was used to working from morning until night. And besides the recent dinner with Eric, he couldn't recall the last time he'd been out with friends. But he'd had two big jobs back-to-back that had lasted seven months without a break.

Mitchell stopped at the door to his room and stood stock-still.

"I've become my father." His stomach clenched at the realization.

"No way in hell."

****

Liz popped the last bite of waffle into her mouth. Homemade waffles created by Mom. "You're spoiling me."

"If I do it well enough, maybe you'll want to move back home."

She bit her lower lip.

"Don't listen to me," Mom said. "Selfish thoughts."

"I know it's hard, being here without Dad."

Mom brushed Liz's hair off her shoulder. "True, but this is my life now."

The urge to move back home intensified. If she returned to Jubilee, she'd know for sure how her mom was coping.

"How are you, Mom?"

"I have my lonely periods. And sometimes I have to push myself. At least going to church helps me find peace. So, let's get going."

"Just have to slip on my dress. I'll be down in ten."

An Epsom salts soak last night left her ankle feeling fine this morning. Hopefully, it would remain that way after wearing her favorite three-inch heeled boots to church.

On the drive into town, Mom said, "Lizzy, I'm happy you're home." The words hung in the air.

"I hear a 'but' coming. What is it, Mom?"

Silence.

"Just tell me."

"When you called to say you'd be staying in New York for Christmas, I volunteered to spend my Sunday evening at Fancy Bluff Retirement Community. I'm sorry."

"No need to be sorry. Just tell me we're having Christmas Eve dinner together with Aunt Marge and Violet."

"Of course we are! Haven't missed a Christmas Eve with them for at least a decade."

And now both Marshall brothers are gone.

"Good, it wouldn't feel right if my cousin and aunt weren't here."

Lunch followed church, and afterward, Mom chose to nap. Liz decided on one more round of Epsom salts. While her ankle soaked in the warm water, she flipped through the *Jubilee Journal*, the local newspaper. It had diminished in size but still carried the flavor of Jubilee in its words about the small town and its inhabitants. On the last page, she read about the caroling-in-the-square event scheduled for that night.

With the right person, that could be fun. Does Mitchell do Christmas carols if he hasn't done Christmas in ages? Probably not.

"Maybe it's time he started."

Chapter Nine

Mitchell had learned one thing for sure during this trip: downtime wasn't his deal. Maybe when he reached his seventies or eighties? His attempt to sleep in on Sunday morning had been a bust, and he'd left the warmth of his bed at nearly half past six to brush his teeth. After dressing, he added a blue jacket and an orange ball cap, a total Mets guy. Now he was ready to greet Jubilee in the early morning hour and make up for the past two days of not working out.

Astonished that the road leading to the town square was traffic-free, Mitchell jogged and was also amazed how the air was devoid of noise. Back home, his environment could be described as boisterous or raucous, but never quiet. He could close it away with double-paned windows, but still, it was always there.

Since the beginning of his run, he'd heard only a lone seagull cawing in the morning air. He did two laps around the square, finally stopping to rest in front of a huge Christmas tree. He bent over, hands on thighs, pulling in deep breaths.

His family had made annual trips to Rockefeller Center to see the Christmas tree. Except for that last year.

His mom had been too sick to travel, and he had never been back since.

Mitchell straightened. "Wonder how it looks all lit up."

He turned and started back through the square. The town started waking up. More than one person had waved or said hello before he turned down the street toward The Sandpiper B&B.

Jogging up the steps, Mitchell stopped to greet the owner, sweeping the porch.

"How are you liking our town, Mr. Lang?"

"It's great. Saw some fireworks last night."

The old man laughed. "You went to the live Nativity. It's not usually that rowdy. Had a couple of ill-mannered preteens disrupt Reverend Angela's production."

"It did liven things up. Hey, I'm looking for a unique place for lunch today. Any suggestions?"

"If you want different, try the Woodsman's Grill down by the pier. They have a variety-type menu and some specialties, too."

"Thanks for the tip."

At half past one, Mitchell entered a log cabin adorned with preserved animal heads on the walls and light fixtures encircled with antlers. Trying something new trumped eating alone. The menu offerings yielded the usual. On the back cover, he saw the wild game listings. Frog legs, gator bites, wild boar burger, fried quail. He'd had bison burgers out West, wasn't too sure about frog or gator. Quail might not be too bad.

When the waitress inquired, Mitchell said, "I'll have the wild boar burger. And a beer."

An old man with a salt and pepper beard approached. "Now that's what I call a man's lunch. Name's Roy Snider." He held out his hand. Mitchell accepted.

"Nice to see a new face in this old place. Traveling through or planning to stay around?"

"I'm here for a few days, then home."

"Enjoy your stay. If you get a chance, you should ride through the wetlands at sunrise. God's gift for sure."

"Thanks, I might do that."

The man walked away, his gait aided by the use of a cane. Mitchell did a quick check of his emails and then set his phone aside when the waitress appeared with his meal.

"Give me a shout if you need anything else."

"Thanks." He studied the food, cocked an eyebrow at meat that was a bit darker than any burger he'd ever eaten. Mitchell breathed and took a bite. A juicy cross between pork and beef greeted his taste buds. The beer proved to be a perfect complement to the burger.

Well, he'd gambled on lunch and come out a winner. Would he be as lucky as Eric if he gave a relationship a chance? Things probably shouldn't cross the friend line with Liz until after Derrick took over the business. But they could continue to get to know each other.

He swallowed his last bite of wild boar burger as his phone rang.

Liz.

Maybe luck *was* on his side.

"Hi there. How's the ankle?"

"Perfect. No more limping."

"That's good news. Since you've recovered, I'd like to ask a favor."

"Okay."

"I want to take a gift to my Aunt Nina. I was hoping you'd help me shop for something unique." He held his breath waiting for her answer.

"You're the negotiating type. I think we can work something out. I'll help you shop *if* you'll go with me tonight to the caroling-in-the-square event. They're holding it by the Christmas tree."

"What if I say no?"

"Oh. Well…"

Her disappointed tone caused a pain in his chest. "Just teasing. I saw that tree this morning and wondered how it would look all lit up. Sounds like I'm going to find out."

"Meet me there at five o'clock. We'll have an hour to shop."

"Will do. See you at five."

****

Liz checked her outfit one more time. She enjoyed wearing her Twelve Days of Christmas sweater. Maybe it would inspire Mitchell to sing tonight.

She sighed as realization hit. "He's not going to see my clothes."

They'd have their coats on during the outside event. She grabbed her gloves from the foyer table before heading to her father's car. Her mom had done nothing with it except drive it occasionally. Did it bring her comfort to have his car sitting in the garage?

As she drove, a peace surrounded her, put a smile on her face.

"Thanks, Dad."

The street to the square had been roped off for tonight's event. Because it was early, Liz easily found parking a block from the stores. Sauntering and window-shopping, she made her way to the tree. A pain squeezed her chest when she realized again there would be no shopping with Dad for Mom's Christmas gift this year.

Liz circled to the front of the tree. Her mood lifted when saw Mitchell admiring the twenty-seven-foot holiday creation.

She tapped his shoulder. "Hi there."

"Hey. This may be only a fourth of the size of the tree at Rockefeller Center, but it's just as impressive."

"I love the color scheme. White lights, green and red cardboard chains, gold and red balls. A tree this large needs simplicity."

"I like the gold star with a comet-like tail. Whoever

roped the strings of lights around this monster is a master. There's not a blank spot that I can see."

"Every step is a team effort. The cardboard chains were made by our kids and senior citizens. Wait until dark—the lights are spectacular then. Are you ready to find a gift for Mrs. Lang?"

"Where do we start?"

"I'm taking you to my all-time favorite shop, Everything Peachy and More. You'll have tons of things to choose from."

****

After making a purchase, they left the shop. Mitchell enjoyed witnessing Liz's exhilaration at being home. She accepted hugs, waved at people, bounced on tiptoes. "Thanks for your help. I know Aunt Nina will love the book."

"You didn't need me."

"Yes, I did. I wouldn't walk into a store named Everything Peachy by myself. So, thanks."

Liz smiled. "You're welcome."

Mitchell soon discovered the caroling was a mix of sacred hymns and secular songs. The night started with "Hark! The Herald Angels Sing" and moved on to "Little Drummer Boy," then "Silent Night," and after that, "Deck the Halls."

After a couple of songs Mitchell couldn't resist joining in. He wouldn't have chosen this activity, but he wasn't sorry to be here. Liz had a beautiful voice. Sometimes he stopped singing to listen to her.

With the ending of the tenth song, Mitchell said, "I didn't know this would be a marathon-long night. Your nose is red like Rudolph's. There's got to be coffee or hot chocolate nearby. I see people with steaming cups."

"That would be Roy Snider's concession. He sets it up every year." Her head tilted, eyebrows squished together. "Can you call it a concession stand if he doesn't ask for money? He does accept donations."

"Let's take a break and find Roy." Mitchell put his hand on her elbow, and they started walking. "I could listen to you sing all night. You have a beautiful voice."

"Thank you. I love to sing." Finding Roy's stand, they stepped in line. "I sang a good bit before I moved to New York."

"Where?"

"Weddings, county fairs, funerals. You name it, I sang there."

"Well, hello there, young man. Nice to see you again. Liz, it's good you're home," Roy said.

"Hello, Mr. Snider. We're here for some of your hot chocolate."

"Two cups coming right up. Did you take that ride through the wetlands?'

"No sir, I didn't get the chance." Mitchell pulled a twenty from his wallet and pushed it into the gallon pickle jar marked "DONATIONS."

"Enjoy the rest of your time in Jubilee."

"I'll do that, sir."

Liz waved. "Merry Christmas, Mr. Snider." And it was truly turning out to be a merry holiday season after all. Could she hope that Mitchell enjoyed the change and even liked Jubilee?

Chapter Ten

Liz took short sips of the hot liquid as they walked toward the giant evergreen. "My mother instructed me to invite you to Christmas Eve dinner. Six o'clock."

"So, your mother wants me there."

"I was going to invite you." She gave him a sidelong glance. "Now you know we both want you there."

They stopped at the back of the crowd. Liz joined in singing "White Christmas" and "Frosty the Snowman," then "Winter Wonderland."

"I sense a theme here," Mitchell said.

"Well, if we don't have snow for Christmas, at least we can sing about it."

"I know where Jubilee can borrow all the snow they want."

Liz laughed. "If only that were possible. I do love seeing snow on Christmas morning." Her face sobered. "Even without the snow, I'd move back home."

The director took the microphone from his assistant. "Folks, we're down to our last song. Thanks for coming out tonight, it's been great. Now, everybody join in." He began singing, "We Wish You a Merry Christmas."

When the song ended, the crowd dispersed like molasses waiting to drip from a bottle.. People mingled, the camaraderie remaining long after the last note was sung.

After stopping by the store to reclaim Mitchell's purchase, they started to the car. When they passed by the gazebo in the square, Mitchell stopped. He took Liz's hand and led her to the picture-perfect spot all decked out with evergreen boughs, ribbons and lights.

"Let me take your picture. You can put it in your album."

"I like how you think." She posed and Mitchell took a few shots.

A lady walked up with a child in tow. "Lizzy. I'm so happy your plans have changed. Your mother never said, but I could tell she was sad about your staying in New York for the holidays."

"Hi, Mrs. Wilson. Meet my friend, Mitchell."

"Merry Christmas, Mitchell, and welcome to Jubilee."

"Thank you. Glad to be here."

"Good. Now, you hand me that phone and stand with Liz. I'll snap your picture."

Mitchell's heartbeat kicked up a notch when Liz waved him over. He would remember this moment forever. He joined her at the gazebo.

"Mommm," whined the redheaded boy.

"Hold on, Gunner. Just taking a few pictures for Ms. Liz."

The boy ran backward and cupped his hands around his mouth. "Back up."

Liz and Mitchell did as he said.

"Move up on the steps," he shouted.

Liz looked at Mitchell. He shrugged, and they complied.

"You're under the mistletoe." He let out a belly-busting laugh. "Now you have to kiss her!" he blurted in a singsong fashion.

Liz gazed into Mitchell's eyes.

Mitchell lightly touched her chin, lifting it until their lips met in a sweet, brief kiss. Her heart beat faster than the Little Drummer Boy banged his drum.

When it ended, she caught her breath. Her eyes widened and so did her heart. Then he followed it with a lengthier, toe-curling kiss.

Mrs. Wilson approached. "Maybe Gunner helped after all? Here's your phone, dear." She winked and looked around. "Gunner, let's go."

"Thank you, and Merry Christmas, Mrs. Wilson. Merry Christmas, Gunner."

She had never known the mischief maker was a cherub on the inside.

Mitchell traced her jawline with his fingertips. "I would say the trick is on Gunner."

"You would?" Her heartbeat quickened. Could he be feeling the same rushed giddiness as she?

"Yes, and I don't waste opportunities when I'm standing under mistletoe." He kissed her again.

Warmth flooded her body, followed by a shiver of pleasure. The reasons to remain in Jubilee were mounting. She needed all her fingers and toes to count them.

However, the small Southern town lacked one thing—and he was standing at her side, giving her ammunition to fight the urge to relocate.

But, if she went back to New York because of Mitchell, it wouldn't last. He was leaving in a few months.

Could Jubilee, her family, and friends bring enough joy for her to come home for good? She needed to give this serious deliberation away from the man who lit a fire in her core in near-freezing weather with his kisses.

When they arrived at the B&B, he got out, then leaned his head inside the car. "I had a great time tonight. See you tomorrow."

She wanted to know where things might lead between them. Could strong attraction and lots of like flip into love? Was she already falling and hadn't realized it? Yet falling for him only to have him leave in a few months…that was too bleak to consider.

"Mitchell, I'm giving my three-week notice. I'm moving home to Jubilee."

****

Mitchell stalked to his room. What was she saying? What was she thinking? What was she doing to him?

Taking short, fast breaths, he paced in a circle.

Where had that come from? Liz appeared to enjoy her job. Loved the animals at the shelter. She had been in New York for several years. Why the sudden urge to return to Jubilee permanently?

He rubbed the back of his neck. Had he put too much stock in their blossoming friendship? "Three weeks' notice?"

His agitation turned to disappointment. He had planned using the time he had left at the company to learn even more about Elizabeth Marshall.

He sat, elbows on knees, face in hands. Eric's advice on joy rang in his ears. His offer of a new direction in his life clanged even louder. If Liz followed through with moving back to Georgia, then his first experience at relationship joy would end as well. There would be no time to grow together.

He moved from the chair to the bed, didn't bother to undress. Lying in the quiet darkness, he pictured Liz. Dressed in red standing by a Christmas tree. Laughing. Blissful. Content. The image remained until he fell asleep.

Mitchell rolled over to the brightness of midmorning. Without intending to, he'd slept in. He sat on the edge of the bed, recalling Liz's announcement. Sudden onset of nausea caused him to press his hands to his stomach. He had to find the words to change her mind.

But a small voice told him her decision was smart.

There was no guarantee their spending time together would develop into a lasting romantic relationship. And he was leaving the company. Leaving White Plains in a few months.

She hadn't given her reasons for moving home. Mitchell was sure part of it was for her mother. After losing his at such a young age, and essentially losing his father, too, he could understand her desire to move home.

What a mess. Three weeks of pretending things were top-notch. Could he get used to the idea of no Liz at work? He couldn't go to dinner tonight and act as though everything was okay when he felt the complete opposite.

He picked up his phone and sent her a text: *I won't be able to make it to dinner this evening. Please give my regrets to your mother. We're set to fly out tomorrow at three o'clock. I'll pick you up at two.*

****

Liz awoke on December twenty-fourth, the excitement of Christmas zipping through her as though she were a child. Then it hit her. Again.

Our first Christmas without Dad.

The ache of that loss mingled with a newly discovered joy. Mitchell's presence in Jubilee had provided a diversion from her sadness. Her exhilaration wasn't about Christmas. It was all about seeing Mitchell today.

Guilt pinched her heart. How could she allow this

elation when Mom was feeling the opposite?

Her thoughts turned to the kisses he'd given her under the mistletoe. A smile blossomed on her face that she refused to repress. Bless that devilish Gunner Wilson.

Then she recalled Mitchell's apathy regarding her announcement. He'd said nothing and raced up the stairs of the B&B. Her impulsive decision took her by surprise, but her gut told her it was the right thing to do, even if it wasn't the exact perfect time to tell him. The words had just tumbled out.

After showering, she hurried downstairs to the kitchen. "Morning, Mom."

"Good morning, sweetheart."

Liz eyed the menu board, reading aloud. "Cracker Spoons with Creamy Pimiento Cheese, Tossed Greens-and-Grapes Salad, Shrimp and Andouille Sausage with Asiago Grits, Red Velvet Marble Bundt Cake, Sparkling Rum Punch. Wow, ambitious."

"I thought we could switch things up a bit this year."

And not make any of Dad's favorites.

Liz picked up a teaspoon-shaped cookie cutter and sat it back on the counter. "Getting an early start. That's smart with a whole new menu. If I'd known, I would have set my alarm."

"I don't like it, but I'm getting used to doing things by myself."

"Maybe you could take in a boarder."

"Heavens, no. I'm doing all right financially. I couldn't have a stranger living here."

"What if she's not a stranger?"

Bewilderment framed Mom's face. "What do you mean?"

"What if I'm the boarder? Until I find my own place."

Mom removed her hands from the piecrust and wiped them on a towel. "Lizzy, what are you saying?"

"I gave Mitchell my notice last night. I'm coming home."

Mom grabbed her in a hug. "That's wonderful!" She pushed her away. "But I won't have you turning your life upside down because of me."

Taking Mom's hands, Liz led her to the table.

"Of course, I miss you, but I'm *not* coming back to be your nursemaid. This is what I want. New York is a fabulous place. I've enjoyed my time there, or I wouldn't have stayed as long as I have. New York is *not* Jubilee, and I want those unique things about this town to be a part of my everyday life. Keeping up with my friends and family through social media is *not* how I want to interact with them. I need face time and not the virtual kind. That's why I'm coming home."

As she spoke, her heart ached because none of the words included Mitchell.

You might be only a blip on my timeline. My family is my life's blood.

Tears shown in Mom's eyes. "Best Christmas present ever."

"Speaking of presents, I'll be bringing yours when I return. I talked to Courtney last night and asked to adopt Tallulah—for you. Mom, she's so sweet and she needs someone. So do you."

"I haven't had a dog in my life since I was a young girl. Might be nice." Mom swiped at her eyes and smiled. "Let's get to work. I want everything to be perfect tonight. Oh, would you call Aunt Marge and ask her to bring her small punch bowl for the alcoholic refreshment?"

"Sure. I left my pocketbook in the family room last night." Liz found her phone on the bottom of her purse. She also found Mitchell's text.

Confusion jolted her as her body temperature rose in the cool room. Like someone had pushed her internal thermostat upward. What would keep Mitchell from coming to supper? He didn't know anyone in Jubilee. Was he angry about her notice?

Her brows knitted, re-reading the message as she entered the kitchen.

"Something wrong?" Mom asked.

"Mitchell sends his regrets. He won't be joining us for dinner."

"That's a shame. Hope everything is all right."

"I guess it is. He'll be here at two tomorrow afternoon to pick me up."

That evening, Liz did her best to bring holiday cheer to the small family gathering. Handpicked wine, handpicked music, handpicked memories. Still, it was tough, each woman experiencing moments of difficulty.

Liz's sadness multiplied by two. Fate had taken her father from her life. Through her own doing, she had displaced a wonderful man from her life. A man to whom she felt a connection unlike any she'd experienced with other guys. But a force inside her insisted this was the path to take.

Leave New York for Jubilee, which meant leaving Mitchell.

Chapter Eleven

On Christmas morning, Mitchell stood outside the Marshall home. It wasn't cold enough from him to be shivering, but the possibility that Liz would turn him away without hearing what he had to say made him cold inside. "I'll never know if I don't try."

He pressed the doorbell twice.

Waited.

And waited.

Mitchell checked his watch. Eleven o'clock. Surely, they were awake.

The door opened. Liz peeked around the edge. "Mitchell." She opened the door wider to allow him to enter. Her hand went to her hair. She tightened her robe across her chest.

Liz appeared uncomfortable, but to him, she looked fabulous. Little bits of butterscotch curls falling from that elastic thing holding her hair on top of her head. A red robe, the same shade as the dress she'd worn in his imaginings.

"I didn't call because I wasn't sure you'd see me after I canceled dinner last night. I thought just showing up was my best option."

Silence.

He leaned in. "It worked. You opened the door."

"Will I not see you at two o'clock today? Or are you here to tell me to find another way back to New York?"

Mitchell paused when Mrs. Marshall entered the foyer. "Merry Christmas, Mitchell."

"Thank you. I—"

"Please, excuse me while I get dressed. We'd love to have you stay for brunch."

When they were alone, Liz faced the window, her back to him

"Liz, please. There are things I need to say."

She didn't move.

"You stunned me with your decision to move back home. I don't want you to slip out of my life."

She swung around. "I've made a decision that removes me from your life, and *now* you tell me this? I told Mom yesterday that I'm moving back to Jubilee. I haven't seen her this happy since—before my dad died."

He clasped his hands together. "Seems I'm always asking for a do-over. I'm sorry about canceling last night. I was reeling from your announcement, needed some space."

Liz moved toward the sofa and invited him to sit. "I admit my notice was out of left field." She sighed. "I made my decision knowing there is a piece of me that doesn't want to give up on what's happening between us."

He smiled. She'd given him the confirmation he needed.

Liz frowned, her face flushed scarlet. "Mitchell Lang, are you making fun of me after I told you my innermost feelings?"

"Not at all. But I'd like to tell you about my conversation with Uncle Walter. The phone call I would have missed if I'd been at dinner last night."

"Tell me."

He took her hands in his. "My uncle is returning as CEO until Derrick can assume the position in late spring."

"Was he upset with the way you handled the Ramsden account?"

"No, he was fine with my decision. I'm leaving the company in February to work with my friend, Eric."

"I'm happy for you, but what has that got to do with me? Us?"

"When I called Eric to accept his job offer, I stipulated my condition—the Southeastern territory."

"What kind of job?"

"Piloting for Eric's charter service."

Liz smiled. "You were happy when you were flying a few days ago. Where is the Southeastern territory?"

"That's the beauty of this whole turn of events. The location has yet to be determined." He stood. "I spent hours last night gathering stats about other charter services in the area."

Mitchell stood and pulled her upright. He whispered in her ear. "The coast of Georgia is looking promising."

She leaned back slightly. Her gaze focused on Mitchell's eyes, then his lips. Liz circled her arms around his neck, pulling him close.

Her kiss started tender but ended with a stirring passion that left her heart racing faster than Santa's sleigh.

"A hem. Well, I see you two don't need mistletoe," Mrs. Marshall said.

Mitchell pulled back. For a second he felt like he'd been caught opening a Christmas present without permission.

"Mrs. Wilson called to wish us a Merry Christmas but didn't hang up until she had informed me of your kiss under the mistletoe in the town square."

Liz reached out and pulled a sprig of mistletoe from a flower arrangement. "How can such a small thing cause such big problems for some people?"

"Really?" Mitchell asked. "Jubilee has mistletoe police?"

Liz laughed and leaned into him. Mitchell liked the warmth and weight of her against him.

"Mrs. Wilson's just kicking up dust. If it had been her daughter, instead of you kissing a handsome man, she wouldn't have a problem with mistletoe."

"If this Georgia coast thing works out, you'll get a chance to meet more Jubilee citizens. You'll see we have a variety of personalities." Liz waggled her eyebrows.

He enjoyed the intimacy of their closeness. He squeezed her waist.

Mrs. Marshall cocked her head. "I seem to be missing something. I'll set the table and y'all can bring me up to speed during brunch."

Mitchell pulled Liz close and whispered, "I promise you, I'll do my damnedest to find the closest location to Jubilee and you."

"And I'll do my best to help you keep your promise." She held the mistletoe over his head and kissed him.

THE END

Rachel's Recipe

Liz's Fruitcake Cookies

1 box vanilla wafers crushed
8 ounces red candied cherries diced
8 ounces green candied cherries diced
2 cups pecans chopped
1 can condensed milk
12 ounces or 1 1/2 cups coconut

Combine all ingredients except coconut. Form into logs and roll in coconut.
Freeze and thaw 30 minutes before serving, then slice.

Rachel W. Jones

Award-winning author Rachel W. Jones wrote her first contemporary romance manuscript at age fifty-seven. She composes stories about strong heroines, heroes with heart, and sweet romance. Her writing reflects her passion for performing arts, and a twenty-nine-year career in healthcare has influenced the threads of medical drama woven into her storylines.

When she's not writing or working as a registered nurse, Rachel loves traveling, sewing, and the music enthusiast in her still believes in practicing her clarinet and piano. She lives in metro Atlanta with her husband of forty years and one spoiled Labrador retriever who has her own full-size bed but sleeps wherever she desires.

Learn more about Rachel at her website: **www.rachelwjones.com**

Christmas Present

By Linda Joyce

Acknowledgments

I'm sending out a heartfelt thank you, though the words feel inadequate, to Leah Noel Sims, Melissa G. Klein, and Rachel W. Jones for their unrelenting support, intelligence, and chuckle-producing humor. We did a writers retreat in April 2018 at the beach on Saint Simons Island and solidified our commitment to bring Jubilee, Georgia to life. I'm blessed to have each of these ladies in my writing world.

A big hug and a huge shout-out to Linda's Lovelies. Your continued enthusiasm, support, and suggestions add a dose of encouragement and fun to my writing world. Thank you.

And a very special thank you goes to my husband—Donald, Don, and other pet names that shall remain private. You help me remain rails-on whenever I'm overwhelmed or need a hug or a pep talk. You are the love of my life.

Christmas Present

Chapter One

Chelsea smiled and hello-ed to folks as she zigzagged a path through the fairground crowd at the tenth annual December fundraising event. The cooler coastal Georgia temperatures and bright afternoon sunshine had attracted a record attendance this year. However, most of the credit belonged to her assistant, Mika, for all her behind-the-scenes work. She'd spun a brilliant PR campaign after snagging a TV celebrity chef as this year's guest of honor—Chef Zachary Tanner. Charming. Creative. Cool under pressure.

But even with him being *all* that, Chelsea worried his star power might not fill the coffers enough to give a Christmas present to every child on the list. Her team had a lot riding on the chef's fans. Uncertainty pinged between her heart and her gut like a tennis ball in a heated match. Everything had to go as planned, because this year, given all that had happened with Momma, Chelsea had no Plan B.

"Smile for the camera, Miss Cooper," a young female reporter with a local paper said.

Chelsea stopped, smiled, and out of habit, posed for a picture. "Thanks. Your newspaper helps spread the word, and that helps us help children. I'm grateful."

"You're welcome. The headline will read 'Former Miss Jubilee Makes Magic Again!' Great turn out. More art, jewelry, and food booths. And you know that saying, 'If you can't stand the heat, then get out of the kitchen,' doesn't apply when Chef Tanner's cooking. He's scrumptious." The young woman fanned herself, and not because Jubilee had a sudden heat wave.

"Get a raffle ticket," Chelsea told the reporter, then continued on her way, wanting a quick exit from the press. "Maybe you'll win a visit to the kitchen of his newest restaurant in Savannah," she called out over her shoulder.

Headlines sold newspapers. Headlines aided her charity event. Headlines hurt her family. She'd learned, over the years, the press was a fickle medium. Reporters flocked to her when she won a beauty contest, when she won Jubilee's artist of the year award, and also when her father divorced her mother several years ago. To an outsider picking up the newspaper, Jubilee might have seemed like Melrose Place.

But the press about Chef Tanner didn't do him justice—at least about his looks and charm. The man wasn't just a name worth a pirate's bounty of gold. His charm shined as bright as a lighthouse on a rocky shore on a dark night. Since Mika persuaded him to appear, she had her capable assistant manage all the hostess duties. She hadn't yet officially met him, although today she'd caught glimpses of him from afar. Grannies nearly swooned when he turned his brilliant, dimpled smile on them He worked the crowd with a down-home touch that made him so approachable. She hoped the charm picked at their heart and her charity would pocket enough donations to help all the kids on the list.

The hike to the large, white tent in the center of the fairgrounds gave Chelsea a chance to stretch her legs. Still, worries shadowed her. For two years, she'd fought with her sister and brother to keep Momma at home. But some days she doubted her wisdom. Like today. Momma's mostly pleasant disposition eroded to petulance. Mrs. Barrentine had stayed behind at Chelsea's booth to keep a watchful eye on her mother, Marlene Mae. Momma's condition was like shifting sands on a beach battered by a tropical storm. Dementia's cruel nature made life unpredictable. Sometimes downright exhausting.

Chelsea entered the large tent, already more than half full of folks who had claimed their seats. Most from Jubilee, but also a respectable smattering of obvious out-of-town tourists in shorts and sandals—so unlike December attire for locals. A handful of reporters rounded out the crowd.

"Chelsea, hi! Over here." Mika waved from the raised stage and pointed to a chair to the right of the podium.

The turnout sparked hope in Chelsea. People had flocked to see the famous TV personality chef—on his show, he cooked with the rich and famous. And Chef had lit a glow in Mika's eyes, like a child in awe on Christmas morning after Santa's visit.

"I need to rescue Chef Tanner from his booth if we want to start on time." Mika hugged her. "I have to tell you, I looove my jooob!" she squeed.

"I love that you love your job." Chelsea grinned and tapped her watch. "Yes, we need to keep to the schedule. So go."

Mika departed, and Chelsea took her speaking notecards from the back pocket of her charcoal gray slacks and then adjusted her soft pink sweater. Placing the cards on the podium, she flipped through each one. There was nothing to be nervous about. She'd memorized what she intended to say. Mika had been thorough in her background check of the chef. Culinary school in France. Several TV shows over the last ten years. He claimed the road was his home. Relocated to Jubilee with a new restaurant opening in Savannah. Co-owner of three other restaurants. Avid activist for clean waters. No family. Never been married. Never even engaged. From the information, Chelsea had written an introduction to speak to the hearts of the people.

She looked up from the podium.

"This way." Mika appeared in the tent's doorway

with the chef in tow. She pointed up the steps to the stage.

Chef Tanner nodded to Mika. "Thank you."

Chelsea shifted her stance when the chef approached. At five foot five, even with an additional three-inch heels on her black boots, she still had to look up to see his eyes. He appeared taller than his bio-stated six feet. Dark brown lashes. His eyes were not just blue, but a captivating silvery blue that sparkled when he smiled, as though someone had bedazzled his eyes. She tottered like an antique Weeble-wobble doll, hating that her heart had the same reaction to his smile as the grannies she'd witnessed earlier.

"Whoa." Chef Tanner grasped her elbow and steadied her.

She planted her feet, willed her spine ramrod straight, stuck out her hand. "Hello. Thank you so much for being our guest of honor." Her drawl had never sounded so thoroughly Southern to her ears as it did in that moment. "It's a privilege to have you here." How she managed to get the words out with her cotton-ball-dry mouth, she didn't know. "I'm Chelsea O'Connor Cooper."

He shook her hand. His gaze locked with hers. "I've heard all about you." His voice carried no accent—no accent at all. Just smooth. Smooth as Kentucky bourbon. Warm as bourbon going down.

She swallowed. Her heart stuttered and then halted when the voice in her head shouted as though through a megaphone.

He's just the kind that loves and leaves. Don't get involved.

Chapter Two

Zachary looked forward to this moment. There he stood with her warm hand in his. His eyes hypnotized by hers. Curiosity and awe blended together as smooth as rich thick sauce. The kick to his heart—unexpected.

"I'll take my hand back now." She gently tugged, and he released it, not the least bit ashamed of the gaffe. It had been his intention to hold her hand for as long as she permitted. It had not been his intention to feel an instant attraction. Attraction was something he usually guarded against. Somehow, her charm snuck in under his radar. Now he wanted to know even more about her.

"Pretty hand. Delicate for pottery."

She raised a questioning eyebrow.

Would she be surprised by the information he'd collected about her? He always investigated anyone he dealt with before getting involved—professionally or personally. It was a precaution that served him well.

"You know about my work?" There was a pleased eagerness in her voice. A humbleness in her demeanor.

He nodded. "In fact, my mother gave me a piece of your pottery a number of years ago. It's one of my most treasured possessions from her."

It was one of his *only* possession from her. His

mother's gypsy spirit had kept her moving. She traveled light. He'd grown up going from town to town, homeschooled by books and life in a motorhome. It could've been worse, but after high school, staying in one place made him restless. However, losing his mother last year had changed all of that.

Chelsea pushed her fingers into her hair and scooped it behind her ears. "I'd like to see it sometime. Maybe I'll remember it."

"That sounds like the makings of a first date."

Where did those words come from?

He stopped himself from looking over his shoulder to see if someone else had spoken the words that had flashed in his mind.

Her expression shifted from what-did-you-just-say to stunned surprise to aloof politeness.

"We certainly can meet *without* it being a date." Her grin was shy. Bashful, almost. So endearing, he wanted to hug her.

"A date—you pick a day and a time and a place. I'll bring the pottery. And I would like to discuss a piece of business with you, too."

A gentleness emanated from her. She was not the Ms. Cooper found in his research of newspaper interviews, archived photos, and YouTube videos of her beauty pageant days. From those sources, he expected a high-heeled woman with a high-maintenance personality.

Instead, a classy girl next door with honey blonde hair, dark chocolate lashes, and sparkling eyes—the color of tawny port—and a true Georgia peaches-and-cream complexion was a pleasant surprise. Even better, she had to have a big heart given she'd hosted this event for ten years.

He liked that she was simply dressed in slacks and a sweater. The only adornment, a string of pearls around her neck and a watch on her wrist. He liked it more that, after looking twice, he caught no glimpse of a ring. Not even a tan line.

"And I'm interested to know more about Jubilee. Who better to tell me than you—your family history and legacy say you're Jubilee royalty."

"Chef Tanner." Mika interrupted, offering bottles of water. "It's time to begin. Ms. Cooper will make introductions. Then it's your turn to wow the audience." She nudged his arm with her elbow. "It wouldn't hurt for us to make this a record-setting fundraiser. There's a reporter over there"—she pointed to the back of the tent—"who wants an interview after your speech."

"I'm here to do all I'm able for this worthy cause." He followed Chelsea up the steps leading to the platform.

Chelsea tapped the microphone. The crowd quieted. "Thank you for coming to the tenth annual Jubilee Winter Festival…."

Her voice is Southern and feminine and captivating.

A woman from the audience shouted, "I love you, Zach."

"As I'm sure everyone here does," Chelsea chimed in. "From his mussels—the kind we find in the shells"—The crowd chuckled.—"to his active voice in supporting clean waterways."

"I'd like him to just whisper to me," a woman in the front row said. She batted her lashes so hard, Zach thought the woman might levitate.

"And on January first, he's opening a new restaurant, which he'll tell us all about. I give you the celebrity chef, chef to the rich and famous, Chef Zachary Tanner."

Chelsea clapped and encouraged the crowd to applaud more. Zach rose and stood at the podium. He had looked forward to meeting the much-written-about Ms. Cooper. Now he looked forward to a mutually beneficial business arrangement. And maybe something a little more, given the way she made his pulse jump.

"Thank you, Ms. Cooper, for that stirring introduction." For some reason, fans liked his cooking puns. This time was no different. They laughed and applauded more.

To think, he'd almost turned down this opportunity. His booking agent contacted him nine months ago about this fundraiser—it was the week before the first anniversary of his mother's passing. At the same time, a counselor had cautioned him not to make major changes for at least a year, but the man wasn't aware of Zach's mother's deathbed confession. Her passing changed much. Her final words had rocked Zach's life.

So instead of saying no to change, he embraced it. Yes to the fundraiser. Yes to moving to coastal Georgia. Yes to discovering his roots.

And for the first time in his life, there was no rush to get to know a woman. He was here for the long haul. Chelsea, and generations of her family before her, lived and breathed Jubilee. Maybe there might be a spot for him in her future.

Maybe.

Chapter Three

Hypnotized, Chelsea pulled up clay with her hands. The mound turned round and round on the potter's wheel. Wet clay. Constant cadence. Her creativity surged.

Nimble fingered, she'd started with a gray lump of clay, and now, something beautiful began to emerge.

Ding. Ding.

"Huh? What?'

Ding.

The interrupting sounds fogged her focus. Pushed her out of the creative flow. She slid her foot from the potter's wheel pedal. The four walls and three windows of her studio pulled her to reality.

Ding.

The elegant vessel in front of her wobbled. Her focus, mood, and vase collapsed. "Dang!" Frustrated, she reached for her phone and read the four messages.

9

1

1

NOW!

"Vic needs me?" The texts brought a punch of adrenaline, a cocktail of worry, fear, and panic. Chelsea wiped her wet hands back and forth against her jean-clad thighs, then bolted out of her studio behind her house. She glanced to the sensible blue sedan parked on the side driveway, to the small boat tied up at a long wooden dock, then up to the December-eighth noon sky and hooded her eyes from the blinding sun.

"Boat keys. Where?" Patting her back pocket, she fished them out. Four on a ring. One for the house, one for the car, one for the boat, and one for a dream. "Mrs. Barrentine, I'll be back in a little while from Vic's."

"Have a good time, dear. Marlene Mae and I are taking tea."

Chelsea gave a quick wave, then cranked the small boat's engine to life.

She couldn't decide if Vic's text or Momma refusing to speak caused her blood pressure to roller-coaster the most. Momma's dementia had made a sweet, tenderhearted girl out of her once powerhouse-of-Jubilee's-Junior-League mother. Even after two years, Chelsea hadn't adjusted to the continuous changes.

"Deep breath. Mrs. Barrentine's as competent as an air traffic controller at Hartsfield International." But every time Chelsea left the house, she fretted about a repeat escape. The next one could be fatal.

She whipped the boat around, pointed the bow up Fancy Bluff Creek to Vic's house. The tide was tugging water to low tide.

So what in all that's red-and-green-about-Christmas

is Vic's problem?

The 9-1-1 call held a shade of suspicion, but neither low tide nor a dead engine would hinder Chelsea from answering Victoria Abernathy's plea. Even if she had to row all the way.

Victoria remained her best friend since kindergarten, back when Chelsea painted outside the lines, put worms on hooks, and paddled a kayak in the creek. Her friend, on the other hand, had strutted first in Mary Janes, later strutted in heels, and these days strutted in stilettos. Now Vic designed clothes and owned a high-end boutique. Whereas, Chelsea made award-winning pottery, started a dementia support group, and cared for her mother. But some day…

"Come on. Come on. Come on." Chelsea opened the throttle when she passed the last neighbor's dock. Three-hundred horsepower on the small skiff mirrored a jockey riding a racing stallion.

Rrrummm the motor sped up.

Her nerves *rrrummm*-ed as though dancing on a delicate thread about to snap.

The boat followed the wide waterway past spartina, the cordgrass of the twice-a-day tides of the marsh. She breathed in brackish scents to calm her revving high-gear nerves. A therapist had taught her breathing exercises to combat skyscraper-high stress. Stress she thought she'd left behind when she bailed from corporate America. But fate had other plans.

"Sand dollars and seafoam green glaze." Her attempt at visualizing the custom-designed wedding pottery taking shape in her studio started to focus in her mind's eye. But thoughts of Vic's texts broke through.

"What has she done this time?" Chelsea tightened her grip on the steering wheel. Her worry moved faster than a gator in water.

She navigated the changing creek, the size of a small river. The boat raced wide open until the curve. Chelsea backed the engine down to half power, but still pushing the limits of safety to reach her friend in need.

A niggling suspicion sprouted in her mind. Vic had only used 9-1-1 three times in all their years of friendship, but last time—she crossed the line. However, Chelsea's fear over her friend's safety was greater than her suspicions.

"Finally." Chelsea shaded her eyes. The dock in Abernathy Cove came into view. She slowed the engine down, down, down.

Victoria Abernathy stood on the back gallery of her large stately home raised for protection from the creek's annual rise. She motioned for Chelsea to go to the front before disappearing inside.

"No blood. Good thing." Chelsea tied off the lines before trotting around the side of the house. Kip Stewart's Jubilee's Jolly Trolley was parked to one side of the circular drive. She caught a glance of a car pulling onto the brick driveway when she reached the bottom step.

Stopping, she took a moment to take in the surroundings. Vic's house belonged on a Christmas card. It was iconically Southern. Like Scarlett's Tara, only on stilts. Evergreen swags draped the columns of the long, wide front porch. Red velvet bows and golden pinecones added pops of color. Little white lights would twinkle after dark—a perfect holiday image.

Nothing suggested a 9-1-1.

Chelsea's pounding pulse downshifted to low. Her suspicions ratcheted up.

The front door opened when Chelsea was halfway up the wide wooden staircase. Victoria and a cast of friends spilled out of the house and formed a semicircle on the gallery. She motioned Chelsea closer.

Every nerve Chelsea had stood on alert. Had she been duped by Vic's 9-1-1 again? Anger bubbled up. She tamped it down. She shouldn't be mad at Vic. Her best friend was trying to infuse some fun into Chelsea's dull days. Days when dementia controlled her every waking minute.

Three steps shy of the top step, Chelsea noticed a kissing ball of mistletoe hanging from a white velvet ribbon dangling from the porch's carriage house light.

A prickling sensation scratched up her arms and up her neck.

What the…is going on?

"Kiss her! Kiss her! Kiss her!" The crowd in front of her chanted.

When footsteps sounded behind her, Chelsea turned to look over her shoulder.

"Kiss her! Kiss her! Kiss her!" The chanting continued.

Chef Zachary Tanner, brown hair lightened from the sun, a shadow of beard on his jaw, and broad shoulders shrouded in a white chef's coat, followed her same path up the stairs. The world shrank. Her heart lurched. Panic stole her breath. She'd never called him back.

Too handsome. Too many people. Too much surprise.

The crowd clapped and shouted. "Kiss her! Kiss her! Kiss her!"

Her thudding heart was a balloon about to burst. Crowds hit her anxiety button. A gaggle of gal pals versus a single body… Retreat was the only option. She turned to run down the way she'd come up. She could throw a block and knock past Zachary, if necessary.

"Kiss her! Kiss her! Kiss her!"

Zach's expression shifted from puzzlement to welcoming. His I-got-this grin softened his mouth.

His smile triggered a storm in her.

The roar of the shouts dulled as dizziness began to claim her.

Her knees wobbled.

Too much. Too much. Too much.

She started to slip. She fought her feet about to float up.

"Kiss her!" Victoria's insistent voice sounded as though it came through a long, long tunnel.

Zachary's strong arms caught Chelsea in a dip as gravity pulled her down. She struggled to right herself, and his lips touched her forehead.

"Aww," the crowd cooed in unison.

Her arms slipped around his neck—to keep her from falling or floating away, she wasn't sure. Her head bobbed. His lips met hers. A warm kiss. A soothing kiss. A consuming kiss.

Shock shook her. She trembled all the way to her toes.

She blinked. Exhaled. Relaxed. Kissed him back.

Not awful.

She kissed him again.

Pleasant.

Deepened the kiss.

Oh, my....Sweetness.

She nearly melted into a faint. She hadn't been this intimate with any man in two years—arms around her, her arms around him, lips touching.

Oh my oh my oh my.

Straightening, he helped her stand. She cocked her head when he licked his lips as though she were something sweet and tasty, and he was trying to pinpoint the flavor.

She swayed. Her protective moat had failed. Her defenses drained. A kiss shifted her whole reality. All that she'd denied for the last two years smacked her heart, her head, her soul.

But this is just one guy. Just a few kisses.

Realization struck like summer lightning.

Just?

Yeah, she could repeat that over and over again, and maybe she'd believe it.

Maybe.

Chelsea locked eyes with Vic, dipped her chin, and flashed the evil eye at her. A threat she'd make good on later. In the meantime, their friends surrounded Chelsea and pulled her up the stairs and into the house.

Crossing the threshold, she glanced over her shoulder. There stood Chef Tanner. Mister Cinnamon and Spice and Everything Nice and smelling like a sexy campfire.

Chelsea mused. Maybe it would be a happy birthday after all.

Chapter Four

Zach climbed the front steps of the house of his first new private client in Georgia. First new cooking job. First time coming…home. A strange word when he'd never been there before, but since arriving in Jubilee, it was as though his old, lucky wheat penny magically shined like new. A good omen. He was a chef, part sailor, and given to superstitions. *This* was the place where he belonged.

"Kiss her! Kiss her! Kiss her!" shouted the crowd gathered on the wide front porch.

Chelsea Cooper stood a few steps ahead of him and still three steps from the top. She turned and looked at him over her shoulder. A deer-about-to-run-into-a-forest-fire look.

Confused, Zach remained where he stood.

She turned, teetered, started to slip.

Mid-tumble, he caught her in a dip.

In the bobbling movement, his lips touched her forehead.

Her eyes grew wide.

"Aww" came in unison from the crowd of women on the porch.

Maybe it was because her arms were around his neck. Maybe because she looked helpless and dazed. Maybe because he wanted to be a white knight. Any which way, his lips found hers.

An innocent kiss.

Maybe another good sign that I belong.

He finally released her but kept his hand on the small of her back to steady her until the group of women pulled her to the porch. They chanted, "Chelsea. Go, Chelsea." All of them teasing and talking and giggling disappeared into the house.

"So *that's* the birthday girl. The talented Chelsea O'Connor Cooper." Zach made a mental note about how perfect she'd felt in his arms. He also wondered why she'd refused to name a day and time to meet. Why hadn't she returned his calls?

Victoria Abernathy, his client, appeared in the doorway. "It's a beautiful day for many possibilities." She lowered her chin and batted her eyes as though flirting with him.

His breath clogged in his chest. He preferred not to mix business and pleasure, no matter how tempted.

Awkward.

Victoria could make things difficult. She wasn't his type. A quick glance said she required more attention than a boat held together with bandages on the river. In his line of work, high maintenance ate in the front of the house, whereas he worked in the back—the kitchen was his sanctuary. Yes, the TV show gave a different impression, but that was all show—except for his actual cooking.

"Don't you think our Chelsea is something?" She winked. "The two of you would make quite a pair. What with her making beautiful serving plates and you making luscious plates of food."

A breath escaped from his lungs. "Oh. Yes." But uneasiness rode up his spine. Had Victoria set him up? She had refused to name the guest of honor. Did the birthday girl know about the party? She looked fantastic in her tight T-shirt and hip-hugging jeans, but very underdressed compared to the rest of the party revelers.

"Come in. Come in, Chef. Let's get this birthday party started."

Chelsea appeared in the doorway behind Victoria. "A moment, Vic." Victoria disappeared inside, and Chelsea slammed the door shut behind them.

Still standing on the steps, Zach let go of a chuckle. "Well, if nothing else, this is going to be interesting."

He climbed the last steps to the front porch, rang the doorbell, and waited for someone to allow him entry for his cooking demonstration—Victoria's birthday present to Chelsea.

"I was wrong"—he shrugged—"I thought peaches, brown sugar, and maple syrup. But"—he closed his eyes, licked his lips, recalling her lips on his—"she's got some added spice—cinnamon and maybe a dash of nutmeg."

The door opened slowly. Victoria scooted into view

wearing a too-wide smile, an arm around Chelsea's shoulder, towing her along. "Chef Zachary Tanner, I hear you've already met my dearest friend, Chelsea Cooper, a Jubilee celebrity."

Stiffly, Chelsea extended her hand. "Hello. Again." Her gaze darted away.

Zach shook her hand, though he was tempted to smooth away a bit of the clay streaked on her cheek. Attraction as strong as a ship's rigging pulled him to her. Something about her uncomfortableness made him want to put her at ease, show her he was a gentleman, or better yet, a gallant white knight here to…to do what, exactly? Cook her a meal? Tempt her taste buds? Steal another kiss or two?

Steady, dude. You're not a white knight, and she's not a damsel in distress. Just the birthday girl.

Just?

There was nothing *just* about Chelsea. She was a perfect crème brûlée—a sugar sweetness but slightly stiff exterior, and flexible, since brûlée could be served hot or cold, and wildly popular—as evidenced by her friends' desire to serve her up a good-time birthday. He'd never wanted his cooking to impress a woman as much as he wanted it to impress the enigmatic Miss Cooper.

His fingers tingled, waiting to make magic in the kitchen.

Now, it was his turn to wow her.

Chapter Five

Chelsea sat in the club chair parked front and center on the opposite side of the marble island from Zachary. She tried not to squirm under his gaze. Even if she wanted a date with him, she didn't have time this month. What with caring for Momma and working to complete the custom order by December 22, there was no time to be wasted on something frivolous. A date. Or this birthday party.

Victoria offered her a glass of bubbly. She accepted it, turned to face her friends, and lifted her glass in salute. "You surprised me. *Completely*. Thank you. I am very touched."

The strawberry resting at the bottom of the glass reminded her of a small red Christmas ornament. Christmas. In only seventeen days. Where had time gone? She hadn't made the first purchase for a present for anyone. When would she have time to shop? She barely had time to sleep. Momma came first. Work came second. But it was a *big* second. Anxiety seized that moment to elbow its way in. She fought to slam the door on the too familiar feeling and relax for a change.

"To Chelsea," the group said in unison, including Chef Tanner, bringing her back to the room and the party and the champagne.

Crystal flutes clinked. Everyone sipped.

Her gal pals—cohorts, cronies, bosom buddies, some classy teetotalers, some vamps, and some tramps, all with a spot in her heart—occupied dining room chairs placed around the island, creating a kitchen theater in Vic's open-concept main room.

"Just wait till she *tastes* her birthday present," one friend behind Chelsea murmured.

"Oh, my. Oh, yes," came the breathless response from a second friend. The air behind Chelsea moved—someone was fanning—and she mused that the last response bent toward a touch of the risqué rather than the wholesome girl next door. Her friends were a smorgasbord of contradictions. She loved them. Depended on them. Trusted them.

But today, Victoria violated that.

Staring straight ahead, acting as though her friends weren't on hormonal overload, Chelsea caught a darting glance from Chef Tanner. One eyebrow lifted. It was barely perceptible. But it was clear he was fighting not to grin.

He heard them!

Her cheeks flushed warm to hot. How awful. He'd been hired to do a cooking demo for a party, not be the kissing appetizer for the birthday girl or the object of leering.

What must he think of me? A thirty-year-old wallflower. That this is less of a birthday party and more of pity-party.

"Oh, yummy," said another member of the group when Chef added shrimp to the large hot skillet.

"The grits are perfectly cooked and seasoned." Chef Tanner laid his tasting spoon beside the cutting board on the counter. "I'll add the roux from the saucepan into the skillet with the other ingredients, and then I'll add a splash of Worcestershire. Stir until all mixed and simmering."

"He's mixing, and I'm simmering," a voice behind Chelsea whispered close to her ear.

"What about the bacon?" someone asked.

Chef Tanner snapped off a piece of crispy bacon and popped it into his mouth. "It goes with everything. I'll crumble it on top, along with a few thin slices of green onions." He licked his fingers. The women around Chelsea sighed.

She had to admit, the man exuded even more charm in person than he did on TV. Okay, she'd confess to late-night watching a couple of his shows since they'd met last week.

Chef Tanner kissed me. THE Chef Tanner. Kissed me.

Chelsea set her glass on the edge of the island. Her hand went to her lips. She tried to make it appear as though she were covering her mouth in case she burped, because bubbly did that to her sometimes, but she was checking her lips for the continued tingling from the kiss. Was it visible to anyone who looked at her? Were her lips literally vibrating?

A Tanner kiss. He could patent it, trademark it, copyright it. Then sell it to women everywhere. Make another million.

Vic sauntered catlike to Chef Tanner's side, draped an arm over his shoulder, like they'd been friends for years. She picked up a piece of bacon crumble and ate it. Licked her lips as though it were... orgasmic.

Chelsea wanted to hide. Had the surprise birthday party been a ruse for Vic to get close to the celebrity cook? He wasn't a stripper dressed as a chef. He was the real thing.

This was only the fourth time in all their years of friendship Vic had flashed their secret 9-1-1 code. The first time, Vic had cut her finger learning to use a mandolin, a potential serious bleed-out situation. Then doubled her trouble by passing out at the sight of her own blood. For sixteen-year-old girls, the sexy ER doc had made the hospital trip worthwhile.

The second time Vic sounded the girlfriend alarm, vixen Vic was stranded in a *haute couture* beaded evening gown on a sandbar with high tide rushing in. Her date, a douche dressed in a tux, left her to *swim for it* as a joke after Vic had refused to "gift" him with what he wanted after a charity event.

On Chelsea's twenty-fifth birthday, she had answered Vic's urgent plea for help. A police officer pulled her over when she arrived in front of Vic's house, saying Chelsea neglected to use her turn signal at the corner. He made her step out. Walked her to the front of the car, made her lean forward against the hood, cuffed her, spun her around, then whipped off his pull-away pants, and began to gyrate around her wearing only skintight briefs.

Vic and all her friends had streamed out onto the wide front porch, cheering, shouting, catcalling. Shocked, Chelsea endured, but heated embarrassment could've melted her into the asphalt. Vic had promised never ever, never ever, to do that again.

First time, shame on you. Second time, shame on me. I will never fall for another 9-1-1 call again.

Chef Tanner stepped away from Victoria and walked around the island. He carried a bowl and a spoon. "I was told this is your favorite. Shrimp and grits. Happy birthday, Chelsea."

She looked up at him. Her mouth opened, then closed. "Thank…you."

He leaned against the island, arms crossed on his chest, barely leaving breathing space between them. "Aren't you hungry?"

She nodded. In fact, she hadn't eaten since…yesterday. She looked from her spoon to the bowl and then back at him.

"I promise it's good." His brows furrowed as if he might be worried.

"Everybody eats now," Victoria called. She motioned to the partygoers. "I'm serving. Come and get it."

Under Chef Tanner's stare, Chelsea scooped a small bite of the grits, a piece of shrimp, and bacon into her mouth. The familiar flavors danced. Satisfied a craving. Many places made the dish, but this had a depth of flavor that rivaled all.

She looked up at him. "Wonderful."

Yummy! The way to a woman's heart is with food that tantalizes the taste buds.

She took another bite.

In the background, the ringing of Vic's home phone punctuated female chattering.

Someone called out, "Whoever it is, tell them to bring more wine." A titter of laughter floated around the room.

"Chelsea," one of her friends said. "It's Mrs. Barrentine. There's a problem with your mom. You're needed there ASAP."

Chelsea shoved the bowl and the spoon at Chef Tanner. "Thank you. More than you know. But I've got to go." She bolted for the door and ran to the boat. Why had she left Momma? Why?

Unmooring the boat, she hopped inside. The motor purred to life.

A florist's boat pulled up at Vic's dock. A pang hit

Chelsea. Flowers reminded her of Liz, now living in New York, who had once again missed her birthday. Just as well, the party was over before it really started.

The crowd of gal pals on the back veranda of Vic's house grew smaller as the boat roared away. Chelsea kicked the motor into a higher gear when she was clear of the No Wake Zone. Victoria shouted something, but Chelsea was too far away to understand. She waved and kept going. Images of Momma filled her mind. "Please, Lord, let her be okay."

Chapter Six

Chelsea paced the hospital's hallway, waiting for the nurse to finish settling Momma in bed. Random beeps from various machines followed her in her trek back and forth down the hall. The colorful art on the walls did nothing to settle her nerves. It was the worst birthday of her life. Worst.

She stopped beside Mrs. Barrentine who was seated in a recliner—the one waiting to be moved into Momma's room—where Chelsea planned to sleep that night.

"Momma could've drowned." Chelsea closed her hands into tight fists. Guilt peppered her. "It's all my fault."

"But she didn't, Chelsea, dear. Again, I'm so sorry." The older woman had ridden with Marlene Mae in the ambulance, which had already left the house by the time Chelsea arrived home.

"Mrs. Barrentine, who could've guessed dementia wiped away Momma's ability to remember how to swim?" She raised her hands in surrender. "Just last week, she and I were racing in the creek together."

It's my fault for leaving.

"I left her for a moment to go to the restroom." The older woman hung her head.

"Chelsea!"

She and Mrs. Barrentine turned in the direction of the offending shout.

"Doesn't he know not to do that?" Mrs. Barrentine sniffed. "Disturbs patients trying to rest."

Chelsea strode down the hall, meeting her brother halfway. "Layton Cooper, where did you leave your manners? This is a hospital."

"How is she?" Worry creased his forehead. "What have you done *this* time?"

"What?" She narrowed her eyes and puckered her mouth tightly. Her younger brother might be a hotshot in the car business, but he needed to keep a cool civil tone with her.

"Momma wouldn't be here if you'd listened to Isabella and me." His accusation cut.

"Show some respect. I will *not* argue with you here in the hall. It's as unseemly as you and our sister wanting to shut Momma away in an institution."

"For pity's sake! You won't even look at the place!"

"Keep your voice down." Chelsea gripped her brother's arm, dragging him back toward the elevator. "Or leave." He might be nearly a foot taller, dressed in a crisp shirt and silk tie, but to her way of thinking, he was not the devoted son he wanted everyone to believe.

"Look, Fancy Bluff Retirement Community has a memory care unit. You have to look at it with me and

Isabella. She's on her way. We're *all*"—he moved his finger in a circle—"taking the tour."

Chelsea swallowed back anger, but fresh frustration brought tears. She blinked them away. "You look." Her voice was tighter than a wrung-out mop. "That's our momma. I'm all she's got since Daddy divorced her."

"Wrong," Layton snarled. "There are two other children. And Dad does care."

"Only about the money he gets every month from her trust fund," she hissed.

Nurse Ahern, their mother's old high school classmate, gave a sideways glance at them and raised an eyebrow. "Let's hope the third one has better sense than the two of you. Quiet down, or I'll call security."

Chelsea's shoulders rose as she sucked in a deep breath. Exhaling, she shook out her hands, hoping to shake off her anger. Everyone in Jubilee knew the Cooper family. One of the founding ones, generations ago. And gossip spread faster than melted butter on grilled fish in this town.

"Children," Mrs. Barrentine said, walking toward them. "The nurse has given permission for visitors now." She motioned to them.

Layton pushed past Chelsea. His leather-soled loafers smacked against the linoleum floor. He skidded to a stop in front of Momma's door, adjusted his tie, and pushed the recliner into the room. "Hey, Momma. How's my favorite girl?"

Chelsea gritted her teeth. Yes, Layton was concerned. But he, like most, didn't understand what she endured to give Momma the most normal life allowable due to dementia. Momma's decline was progressive. Some days were good. Some sunk to new lows, and most recently, the new lows had become the new normal. But that didn't mean Momma was ready for an institution.

Memory care unit my...

Standing where two hallways met perpendicularly— Momma's room three doors down in one and the elevator in the other—Chelsea couldn't decide whether to leave and come back after Layton's visit or stay. He rarely lasted more than thirty minutes. Or she could run like a boat on open full bore and leave the problem of Momma's dementia to Layton and Isabella to handle. Over the last two years, all they'd done was complain, find fault, criticize.

The elevator dinged. The doors opened. Here was her chance to go.

But Chelsea took a step toward Momma's room, rather than away. No matter what, Momma came first.

The sound of high heels tapped behind her.

"Chelsea, girlfriend, I brought coffee."

Turning, Chelsea found a cup of coffee pushed toward her. "Oh, Vic, thanks. I really needed this."

"Almond milk mocha. The largest size they have."

Victoria held her coffee cup out to the side and scooted in close for a one-armed hug. "I got your back, sistah."

Chelsea linked her arm with her friend and guided her toward her mother's room. "Is that what you call what happened earlier today?"

"*Moi*? I gave you a surprise birthday party. And a little gift. By the way, all the presents are in my car. And Chef Tanner insisted on taking some of the shrimp and grits with him."

"He's who I'm talking about."

Victoria winked. "I thought you could use a good home-cooked meal…and maybe some dessert later. Something sweet."

"Well, nothing will come of that. I was Cinderella at her own ball. Me in jeans and a clay-stained T-shirt. You and the others in fashionable frocks."

Victoria pulled back. "Let's get one thing clear. I. Do. Not. Frock. That red and green taffeta dress was seven-hundred dollars. Not a frock. High holiday fashion, yes. Frock? That's a definite no."

"Whatever." Chelsea shook her head. "Besides, that man can have his pick of dessert. I'm not on the menu." She paused outside Momma's door. "Let's wait here for a few minutes. I'm certain Layton won't be too long. Hospitals give him hives. Or so he says."

"When will the Isabella cavalry arrive?"

Chelsea shrugged. "I left my phone at home. Hopped

in the car and came here." She leaned in close and whispered, "I didn't bring my wallet. Not even my driver's license."

"*I'll*"— Victoria tapped her own chest—"chauffeur you home."

"Thanks. As for Isabella—haven't spoken to her—the one-woman army that she is. However, Layton assured me she's on the way."

They lingered outside Momma's room. Chelsea overheard bits of Mrs. Barrentine's good wishes and good-byes. The woman departed shortly.

Layton's voice drifted from beyond the drawn curtain of the two-bed hospital room. "Momma, tomorrow is going to be a good day. Isabella and I are going to move you to a good, *safe* place."

"Who are you? What's your name?" Momma asked.

Chelsea's heart sank. Not just for Momma and her condition but also for the pain those words had to cause her brother. Yes, they had differing opinions, but the words still had to be a knife to his heart. He was the only boy. Twenty-seven, working for their father at his car dealership in Savannah, a successful car salesman since college, and Layton remained Momma's favorite…when she remembered him.

"I'll be back in the morning"—Chelsea heard Layton tell Momma with a warble in his voice—"after you're released. I'm going to go now."

He bumped into Chelsea when he bolted from the room. Coffee sprayed up through the small hole from the cup's cover and splashed her T-shirt.

"Sorry 'bout that. Hey, Vic."

Chelsea wiped away the dots of coffee, then put her hand on his arm. "I know it's tough. I know it hurts. I know she might need more care. But a memory care unit? Not yet. I can adjust things to ensure there's no repeat of today."

"Sorry, Chelsea. That's what you said when she wandered out of the grocery store and was nearly killed by a car. I'm in Camp Isabella on this one. Mom is moving if we have to get a court order and fight you." He patted her hand and then moved down the hall in the direction of the elevators.

"I don't know what to say to get through to him, or Isabella."

Victoria shook her head. "Why don't you say your good-byes to your mom and let me take you home for a while? You can come back tonight. Let's salvage a bit of your birthday."

Chelsea couldn't leave Momma. That's why the recliner had been brought up. She'd sleep here to guard her from wandering, hurting herself, and any actions that might not be able to be undone. "Can't."

Heels clicked down the hallway. Drew nearer. "Yes. You. Can." Isabella, Chelsea's older sister, appeared.

"How did you get here so fast?" Chelsea took a sip of coffee to fortify her courage. Prepared to do battle. She and her older sister looked a lot alike. But no one *ever* confused them.

Isabella's barely-there makeup showed off her flawless complexion. She nearly always wore a suit: navy, gray, or black. High heels—high enough to be sexy but low enough to still be sensible. And a silk, button-front blouse. The expensive jewelry she dangled around her neck added fashion to her outfits. Isabella called them "statement pieces." However, Chelsea had checked. They were "investment pieces" with lots of zeros to the left of the decimal point.

But it didn't matter, Isabella could wear a muumuu and still convey authority.

"Corporate jet at my disposal. Now, happy birthday. I see you haven't been home to accept my present. You can thank me later. Please say good-bye to Momma. I'm taking this shift tonight."

"No." Chelsea shook her head. "I don't trust you. I'll come back in the morning, and Momma will be gone. You'll have shoved her aside, shoved her out of sight, shoved her quicker into a grave."

Isabella leaned in for a hug. That caught Chelsea by surprise. Victoria took the cup of coffee from her.

"Sis, I've been doing research. Talking with doctors. I understand the situation much better than you think. Let me help. I promise. Promise. You come back at eight in the morning. Momma and I will be waiting for you." When Isabella finished speaking, she released her from the hug.

Weariness settled over Chelsea, but she didn't dare leave. After all, what happened to Momma was her fault. She should be the one to stay in the recliner by her side all night.

Chelsea blinked when her sister shoved her. "Go. Victoria, take this barely-standing, extremely-stubborn, obnoxiously-dressed sister of mine out of here. Make her a good memory for her birthday."

Chelsea caved to her sister's demand. It was a kindness, really. And she could use a break—birthday or not. Never before had Isabella offered to stay with Momma. She didn't trust her sister's motives, yet recognized her caring. "Let me say good night to Momma."

At her mother's bedside, she pulled the blanket up to cover her mother's shoulders, like her mother had done with her when tucking her in as a child. Momma was pale, wearing a new fragility that hadn't been there this morning. Caring for Momma came from a place of love and deep affection. Chelsea kissed her forehead. "I'll see you in the morning."

Momma's expression altered to concern. "That's what that young man said. Is there going to be a party,

Chelsea?"

"Yes, Momma. A party of sorts."

She walked out of the room and scrunched her eyes shut. Isabella squeezed her shoulder before entering their mother's room.

Victoria linked arms with her and said, "Let's go." Twenty minutes later, Victoria pulled her Mercedes onto the driveway at Chelsea's house. A box sat by the stairs—probably from Isabella. On the front gallery, Chef Tanner sat with a small cooler.

Victoria patted Chelsea's arm excitedly. "I'll bet he's got something in there for you. Hop out. Go."

"You can't leave me here with him," Chelsea hissed.

"I'll bet he's good with dessert." Victoria wiggled her eyebrows. "Let's get these gifts unloaded, and *then* I'll go."

Too tired to argue, Chelsea exited the car.

Chef Tanner rose as she climbed the stairs. *Déjà vu* hit her. Her climbing stairs. Her wobbling. Her with her arms around his neck. Her gaze narrowed on his lips.

The urge to kiss him rolled in a wave, one the size of a tsunami. And she hoped that should she kiss him again, he'd make her lips tingle. A quasi-date with a celebrity chef would certainly be a highlight to her otherwise dull diary entry for her thirtieth.

Another kiss would be a great birthday present.

Chapter Seven

Zachary carried the last of Chelsea's dozen-plus birthday gifts from the trunk of Victoria's car. The sun had dipped below the horizon, and the first star twinkled in the inky blue sky. The exterior landscaping lights around the house popped on, giving the place the look of a private paradise. Palm trees. Oak trees. Dripping Spanish moss. As he walked up the steps to Chelsea's, Victoria hurried down.

"You're leaving?" He met her in the middle of the dozen stairs.

Victoria ran a finger down his arm. "My busy holiday season. I have a trunk show tonight." She winked. "You could come. Cause quite a stir. A few nice words from you might up sales of my clothing line." She eyed him as though fitting him for a suit. "I've not designed for men before, but you could be a muse, my inspiration."

He'd never met a Southern woman as bold and forward as Victoria Abernathy. The more he got to know her, the more he was certain he needed to run—run like Forrest Gump. But he certainly admired her devotion to her friend.

"Aww, don't look so panicked." She grinned. "You're not my type either. I just love stirring the pot."

She crooked her finger and motioned him closer. He leaned in, and then she said, "But I promise you, you hurt my friend"—she thumbed behind her in the direction of Chelsea's door—"and we'll be having some Tanner oysters at our next low country boil. You get my meaning?" She raised an eyebrow.

Zach drew back. He was more than a little offended. "Victoria Abernathy, I do not kiss and tell. I do not sleep and talk about it. I do not take orders about my personal life from you. Retract your claws. Pull in your fangs. Do we understand each other?"

Victoria chuckled. "You're perfect for her." Then she descended the stairs, leaving him alone. There was a time when he might have considered giving Victoria a second thought—witty, stylish, she-devil—but age and maturity had set him on a different course. Now, it was the demure, artistic Chelsea who captured his full attention. She could calm the roughest of seas with a kittenish glance and a soft smile. His heart swelled thinking of her looking at him that way.

He entered the house and deposited the gifts with the others on the dining room table.

"Thank you for helping with the packages." Chelsea was sitting on the couch, her feet resting on a leather ottoman, her head back, eyes closed.

"I have some shrimp and grits for you. A nice bottle of white Georgia wine. Baguette of French bread. You've had a rough day. Let me heat this up for you."

"Wine would be nice. I'll get up in a moment for glasses and the opener. Why don't you take a seat by the hearth?"

He wanted to cook for her. Did she ever allow anyone to take care of her?

He took a seat in a wingback chair near the lit fireplace. "Are you hungry?"

Shadows beneath her eyes hinted at weariness. Yet still so beautiful. He recalled their earlier kiss and then learning how she cared for her mother with dementia had touched him deeply. It was as if some part of his soul had locked with hers.

"Chef Tanner, I appreciate all you've done. Yes, shrimp and grits are my favorite, but I don't want to inconvenience you."

"Zach," he said.

"Zach?"

"Short for Zachary. My friends call me Zach. Some call me Tanner. The professional world calls me Chef or Chef Tanner."

She opened one eye and looked at him. "What does your family call you?"

"Family?"

"Aren't you related to the fishing Tanners? The ones with the fleet of shrimp boats?"

"Maybe." He wasn't yet ready to talk with her, or

anyone, about what brought him here to Jubilee, Georgia. Or what he had learned about his father—and how little he knew.

Chelsea's feet plopped to the floor. She leaned forward. "There's a story in there somewhere, and I want to hear it. I'll get those wineglasses and the opener now."

"Why don't you let me heat up this food? We can have dinner on your porch. Through those doors looks like a great view of the water." He wanted to distract her from the subject he wasn't ready to discuss.

"Why not? I'll turn on the torch heater outside. Where's that bottle of wine you promised me?"

He grabbed the cooler he'd left by the front door and brought it into the kitchen. The space was small, perfect for two. But the nearness of her made him all the more aware of the curve of her neck, the gracefulness of her fingers when she reached for two wine glasses, her gentle blonde waves cascading down her back, windblown-sexy with the scent of salt water and sunshine. She had all the sweetness of a peach.

Chelsea handed him a pan. "This is for the shrimp. And over the microwave"—she pointed—"there's a bowl to heat the grits. I'll grab some butter for the bread."

He began heating the food while she took the bottle and glasses to the opposite side of the kitchen island. She attacked it, stabbing the cork with the corkscrew.

"Wait." He wiped his hands on the nearest towel.

"Please, allow me." He uncorked the bottle and handed it to her.

After pouring a small amount into a glass, she offered it to him. "Taste test, Chef?"

He took the offering. He'd discovered Georgia's wine highway and attended a tasting to select wines for the wine cellar of his new restaurant. "A Viognier grape pairs well with seafood."

"I'm sure it will pair perfectly with your meal." Her amused grin hinted at mischievousness.

"What?"

"I kinda like having a man in my kitchen cooking for me." She sipped her wine, then traced the rim of the glass with her finger. "The last man in my kitchen—he came to unclog the garbage disposal. Momma stuffed a whole head of cabbage in there."

"How long has your mom had dementia?" He stirred the broth as it simmered before adding the shrimp to not overcook the shellfish.

"So you know. Vic must have told you." She sighed. "Twooo looong yearsss—since she started forgetting people. Since my dad divorced her. Since she starting living with me."

She strung out the words, as though it were a lifetime.

"Two years since I had a date. Two years since I had a vacation. Two years since I've been away from home for more than a few hours."

The microwave dinged. The grits were ready. And he was ready to know more about Chelsea. What made her tick? What made her tingle? What would make her take a chance on the chemistry brewing between them?

"Bowls are behind you, to the left of the sink." With the wine bottle tucked under her arm, two wineglasses in one hand, and a bread plate in the other, she headed for the French doors leading to the back porch.

A few minutes later, once all the food was before them, Zach lifted his glass. "A toast."

Chelsea lifted hers.

"To the birthday girl. May life grant you your fondest dreams." Zach clinked his glass against hers. Two years since she'd had a date. Why? Were the men around her blind or just dumb—the stupid kind?

"Thank you. To dreams." She sipped and cast her eyes downward. It was as though dreams were something too far out of her reach. Maybe in time, he could uncover what she wanted most. In the meantime, the energy between them was easy, breezy, and growing more alluring. If he were a fish, he'd want her to reel him in.

Over dinner, they talked about things they had in common: a love of smooth jazz, opalescent sunsets, and seafood. Her eyes were lit with a glow from within. Hypnotized. That's what he was. They also spoke about things they didn't like: bad drivers, too sweet wines, and Daylight Saving Time. The topic they never discussed further was family.

Until a year ago, he hadn't known anything about his. His mother was an only child from Kansas whose parents died before he was born, and his mother had always refused to speak about his father or explain why she kept all information about him secret—the man wasn't even listed on his birth certificate. Revealing secrets became her deathbed confession...his curse and blessing.

But Chelsea's family—they had history written up in books that revealed skeletons and scoundrels and scandals. News stories chronicled her life: first ballet recital, Girl Scout cookie seller, artistic talent with a full art scholarship. And all her volunteer work. She had a good heart. Had compassion for people. People who were flawed. People like him.

"Last sip." Chelsea lifted her glass. "Thank you for a wonderful birthday dinner."

He hoped, over the course of the evening, she'd enjoyed his company as much as he enjoyed hers. And it made him consider the days ahead. Of Christmas. His wish would be to see her face lit with joy. Some quiet time with for the two of them. Contented. Fulfilled. And maybe a little in love.

Maybe.

Chapter Eight

One day blurred into the next. While Momma remained in the hospital, Chelsea found a new rhythm of working nearly around the clock. The tiring schedule wouldn't beat her, not with her business reputation to protect.

The only moment of joy she had allowed herself was to open one birthday present a day. It had been kind of Vic to bring them to her and kind of Zach to tote them into the house. One present a day brought levity to the sad upheaval in her life. "Dang dementia. I hate you."

On Wednesday, the doctor called an afternoon family meeting. A perfect December day. Blue sky, seagulls calling to each other, and no humidity. With uplifted spirits, Chelsea bounded into Momma's room where everyone had gathered.

"Let's talk in the hall." The doctor led her, Isabella, and Layton out of Momma's earshot.

"She has a urinary tract infection. A UTI." The doctor determined it was brought on by dehydration. But a combination of symptoms had caused Momma's crazy behavior.

"I don't know how to force her to drink more," she told the doctor, feeling as though she were being blamed.

"Maybe it's time to consider a different kind of care."

He'd played right into her sister and brother's plan. Chelsea fumed.

"We're going to keep her for a few more days. Start an IV with antibiotics. We'll see what's next."

Chelsea returned to Momma's side, but she'd fallen asleep. Ignoring Isabella and Layton, Chelsea left the hospital. Pottery didn't make itself. She needed to work.

That evening, Zach appeared with hot, homecooked food for a late-night meal. A pleasant surprise. She briefly showed him around her studio before they ate.

"We haven't had a chance to talk about business. I have a plan that might be mutually beneficial for both of us," he said.

"Oh, Zach. Business is going to have to wait. I'm overwhelmed as it is, but I promise, someday soon we'll have that chat." Concern tugged at the corners of her mind. Mixing business and pleasure—not a good idea. But that didn't matter, because what was happening between them was neither business nor pleasure, just friendly, though her mind caught the rapid beat of her heart sending a Morse code message about there being something more.

The chardonnay and smooth jazz flowed. Flickering candlelight danced. She sat with a man cocooned in a world she'd forgotten existed: a place of civilized conversation. A beautiful view of the bright white moon. The comforting sound of a boat puttering on Fancy Bluff

Creek.

And flirtation fanned the flames of desire.

Chef Zachary Tanner was one hot dish.

Chelsea stifled a giggle. He'd probably heard that before. The man had cooked all over the world for some of the most glamorous celebrities. So what in the world was he doing here? With her? She didn't have time to ponder that. She had to get back to work.

By Saturday, Chelsea fumed. Her emotions were a hurricane. "She needs memory care." The doctor's words made her inner landscape dark, matching the rainstorm now drenching Jubilee. A miserable Saturday afternoon. She'd been surviving on fours of sleep a night and a few catnaps. But before she found a bed tonight, she needed to finish glazing. Tomorrow, she'd stack the last load into the kiln. At least Mika had the Christmas present buying and distribution to the children under control.

Mixing seafoam green glaze in a five-gallon bucket, Chelsea seethed. "We're not ready for that. Assisted living." She snorted. "No. And no. I'll fight Isabella and Layton."

Yet guilt settled heavy like an anchor on her chest. Maybe Momma needed more supervised attention. And with her gone, she'd had uninterrupted work time for the special order due next Saturday. If Momma hadn't ended up in the hospital, she might have had to disappoint a bride. That would have been bad for business and bad for her reputation.

She heard a knock at the studio's open door.

Zach filled the doorway. She squeezed her eyes tight and then blinked several times. A denim blue shirt, cuffs rolled up, faded jeans. Those blues brought out the blue in his brightly shining eyes. And he directed that shine solely at her.

"What are you doing here?" She wasn't a hundred percent sure she hadn't conjured him up due to her exhaustion.

"Why, hello, Zach. It's nice to see you. Dinner? Of course. Now would be great. I haven't eaten since…" Zach gestured to her to finish his sentence.

"Since…I can't remember. I think I ate something at noon." She instantly recalled their last dinner together. Lighthearted. Engaging. Purely platonic. Fish so fresh it could nearly jump back into the sea. And a bottle of wine—not enough to reduce her inhibitions, but enough to make her consider kissing him again.

No. No. No time for romance.

"I actually arrived about an hour ago. Dinner is ready. And frankly, my dear, you look ready to drop. Food first. Sleep next." His gaze bore into hers.

"You're pretty gutsy. Did a B&E in my house."

He chuckled. "No cop is going to believe that. Not when you don't lock your door. Besides, I texted I was coming. You never responded. I took silence for a yes."

"I have to work." Tension put her nerves on alert. Momma wasn't home. Work had to come first. But drinking in the sight of him, the storm he caused, and the chance of another dinner with him...did she have the defenses to resist?

"Chelsea"—he reached for her hand—"take thirty minutes. At least eat."

His voice smoothed over her. The heat of his hand. The gentle tug he gave. All so persuasive. "So, Chef, what's for dinner?" She stepped out of her studio and ran through the rain to the covered back porch. "Last one in has to pour the wine."

Chelsea headed for her bedroom to find something clean and dry to wear. Pulling the stained T-shirt over her head, she tossed it on the floor in the bathroom, washed her face, and for a brief second, considered crossing the line into something more than friendship. Instead, she pulled on a scoop-neck blouse, scooped her hair into a twist, and scooped up her quaking nerves. Taking a long slow breath, she blew it out even slower. She mentally grounded her feet and drew up the drawbridge to protect her heart—Zachary Tanner had a way of making her feel as though she floated, untethered to the earth.

Finally, she entered the kitchen. Zach lifted an eyebrow but didn't comment. Did he have any idea how she felt about him? She paused. Exactly how did she feel? Breathless. Giddy. Hopeful. And that last emotion made him dangerous.

"Dinner is served on the back porch. I'll get the wineglasses. You go have a seat."

Chelsea settled into a chair at the table. Soft music swirled around her. The elegant table setting featured china from Zach's new restaurant with his starfish logo. The silverware shined. Ice water already poured in water glasses showed the logo etched into them. A salad had been tossed with vinaigrette. She lifted the lid of the serving dish—seafood fettuccini. The heavenly aroma nearly lifted her from her seat.

Zach set a wineglass in front of her and poured the wine. "An Italian Pinot Grigio to go with dinner." He seated himself across from her and poured for himself.

"You've gone to so much trouble."

"No trouble. I wanted to spend time with you. I can't get you to call me, so I'm making my own opportunity." His smile was devilish and she liked it.

"A toast." He lifted his glass. "To celebrating new friends becoming good friends."

She clinked her glass with his.

And a realization dawned.

Her heart had tripped, flipped, and flopped.

She wanted to be more than *just* friends.

And for a little while, over dinner, she could pretend they were destined for more.

Dinner was delicious. The conversation was a volley

of double entendres. The pull of attraction netted her like a crab caught in a trap. And she didn't want the night to end.

A little while later, she tipped her wineglass up to empty the last drop and set it on the table between them, creating a boundary. He had his half of the table. She had hers. Reality had come knocking. She had to work. He had to go. To distract her from the magnetism pulling her in his direction, she moved her fingers to the music as though playing the piano piece along with David Benoit.

Zach's hand crossed the imaginary boundary.

She cocked her head to study him but kept playing.

Her heartbeat changed from a flutter to the banging of a bass drum when his hand inched closer to hers. He stretched his finger out to rub the top of her hand.

That stilled her fingers.

Her breath caught.

The scorching heat of his touch startled her the way a sudden jerk on a fishing rod signaled a hooked fish too big to land. She stood abruptly. "I'm really sorry, but I need to call it a night. I have to work and must be at the hospital early in the morning."

Zach didn't move. He looked up at her. "What about a late lunch tomorrow?"

From her vantage point, she thought his face was even sexier in candlelight. She shook her head and rubbed her hands together. "Can't. I've got to work."

"Ah, the artist's soul never rests."

"I have a special bridal order that must be completed for a holiday wedding on December 22. It's the same day as the live Nativity, which I haven't missed in years."

"How about dinner? Same time. Same place. I'll bring the food."

Lord-o-mercy, the man was persistent. A welling deep in her gut pushed up, and the words, "Yes, I want to have lunch *and* dinner with you" fought to get out. She quelled the riot by standing straighter. "How about I call you when I have some time?"

He leaned back and chuckled. The smoothness of his laugh rose over the velvety smooth jazz that no longer soothed her paper-thin defenses.

Zach rose. Came around to her side of the table.

Chelsea faced him, remaining rooted to her spot. Her gaze darted from side to side. She didn't dare make eye contact with him. Her heartbeat quickened.

He lifted her chin.

Her every nerve froze.

He lowered his lips to hers. Pressed a light kiss, then deepened it.

She trembled.

He lifted her arms and placed them around his neck. Pulled her closer and kissed her more.

Lost, she melted into him. The heat of him. The smell of him. The feel of him.

When he broke the kiss, he stepped back, taking her

hands in his. "Chelsea Cooper, I didn't get to be successful by following rules. I blazed trails where others didn't. I'm a man who's totally fascinated by you. But I sense your reluctance. And though I've always been a gentleman, I've recently discovered my Southern roots, so I have a lot to live up to—being a *Southern* gentleman. But make no mistake, this man is very interested in you."

She nearly swooned.

He held her hand, tugged her along through the house to her front door. "I'll say good night, now. And I'll call you tomorrow. You can tell me then what time for dinner. I understand work. Even now, my staff is practicing our menu. It takes time and patience. I've got a boatload of that." Zach kissed her hand. Opened the front door. Descended the stairs.

Dazed, Chelsea watched him go. No false male swagger. No bravado. Just confidence.

A man who scared the heck out of her.

He waved as he pulled away. She waved back, then closed the door and headed for a cold shower—because she was like melted butter and there wasn't a freezer big enough to cool her down. The man's touch was on her skin, seeping through her pores and igniting hot sparks in her bloodstream.

He needed to go about his life. Even if they had a chance to build common ground, he would leave the way Simon had, her father had, some of her friends had…because Momma always had to come first. There was no room in her life for a man. Even one as enticing as Zach.

The heartache of Momma's slow slide into deepening dementia had wrapped her heart tight. The metronome of her life ticktocked. It was only a matter of time before a man as wonderful as Zach would grow tired of her priorities and leave.

In the shower, cool water sluiced over Chelsea. She sat on a teak stool and cried. Salty tears mixed with the water. She was thirty. Unmarried. Undating. Unattached.

"Enough pity-party time. You have things to do before falling into bed." She dried, pulled on a T-shirt and jeans. Heading to her studio to work, she snagged the empty wine bottle. Maybe she'd paint Zach's name on it as a reminder of the most romantic evening she'd had in years.

Thoughts of Zach stirred her heart and her blood. Anticipation was a heady cocktail. But…her father left her mother because of her mother's condition. Simon left her because of her mother's condition. Men promised many things. Didn't deliver on much. And after a perfect evening, she wasn't willing to risk ruining the memory. This was the highlight. Her one night to remember. Just one night.

She focused on glazing plates for the wedding order. Shut everything else out. Later that night, she'd load the kiln. Then, she could cave to sleep.

At midnight, a text from Victoria dinged on Chelsea's phone.

Wishing you many more dinners…with Zach.

Vic included a smiling emoji with red hearts for eyes.

Chelsea replied.

Fiddledeedee. What could you possibly mean? Good night, Vic.

Even later, in the wee hours of Sunday morning, she couldn't resist a glance at the moon before sliding into bed. "Is he watching you, too?"

A longing ache over what was lost before it ever began chained her heart.

Chapter Nine

The next morning, Chelsea dressed for church in a red wool skirt and sweater. Her black knee-length boots and black Chanel purse were gifts from Isabella. She stopped at the hospital for a visit with Momma, carrying hope in her heart that everything would shake out, smooth out, and work out. They'd have another wonderful Christmas.

Chelsea planned to stay until it was time to leave for church and then return afterward with fried chicken, potato salad, and coleslaw from Ruby's Restaurant. A picnic in the sunshine-filled hospital room—unconventional, but the food and company would be first-rate.

A text dinged on her phone.

Good morning. I'm in need of some authentic Jubilee advice. How about lunch or dinner? What will it be?

She smiled at Zach's request. His persistence could melt an iceberg. It was nice to have a man, not just any man, but a man as charming, accomplished, and handsome as Zach interested in her. Yet, the flirtation was over. Momma would be coming home. He'd have to understand Momma came first. And once that message sank into his brain…she'd be alone, just like when Simon had declared he wasn't engaged to her *and* Momma, too.

She exited the elevator and turned right. The hospital

floor was by surrounded quiet, like a morgue rather than a place designed to heal the sick. She shook off the momentary attack of melancholy. Her heels tapped against the linoleum floor, a lonesome sound. She decided to focus on the positive, and her spirits buoyed.

"Knock. Knock." Chelsea rapped quickly on the door.

"Who's there?" Momma's voice was filled with suspicion.

Chelsea nodded to Mrs. Barrentine, stepped to the side of Momma's bed, and reached for her hand.

"She's had a fitful night, dear," Mrs. Barrentine said. "I'm going to step out for just a minute."

Chelsea leaned to plant a kiss on Momma's forehead, but Momma's eyes widened wild with fear. She tugged the sheet over her shoulder, covering her arm, her hand, and scooted to the opposite side of the bed. "*Who* are you?"

Chelsea's breath caught. "Momma, it's me, Chelsea."

"Momma?" Her voice pitched up an octave. "Momma?" she screeched. "I don't know what you're talking about. I'm a good girl. I'm only fifteen. I'm not anyone's Momma. Certainly, not yours. Who. Are. You?"

Nausea splat in Chelsea's stomach and then rolled like a boat pitched in high seas.

"Chelsea O'Connor Cooper. Your second daughter." This disorientation had to be the side effects of medication the doctor had prescribed. When Momma knew nothing else—Momma always knew her. Chelsea's knees wobbled. If she hadn't steadied herself against the bed, her boots would've been heels up.

"Get out! Get out! You can't come to my sweet sixteen party. You're not invited. Don't try to steal my dress."

Shock cemented Chelsea's feet to the floor. Her nerves pinged like an old-fashioned phone board lighting up.

"Leave?" she squeaked.

"Maybe you should go." Mrs. Barrentine squeezed her shoulder.

Chelsea leaned in Momma's direction and peered harder, looking for recognition. "Momma, it's me. Chelsea. You live with me. We have tea parties and swimming races and boat rides up Fancy Bluff Creek."

How can she NOT remember ME?

"Get out! Get out! Get out!"

Chelsea clutched her purse. Her knuckles whitened. A nurse rushed past her to her mother's aid. Chelsea left the room. In the hall, she leaned against the wall, sank into a squat.

"I know how much this must hurt, dear." Mrs. Barrentine had followed her into the hall.

Chelsea clutched her chest. "I've explained dementia to so many people. People Momma no longer recognizes. I tried to lessen their angst when she couldn't remember them. Now, all I feel is…shock…despair."

"Honey, you're worn out. You're not looking at life clearly. You cannot care for your Momma alone. It's not about your love, dedication, or tenacity. The level of care she now needs exceeds what you can give."

Numb, Chelsea returned home. She had to be alone. No church. No Zach. No emotional ties. Dementia left her dangling. Momma wasn't the only one impacted by the dreadful disease.

She peeled off her clothes and left them on her bed, then slid into flannel pajamas. Today, she would hide. Lick her wounds. Tomorrow she could start again. A full-on pity party day was what she needed.

She wandered into the dining room. The last of her birthday presents remained. A box wrapped in shiny white paper and topped with a pink bow as large as a cluster of hydrangea blossoms. She couldn't bring herself to open it. Wasn't ready for a moment of joy. It would be incompatible with the grief seeping from her heart.

Momma had always taught her to make lemonade from lemons. Her life was now a bushel full of the fruit, but she had no energy to change anything. Her mother had been her biggest cheerleader, biggest supporter, and one of her best friends. Pulling the knitted coverlet her mother made years ago over herself, she scrunched down on the couch and covered herself. And slept.

Bringgg. Bringgg. Bringgg.

Pulled from a deep sleep, Chelsea rolled over,

reached around for her phone, then opened her eyes. The dang noise made her want to fling the thing into the river.

"Yeah," she answered, her voice as flat as she felt.

"Chelsea? That you?" Angie asked.

"Yeah."

"Are you okay? You don't sound quite right."

"Bad day." Her old friend and minister, Reverend Angela Duncan, would understand.

"I'm sorry. I heard your momma's still in the hospital. Missed you two in church the last couple of weeks. I'm going to swing by and see her. Should I come see you, too?"

"Don't bother. On either account."

"What's wrong?"

Chelsea sat up, anger propping her up further. "Wrong?" Her voice hit a wobbly high note. "Momma doesn't know me. My mother won't *know* you if you go. In fact, you may upset her, which in turn will upset you."

"The dementia has gotten worse." Angie's tone was full of compassion.

"Fatally so for me."

"I'm here to help."

"Then find a cure for dementia. Now!"

She shouldn't shout at Angie. Her friend was only doing what came naturally to a minister—visiting the sick and saving souls—but unless she had a miracle cure mixed in a cocktail of prayers…there was no hope for Momma now. The dementia ship that Chelsea believed would be Momma's slow ride across the sea had morphed into a speedboat and whisked her away.

"Chelsea," Angie whispered, "if I could. I promise, I would. But what I can do is pray. And come see you."

"I'm sorry. I shouldn't have yelled. I'm just so dang…angry. Frustrated. Feeling so guilty. After the live Nativity next Saturday, we'll make plans. I promise. And maybe Momma will be home by then."

A text dinged on her phone. She ignored it.

"How about if we go see your momma together?"

"No. I can't. Isabella's with her now. Layton will spend the night. I have no objections if you visit, but I can't take any more right now. Angie, I've got to go. Someone keeps texting me. Technology is impatient." It was a lie, but only a little white lie.

"I'll check on you tomorrow. But I am going to see your momma. Besides, I haven't seen Isabella in a while. She never comes to church when she's home."

"We'll talk again soon. Bye." Chelsea ended the call quickly. Angie meant well.

The phone dinged again.

And again.

Chelsea reviewed the text messages. All from Zach.

Dinner. I'll pick you up in thirty.

Casual dress.

I'm down the street. Arriving early.

Chelsea jumped up from the couch, pulled on a jacket, slid her feet into sneakers, grabbed her keys and her regrets.

She headed for the boat. A ride on the creek would help clear her head. The last thing she needed was someone trying to make her feel better. Someone who made her feel things she hadn't felt in a while. Someone with whom she wanted to spend more time...but the past had ruined that.

Zach, sorry. Can't make it.

Maybe after Momma came home from the hospital, after she settled into a new routine, after Isabella returned to Tampa, then there might be time.

Maybe.

Chapter Ten

A few days later, the sun cast fresh light on a hopeful day. A day to put away gloom, regrets, what-ifs—like Zach—to officially begin prepping for the holiday. Trees. Lights. Ornaments. Music. Chelsea tingled with anticipation.

She arrived at the hospital dressed in a red silk blouse—the only silk one she owned—black slacks, and low heels to match. Momma liked it best when she dressed up, and she wanted to make her happy. And fingers crossed, maybe Momma would remember her today.

The doctor had arranged for her mother's release. Less than a week before Christmas. Despite the chaos of the month, there was still time to salvage Christmas.

And she'd pulled *everything* together. The special bridal order was finished on time. Today, they'd get a Christmas tree. Tomorrow, she'd box the bridal order. Saturday would be the live Nativity at church. Maybe a buffet dinner afterward for her friends. They'd all light sparklers on the dock, wave them over the water, and watch the flashes of silver light dance. Talk. Make merry. Just as the holiday should be.

Once she rounded the corner after leaving the elevator, Isabella and Layton waited for her. Their heads close together, whispering, conspiring, and conjuring something. She sensed an ambush. "So what's up? You're like two pirates cooking something up."

Probably want me to walk the plank.

Layton nodded stiffly. Isabella cleared her throat. She'd never seen her sister hesitant, at least not like this.

Dread inched up Chelsea's spine. She tried to swallow, but it was more of a gulp.

"Chelsea, I...we"—Isabella nodded to Layton— "hope you'll agree with the doctor and the psychologist that it's best for Momma to be moved to a memory care unit. You refused to look at the places we picked out. You have Momma's best interest at heart, but for some reason, you're blinded from the truth. The doctor has certified she can't live alone—"

"She doesn't," Chelsea snapped. "She lives with me."

"And she needs more care, more specialized care with certain types of stimulation, like group activities. Can't you see?"

"No."

Layton stepped forward and shoved some folded papers in her hand. "We've filed for guardianship. You don't have final say about Momma. The law is on our side."

Chelsea gripped her stomach. "What *have* you done?"

She held her breath. They were pirates. Robbing her of her mother.

"You made us do it," Layton sneered between clenched teeth. "People are just going to love that we're airing dirty laundry in public. This could be bad for my business."

Isabella put her hand on Layton's arm and reached out, but Chelsea backed out of reach. "You…you…don't understand. She can't be in a home. No strangers caring for her."

Bile roiled. She fought to catch her breath. She tried to clamp down on emotions erupting. She would not lose her breakfast. Not humiliate herself and her family. The gossipmongers of Jubilee would love spreading that news. She opened the papers and began to read.

Guardianship granted blared like a flashing yellow highway sign in the dead of night.

"This is what's going to happen." Isabella's voice rang with authority. "We are all going to take Momma to her new place. Then Chelsea and I are going to meet the movers, load furniture, and take it to Momma. Later this afternoon, we'll get a Christmas tree and decorations. We'll decorate like we always do. Oh, and Daddy bought a sofa sleeper for us so we can spend the night when we need to."

Chelsea flung the papers at her sister. "I'm going to fight you. *I'll* get a lawyer. Momma will be back home with me by New Year's Day." She ran into her mother's room.

"Chelsea, dear." Momma smiled. "I can't believe we're so close to Christmas. This will be the best one yet."

Momma knew her. Her eyes had lit up.

"Momma, I believe you're right." Chelsea blinked her watery eyes. She swallowed and blinked again. She would not cry. Would not.

Every year, her mother exclaimed how it was the season of joy. Gratitude. Blessings. Every day was a gift. And she hated to miss those moments.

Momma clapped her hands. "Fraser fir. I want one at least eight feet high." She raised her arm high. "At least this tall."

Chelsea turned when she felt a touch on her arm and faced Isabella. "Honey, that might a bit too big this year. But we'll have a beautiful tree."

"I think eight feet is perfect, Momma." Chelsea flashed a you-can't-control-me grimace at her sister.

"We're going to help you get dressed. Then we're all going to a…new community." Isabella's voice was gentle. She moved close to the bed and held Momma's hand. "I arranged for you to have a special room there. We'll get a tree. We'll decorate. We'll get ready for Christmas."

The rest of the day was a haze of activity. Numb from her siblings' deception, Chelsea complied with the plan, not wanting to do anything to upset her mother. As soon as she could, she'd consult an attorney. And as quickly as she could make it happen, Momma would be back home.

Layton stayed with their mother while she and Isabella met the moving van. She packed her mother's belongings while Isabella directed the movers. Chelsea could barely swallow past the huge lump in her throat once her mother's room was emptied.

"I'm going to follow the van over. Why don't you take the pickup and get a tree for Momma? Can you grab some decorations out of storage, too?" Isabella climbed into her car and drove away without Chelsea ever uttering a word.

"I hate dementia. I hate dementia. I hate dementia." Chelsea screamed. Tears flooded down her face.

It was dusk when Chelsea arrived with a small tabletop-size tree and a couple of boxes of decorations. Her footsteps slowed as she carried the tree into the lobby, down the hall, and into her mother's room. She would never admit to her sister and brother that the place, with a small living room, refrigerator, cabinets, separate bedroom and bathroom, wasn't quite as hideous as she had anticipated. It was clean, bright, welcoming, and almost spacious.

Layton nodded at her and left the room. He returned a few minutes later with the boxes of decorations from the back of the pickup.

"Let's decorate the tree." Isabella guided Momma over to the boxes. "Where shall we start?"

"Isabella," Momma admonished. "I'm not an invalid

or a child."

Isabella nodded and turned the TV to a music station playing Christmas music. Clearly, her sister had thought of every detail. Had plotted and schemed behind Chelsea's back. Anguish burned in her chest. She both loved and despised her sister. The duality of feelings made the emotional haze she'd battled all day settle in deeper.

Chelsea dropped to the floor, unwrapped Christmas ornaments, and handed them to Momma to hang. "Do you remember that one?" A red velvet ribbon with a sterling silver bell with a date engraved on it.

"Of course." Momma's grin was soft. "It's the one I got for your first Christmas. You were barely weeks old."

"And what about this one?" She held up a small, hand-carved rocking horse.

"That was Layton's first ornament."

Chelsea unwrapped several more ornaments. "I can't seem to find the one for Isabella."

"Oh. I remember," Momma said. "Last year, when we took the tree down, she took all her childhood ornaments."

"Why?"

Momma looked left to right. She took a step closer to Chelsea. Her eyes flashed with wariness. At was as though a light had dimmed. She whispered, "I can't remember." She flopped onto the couch, stared, moved her fingers back and forth in front of her as though reading.

Chelsea straightened. The momma who had come

from the hospital and applauded when the tree lights glowed was not the same woman with her now.

Chelsea's heart seized. Pain so vivid she hugged her chest and fought back tears. Her dearest hope was that her mother wasn't suffering inside in some quiet way.

Please, let us have this Christmas together.

Then her phone dinged. Startled, she jumped up. She read the message from Zach.

I'm trying again. How about dinner?

She shook her head.

I think I've apologized to you more than any person I know. I wish I could, but I can't.

His reply came quickly.

No fun in that. What's your favorite color? What's your favorite song?

Her emotions spun. She wanted him to leave her alone. Her heart couldn't handle the hanging threat of more hurt.

Blue, the color of the sky and the sea near Jubilee. Don't have a favorite song.

To everything there was a season. But this wasn't a season for her to allow a man like Zach into her life.

Sorry, got to go. Flare-up in kitchen. Training before opening.

"Favorite song." She tapped her finger against her phone.

"I'll Be Home for Christmas"

...if only in my dreams.
Then she deleted the message.

Chapter Eleven

Dawn broke Saturday morning, an hour after Chelsea rose and began working in the silence of her studio. All the times she'd craved silence when Momma was having a bad day—she wished for them back. Now the silence was deafening.

Last night, when Chelsea had tucked Momma into bed, her mother had been quiet and still disoriented. She'd eaten little. Getting her to drink all of her sweet tea—her favorite drink—proved impossible. How did she keep someone hydrated who refused to cooperate? Somehow, Momma's mind got stuck like a race car making laps around a track, and repeatedly, she asked for her husband, Layton, Sr. That old repeated request caused more scar tissue to bind Chelsea's emotions into a knot—big, hot, and angry.

Layton insisted on spending the night with Momma. He'd barely said more than a handful of words to her since thrusting legal papers at her.

"Chelsea?"

She jumped. Isabella called her name. Her sister had some audacity to invade her private sanctuary. "What?" She returned to boxing plates for the bridal order.

"Could you at least look at me when I'm speaking to

you?"

"I'm working. I have never barged into your office, scared you out of your skin, and demanded to talk to you."

Isabella chuckled. "Good point. I apologize. However, will you please talk with me?"

"No. Please leave. I'll give you my attorney's name when I get it. Anything you have to say, you can do it through that channel."

"Aww, Chelsea. Please. Look, you've done a great job." Isabella's tone was conciliatory. "An excellent job. But the changes our mother is displaying—the consequences could be fatal. I'm not judging what you've *already* done. Momma has had a wonderful two years because of you. But time has changed things."

Grabbing ribbon, Chelsea tied a seafoam green box with wide white satin bow. "You put Momma in a dumping ground. What did grandpa use to call it? Oh, that's right. Heaven's waiting room."

Chelsea felt the warmth of Isabella's hand on her back. "Please," her sister said gently. "Please. Just give this a chance. In three months, if you can't see this is the best place, the best thing for Momma, I promise, we can talk about what to do next. Let's not waste time, money, and create hard feelings. We're still family."

"Isabella, you showed yourself in. Please show yourself out." Chelsea turned her back on her sister. Isabella's words stung. All night, Chelsea tried to wrap her head around what they'd done to Momma. And a niggling voice, one that grew louder and drove her from bed before dawn said, "*Maybe it is for the best.*"

The words rang foreign in her ears. She entirely disagreed with that sentiment.

Around 10:00 a.m., after the final box was wrapped and loaded into her car, she showered and dressed. Sensible walking boots, jeans, a red and white checked shirt with a silvery thread running through it, and a jean jacket. She had to make her delivery, grab a bite to eat after that, then visit Momma. It hurt that she couldn't take her mother to the live Nativity.

Pulling into the driveway of a quaint cottage on the outer edges of town, Chelsea noticed several cars, including one she hadn't expected to see.

"Hello," she called through the side screen door. The house belonged to the bride and groom who were exchanging their vows at one of the historic houses on Jekyll Island.

"Miss Cooper, sorry about the wait. I'm Sarina, the wedding planner's assistant. Come in." A young woman, barely legal drinking age, waved her inside. "This is kind of a different duty for me. The mothers of the bride and groom got together and had a decorator make a mark in here." Sarina gave a Vanna-White flourish of her arms at the coziness.

"Nice. I have the special order dinnerware." Chelsea

tried to surreptitiously peek around the corner. Someone was in the kitchen cooking. The aromas were heavenly. Her stomach growled, unhappy that it hadn't yet been fed.

"It's a really nice thing their mothers are doing. They hired Chef Tanner''—Sarina leaned close to Chelsea—"to cook and stock the fridge with food. Must have cost a fortune. The honeymoon is only going to be two nights. They'll come home to gourmet food."

"That's some kinda mother's love," Chelsea said, feeling the sadness of her mother's situation. "Do you think Chef could spare a minute to help us unload my car?"

"Yes, I can help, Miss Cooper," Chef Tanner called from the kitchen.

"You know him?" Sarina asked.

Chelsea nodded.

Not only do I know him, but I keep turning him down. Why?

The three of them made quick work of the task.

"Thanks for the help. I hope the bride loves the dinnerware." Chelsea headed for the front door.

"Let me walk you out." Zach fell into step beside her on her walk to the car.

After a moment of uncomfortable silence, Chelsea asked, "Did you know there's a live Nativity tonight? Would you like to go?" She didn't want him to think it was a date, so she quickly added, "There's a group of friends going."

Zach's smile widened. "I'm definitely a friend."

"Yes. You. Are." She laughed.

"As much as I would love to go, I'm not able. Though, would you meet me for a late dinner afterward? I think I *might* need a friend then."

His words struck her as odd. As though something might happen to him between now and then. Was this a planned 9-1-1 call from him?

"It would be a favor and mean a lot. I'm…headed into unknown territory this evening. It will be good or not so much. Either way, afterward, a friendly face would be helpful."

The man was clearly being vague for a reason. She wouldn't pry, but he'd certainly piqued her curiosity.

"Additionally, we've never had a chance to discuss my business proposition. Tonight would be a good time." He raised an eyebrow.

Her special project had been delivered. Time permitted her to consider new options, now that her sister and brother made it so she couldn't provide Momma's care.

"It's a meeting." She offered her hand.

"No, it's definitely a date." Zach pecked her cheek and jogged back to the house. "Nine o'clock. At the Seafood Shac in Stiltsboro. I need a little grease and a beer.

Later that evening, Chelsea arrived at the live Nativity and waved at Reverend Angie, who moved about the set with a spirit of determination, directing the animals and the cast just as the performance began. Chelsea gathered with Vic and a few other friends. She smiled, hugged, kissed the air beside cheeks. No one would feel sorry for her tonight. She wouldn't allow it, putting on only a happy, brave face to the world.

The children began to sing "Away in a Manger." Chelsea whispered along.

Sadness, joy, hope, grief, all swirled as she continued to watch the program. Angie had clearly worked hard to get all the cast and crew to hit their marks.

"Oh, look. It's Liz. With some *hot* guy." Vic's eyes narrowed in appreciation. "And... Oh, *no*." This time her words came out as a threat. She turned sideways, blocking Chelsea's view.

"What are you doing?" Chelsea asked.

"Nothing. Nothing at all."

Obviously nothing was something. A big something. She stepped around Vic and caught movement in the crowd across the way. Zach was hugging a young woman. Shaking hands with a man and another woman.

Boom! Fireworks went off.

The sight of Zach zapped her. Shock as big and loud and startling as the *Boom*!

The spark for Zach she'd tried to bury burned her

now. Hot and fiery.

Chelsea turned. Vic grabbed her hand. "Don't jump to conclusions."

"Right," Chelsea snickered. "That's what you did. Not jump to conclusions. I'm going home. I'm tired. I can't take any more heartache."

Turning into the driveway, Chelsea nosed the car close to the garage. She couldn't bear to go inside. Dark. Lonely. Too quiet. For a few minutes, she'd been carried away by the holiday season. Now, she and Zach were only destined to be friends. She would spend Christmas Day with Momma, Isabella, and Layton. Nothing would ever be as it was.

Nothing in her life would ever be the same.

Chapter Twelve

Chelsea had woken hours ago—when good little girls and boys were fast asleep waiting for Santa Claus to arrive. She ached to experience that joy again. Of the family waking to scents of hot chocolate and pastries baking—Momma had made them every year when they gathered in their pajamas to open presents, back when they were kids. The tradition continued until Layton went away to college. After that, the whole family wasn't often together on Christmas morning, just for the feast at noon. Every year, until her father had left because he couldn't handle Momma's condition.

Dementia. It claimed her mother and left behind someone who looked like her, spoke like her, but was never fully present. Crushing reality squeezed tears from her eyes. George Winston's "December" played through her earbuds. Nice, but not entirely distracting.

Christmas morning with no hot chocolate and baked pastries. She'd wanted to bring some to Momma at sunup, but the director of nursing had said that while she was welcome, right now, Momma needed more time to acclimate to her new environment and follow a schedule. Late morning would be better than early.

Sunlight slanted through the shutters, cutting light

across the room and directly into Chelsea's eyes.

A knock sounded at the front door. It grew more insistent.

"I'm coming," she shouted and pulled on a long robe over her flannel pajamas. It was too warm in South Georgia for them, but Chelsea wanted to hang on to traditions.

The knocking turned into banging.

"What!" she demanded as she flung the door open.

Standing in the doorway in faded jeans, a long-sleeve knit shirt, a Santa's hat trimmed in white fluff, waving a plate under her nose—Zach. He held up a thermos, and two mugs dangled from his fingers. "Merry Christmas!"

He took a step closer.

She took a step back.

He raised his eyebrows. "May I come in?" Zach moved closer, until he stood halfway in and halfway out.

She motioned him inside, then pulled her robe tightly closed around her neck to cover up the vulnerability she was certain was seeping out.

He carried his offerings through the house to the family room and set them on the coffee table in front of the fireplace. "I'll be right back."

Chelsea turned on the Christmas tree lights and gas fireplace for ambiance. Given the effort he'd gone through, she could at least act as though she appreciated it. And she did. But... why was he doing this? She hadn't returned any of his text messages since...since she watched him hugging another woman. She'd replayed it in her mind. Over and over and over. The hug had been a tight embrace. An enthusiastic embrace. A meaningful embrace. He'd never hugged *her* like that.

But you never let him.

Not sure what to do, she sat on the couch and covered her lap with Momma's throw.

The front door banged closed. Zach returned with his arms laden with presents. "I have a Christmas picnic in a basket for our dinner. I set it on the counter in the kitchen. When do you open your presents? In the morning, like now? Or later in the day? Or what's your tradition?"

"A Christmas picnic?" That wasn't Christmassy at all. She twisted her mouth to one side. "All traditions have dwindled away."

"So let's make new ones." Zach placed his packages under the tree.

"Easier said than done." She picked at the stitches of throw in her lap.

Zach took the seat next to her. So close, she could feel joy vibrating from him. He opened an insulated flask, poured hot chocolate into both mugs, and handed one to her. Then he lifted the plate. "Christmas cookies. The first time I've made them in years."

A smiled played at the corners of her lips. Vic must have told him. She loved cookies with green and red

M&M's. He'd put forth a lot of effort to make this for her.

Chelsea's stomach grumbled. No matter what else she might feel, her stomach made its preferences clear.

"Mmmm," she said, tasting Zach's confectionary work.

He leaned over and kissed her. Then licked his lips as though she were something sweet and tasty. "My taste buds are doing a happy dance. And my heart is doing the same."

She set the plate and mug on the table. "Zach, I don't understand. Why are you here? I saw you hugging that woman the other night. I know I've put up a stop sign between us at each of your advances…but I'm not going to be anyone's second thought."

He leaned back. Folded his arms over his chest and propped his feet on the coffee table. "So that's why the arctic chill came to Jubilee."

"I *wouldn't* say I've been chilly."

"Downright icy. To completely ignore my texts and phone calls—why? Honestly, I expected more from you. But would an explanation warm the air?"

"Maybe." She hung her head. Folded her hands in her lap.

"Remember how you asked me about my family? We never talked about it."

"That's what gave me the impetus to ask you to stay, the night of my birthday."

"It's an odd story, but I might have a happy ending. We'll have to wait and see. The truth is, I had never met my father before. He and his wife invited me to join them at the live Nativity. A public place where nothing could get out of hand." He laughed. "Well, except it seems everything did *that* night."

His words were in English, but the context confused her. "You had never met your father before?"

Zach's shoulders heaved up and down. "Long story short—Mom never told him about me. Never told me about him—anything—until she was dying."

"She died?" Chelsea's heart lurched. Spasmed. Seized. Split. Zach had lost his mother?

"My mother died a year ago…on December eighth."

"My birthday…" she whispered. How sad for him. To deal with that, and at the same time cook for someone's birthday. Then the full realization of his words hit her—a *thunk* to the forehead. His mother never…never…told him? She died. As in dead. Stunned, Chelsea's mind tilted off-center trying to process the information. Her personal pity party about her own situation took on a new light best described as self-indulgent misery. At the very least, her mother, dementia and all, was still alive.

She'd been raised in a loving family. Had an ocean of memories. Whereas, Zach was meeting his father for the first time. The celebrity chef always seemed in control, forthright, invincible. A man of many accomplishments.

Their upbringings couldn't have been more different.

"You saw me hugging Jessica—that's what this is about, correct?—she's my younger, half sister. Younger than me."

Embarrassment burned in her gut, and from the way her cheeks heated up, they had to be flaming. "I'm embarrassed. I'm sorry. I apologize for jumping to conclusions."

Zach's feet moved to the floor. He reached for her hand. "Apology accepted. Actually, I'm not unhappy about the turn of events. I now have a father, stepmother, and sister to claim as family. But the best thing of all is the Christmas present you gave me."

She eyed him, unsure of his meaning. His present was wrapped and under the tree. A gesture of the heart even when her head told her to forget it. "And what present is that?"

His broad grin widened, his dimples nearly irresistible. His hands cupped her face. His lips moved within a breath of hers. "Now I know you care, maybe as much as I care about you."

His kiss was warm and gentle. She kissed him back. He was right. She cared. Cared a lot. Her heart fluttered. Giddiness spread all the way to her toes. She kissed him again, enjoying being carried away on a tide of happiness.

"So…I think we need to start our own tradition." Zach kissed the palm of her hands. His look of satisfaction made her smile. He truly cared about her.

"Traditions," Chelsea said. "How long does someone have to do something before it becomes a tradition?"

"Twice."

"Only twice?"

"Yes. That's my rule." He sat and draped his arm around her shoulder. "You can help make the rules. That's what a relationship means to me. Teamwork... and kissing." His quiet tone carried humor and reassurance. "Why don't we go visit your mom, but first, since we're building a relationship, we have to make a few traditions starting now."

All lingering anxiety slipped away. Warmth heated her. Hope filled her, head to toe. She eyed him. There were other places he could be. Other things he could do for the day. Other people he could share the holiday with— especially since he now had a family. But he'd chosen her.

Her heart opened more. Sadness faded. Now was the time to begin new holiday traditions. With Zach.

"My first rule—kissing before anything else on Christmas morning." Chelsea curled into him, lifted her chin. Without a recipe or instructions, Zach did exactly as she expected. He kissed her back.

It was a merry Christmas after all.

THE END

Linda's Recipe

Chelsea's Christmas Cookies

2 1/4 cups all-purpose flour
1 teaspoon baking soda
1 1/2 teaspoon salt
1 cup softened butter (2 sticks)
1 cup granulated sugar
1 cup packed brown sugar
1 1/2 teaspoon vanilla extract
2 large eggs
2 cups of red and green M&M's

Preheat oven to 375° F.

Combine flour, baking soda and salt in small bowl.
In a mixing bowl, beat butter, granulated sugar, brown sugar, and vanilla extract until creamy.
Add eggs, one at a time, beating well after each egg.
Add flour gradually. M
Mix until all ingredients are thoroughly combined.
Gently stir in M&M's.
Refrigerate dough for at least an hour.
Drop by rounded tablespoon onto ungreased baking sheets.

Bake for 9 to 11 minutes or until golden brown. Cool for 2 minutes.

Linda Joyce

Amazon Best Selling author and multiple RONE Award Finalist Linda Joyce writes contemporary romance and women's fiction featuring assertive females and the men who can't resist them. She lives with her very patient husband in a house in Metro Atlanta. Linda is a closet artist who paints with a brush, yet longs to finger paint...but hates getting her hands messy. She's addicted to Cajun food and sushi. Linda will deny she only leaves the house once a week and only then to get criticism from three other authors.

Website: **http://www.linda-joyce.com**

A Farmhouse Noel

By Leah Noel Sims

Leah Noel Sims

Acknowledgments

With enthusiastic and heartfelt thanks...
To Rachel W. Jones, Linda Joyce, and Melissa Klein, for your insights and friendship. Our meetings around the kitchen table are one of the highlights of my week. Here's to more journeys into Jubilee!

To fellow author Connie Lacy, for your precise and thorough feedback and encouragement. Your perspective is invaluable. Your friendship is a treasure.

To Mom, for being the living proof that some people really do just wander around in costumes. For tending the garden of my imagination all my life.

To Dad. You were the original person in my life to urge me to go for my dreams—and you backed up your words with actions. (No matter how tired you were, you were at every single performance of Agatha Christie's *The Mousetrap*.) Your encouragement is more powerful than you'll ever know.

To Brittany Taylor-Reynolds, Babysitter Extraordinaire, for loving on my kids and doing awesome things like making homemade ice cream with them while I write and edit. A certain two-year-old may get persnickety, but I'll speak the truth whether I get a good nap or not: You're amazing!

To my husband, a one-in-a-million man, Andy. You always cheer me on, read my work, and show me in word and deed that you believe in me as an author. For that...no words exist to express my love and appreciation.

Finally, to my own old farmhouse.

They say you should write what you know. I may not know about caring for horses, donkeys, goats, or sheep. I have no clue what it's like to be an equestrian. But if there's one thing I do know, it's sprawling land and shiplap walls. It's a front room facing the sunrise; the creak of an old weathervane in the wind. It's the love of home and all that happened while we lived in it.

A Farmhouse Noel

Chapter One

Tabitha Larsen would never get any work done if she was afraid of a good rain.

By the time she adjusted the LARSEN LIVESTOCK baseball cap on her head and put her tractor in park, the sprinkling raindrops had grown into assaulting pellets. But Paul, John, George, and Ringo expected their hay rain or shine. The horses trotted from the far end of the property, and Tabby climbed over the tractor and onto the trailer. She hefted the first bale and waddle-carried it into the barn.

"Back! Back! I gotta bring 'em in first, you clowns."

"Tabby, I'm talking to you!"

Tabby dropped the bale inside the empty stable at the back-left of the barn and secured the wireless earbuds in her ears. "Sorry, Mom. I've got you on Bluetooth while I unload the hay. I've lost a lot of time shoring things up thanks to Alexander. Only his first week here, and he's taken every opportunity to escape."

"Alexander," said Mom. "New boyfriend?"

"New *donkey*." Tabby rolled her eyes. "Thanks a lot. I bought him specifically for the live Nativity Jubilee Community Church is putting on in two weeks. If he doesn't shape up, I'll sell him immediately after."

As she spoke, the donkey moseyed up, eyeing fresh hay. The horses flattened their ears. They hadn't taken well to the mischievous newcomer.

"Anyway"—her mother audibly yawned—"it may be mid-afternoon for you, but it's almost nine o'clock in Italy, so let's wrap this up so your father and I can turn in."

Tabitha sucked in a breath and hoisted another bale. "Since when do you party animals turn in at nine?"

"Since we were out until 4:00 a.m. Rome never sleeps. So, our flight back into Savannah lands on Christmas Eve at 9:18 p.m. You can get us then?"

"Whew. That's late—and it's more than an hour each way into Savannah." Tabby released the bale and scratched her head through her baseball cap. "Um, yeah. The F-250 has been finicky, but I'm planning to get it in and out of the shop before then."

If the holiday break doesn't have them backlogged. Only sixteen days until Christmas Eve.

"Great. Obviously, your dad and I won't be able to bring anything for Christmas dinner. We'll be lucky to be awake."

"Waffle House it is, then."

"Don't joke."

"I'm almost not." She pulled a pair of scissors from her back pocket and clipped the twine on one hay bale. It fanned out into small square sections. "My to-do list is longer than our driveway, and I've never been much for the kitchen. I wish you and Dad could come sooner."

In the background, she heard her father. "Deb, pass the phone. I need to—"

Her mother hushed him. "I wish we could, too, Tabitha. We can't wait to see what you've done with the old place since last Christmas."

Tabby bristled. From her position in the center of the barn, she could clearly see the 200-year-old family farmhouse...and its rusted metal roof, chipping paint, and rotting porch beams. A hundred strands of garland and twinkle lights couldn't cover that mess. "Are you being sarcastic?"

"I don't know, sweetie, am I?"

"I'm just one person, Mom."

With an old house, ancestral farm, and my own business. Even Michael Phelps would drown in all this.

She fought to keep her voice from breaking. "I thought you and Dad—or especially Hank or Cashel—would've visited more. Helped more."

Mom puffed a loud sigh.

Tabby braced herself for her mother's calm—grating—lecture voice.

"Tabitha, this was *your* choice. We offered you kids

money or land. Hank chose money. Cashel chose money. You, my little South Georgia homebody, *chose* land—ten acres, not even the original forty."

Heat purled through her like an oven broiler set to High. Her beloved farmhouse sat between a lone ranch home to her left and a one-street eyesore of a neighborhood to her right. Sandwiched since 1993, when her parents sold thirty of their original forty acres.

They're probably drinking two bottles of fine Italian wine tonight with the cash from that betrayal.

She seethed a careful breath. "And let's not talk about that."

"Well, apparently you should thank your lucky stars you don't have the original forty. Imagine how stressed you'd be then."

"Thanks, Mom." Tabby flung a flake of hay into Paul's trough. "Always one to point out the silver lining."

Mom's laugh was airy, dismissive. "I'm glad you chose the land. I really am. It means so much to me to know that your Dad and I can travel in our retirement but visit whenever we want—"

"Once a year."

"—and it brings him comfort to know that it's still in the family, even though he wasn't up for that life anymore. But we told you it would be a lot. We did tell you that. At great length. Do you still love it?"

"Of course I do. The land's been in our family since

the seventeen hundreds. I can't imagine giving it up."

"Well, love is one thing. But now that you've had it all to yourself for five years, are you sure you can handle it?"

"You always ask me that."

"And I can never tell if you're trying to prove your capability to your Dad and me or to yourself."

Tabby winced and forced herself to remain silent.

To all of the above.

"You know what they say, then." Mom sighed. "Where there's a will, there's a way."

Tabby pulled the remaining half of a fig bar from her back pocket. Fastening it between her molars, she yanked off a chunk. Chewing, at least, kept her from saying something she'd regret. She chucked the final flake of hay into Ringo's trough.

"Can't wait to see it, Tabby. And you."

"You'll be impressed. I promise." Ringo walked into his stall, nosing Tabby in the chest. Stroking his silky cheek soothed her frayed nerves. "I miss you all."

"And you miss your dad and brothers fixing up the house and land. Goodnight, Tabitha."

"Goodnight." She yanked the phone from her pocket and stabbed her forefinger on the red button to end the call.

And why shouldn't I miss their help as much as their company?

A two-century-old farmhouse—and all the issues that came with *that*—plus ten acres, four horses, three goats, two sheep, and one stupid donkey—all to herself.

"And a friggin' partridge in a pear tree." She stroked Ringo's onyx mane. "You're my boy, though. What do you say we ride? Between your new friend and my family, I say we need it."

Alexander sauntered into the black gelding's stall, nosed the trough, and brayed. The sound scraped like sandpaper to her eardrum. Tabby cringed. Ringo stamped his foot.

"Right? I know what you mean. Let's get out of here. Run in the rain."

Tabby coaxed the horse out of the stall, then stepped into the tack room, returning with a bridle. Talking to her favorite horse brought her comfort, a salve over the sting left by the conversation with her mother.

She walked to his side, launched herself onto his bare back, and leaned down to whisper in his ear. "I promise, I only got him for the live Nativity. No matter what I said, the church wouldn't let Mary and Joseph ride a horse. I know, I know. He's a pain in the—" She straightened and nudged him with her heels. "God, everything I say just sounds like a pun, but it's true."

Drops pelted when Tabby raised her face into the rain, reveling in the sensation of wind and water droplets. A good ride always cleansed her mind and lifted her spirits. Even if she only enjoyed the final quarter of her family's land.

Now, instead of forty sprawling acres dotted with pecan trees, the house sat in the front-center of a narrow, ten-acre rectangle. Ringo and Tabby circled the property, and Tabby's thoughts circled with them.

"Land, house, animals—none of it ever felt like work when we were doing it together," she said to the horse. Before Dad retired, before her parents left for parts unknown, before her brothers moved to opposite coasts, Christmases were spent working and celebrating side by side. They ended their days sweaty, dirty, but singing their hearts out in the house's front room, with Tabby playing carols on the piano, Cashel strumming his guitar, and Hank changing up the lyrics just to make them laugh. That was Christmas.

But for the past five years, the season was marked by stress. Tabby crammed her schedule chock-full of festivals, petting zoos, and birthday parties just so she could write a check to her older brothers that wouldn't bounce. Life was marked by late nights as she struggled to get the house in a condition that showed her parents—and herself—she was up to the responsibility and capable of keeping her dream home all on her own. It was marked by insomnia. By Ambien on her nightstand.

At the beginning of the year, she had promised herself: This year will be different.

Now, at the end of it, she knew: It would be worse.

The thought of facing her family—telling the truth—filled her with dread.

Ringo traveled at a trot, and Tabby chafed at the sight of the identical white boxes forming the little street of neighbors she'd never met. Spotting a silhouette standing in one window, Tabby waved. The blinds flicked closed.

My family left me, and I'm left with that.

From the main road, the telltale sputtering of a beat-up '96 Bronco sounded, underscored by the blaring bass of blasting music. Ringo's ears twitched. Simon and Garfunkel—the two sheep—startled and ran from the front of the property toward the barn, as usual.

"Great," Tabby muttered, spotting the faded red vehicle as it slowed, turned, and struggled up the driveway leading to the lone ranch home. "Here comes our noisy neighbor, just to add to it all."

Nights and weekends, nights and weekends. That blustering old Bronco had shattered her peace on nights and weekends ever since its owner moved in at the beginning of the year, and this Saturday was no different.

She nudged Ringo faster, closer, so she could watch the Bronco's driver enter his house. Hey, if he could be a noisy neighbor, why couldn't she be a nosy one? She could use a good laugh, after all, and Ringo needed a cool-down walk. They trotted past the barn and to the fence before Tabby dismounted. Tugging her baseball cap down, she led Ringo by the reins.

Suit and tie? Tails, top hat, and cane? Breeches, jerkin, and tricorne hat? What would he wear today? Tabby pressed her lips together to hide her smirk.

The music cut off.

The Shins. Add a point for music taste, at least.

The engine cut out. The driver side door opened. Thick black and white stripes unfolded from head to toe as he exited the vehicle. Tabby stifled a giggle. The prisoner costume could've been ordered straight from Looney Toon's ACME catalog.

Worth. It.

Fervent bleating—followed by incessant braying—pushed her panic button.

Tabby spun. "What the—? Alexander!"

She rushed to the barn with Ringo close behind. Alexander stood by the tack room—door shut and latched—shaking his head and snorting. The sheep's bleating escalated to panic level.

"Oh my gosh, donkey! Did you shut them in?" She grabbed him by the mane—"All right, party's over. In you go, now"—and urged him into the stall, latching it shut.

Once the furry perp was corralled, Tabby opened the door to the tack room. Simon and Garfunkel tottered out, fussing. She hugged each of them and scrubbed their wooly heads.

"I'm so sorry, guys. Take some extra alfalfa, on me."

The sheep gobbled out of her hand. "I'll work on him." She straightened, lifting her chin. "Right, donkey? You kick me, I'll kick you back."

Alexander hee-hawed and pounded his hooves against the stable doors, protesting against confinement.

She rolled her eyes and gave the sheep one more pat. "Okay, I got stuff to do. He's in ass jail now and unlikely to receive parole for the rest of the afternoon, so don't you worry."

As she strode across the property, the horses—her Beatle boys—pranced toward her like they were compass needles and she was due north. She ached to spend the afternoon with them, but she'd made a promise to her mother that the place would look impressive, and she intended to keep that promise, at least. Even if it meant staying up at all hours to finish her to-do list.

The crooked steps to the back porch creaked under her weight. She jimmied the bent-up, rusted storm door— *yet something else that must be replaced*—then opened the wooden back door, entering the living room.

Her willpower deflated like a popped balloon at the sight of paint cans, rolled-up drop cloths, trays, and rolls and rolls and rolls of painters' tape. Every single shiplap wall—from the eat-in kitchen, to the front room, to the three bedrooms and two bathrooms—needed a new coat of white paint. It would make all the difference, when the time came. But she was—as she told her mother—just one person.

It would be a very late Saturday night, and not for any fun reasons.

Tabby stepped over the rolled-up drop cloths and trudged to the coffeemaker on the counter. Dumping out the old grounds and brew, she washed the carafe and started a new batch.

Sixteen days from now, Mom and Dad would arrive from Italy. Hank and Yvette from New York City. Cashel and Lila from Los Angeles. The Larsen family farmhouse would be pristine, fresh coats of paint inside and out. Every drain would be clear, every leak fixed, every rotten porch beam and light bulb replaced. She would put a Christmas tree in the front room. Colored lights, like old times. Garlands would drape from every conceivable surface.

Ready for her family. Ready for...

From the doorway that led from kitchen to front room, Tabby spotted it. The glossy cardboard she'd shoved behind the piano now stuck out, mocking her. Over the gurgling of brewing coffee, she walked to the piano, picked up the cardboard, and brushed off the dust that had accrued on its letters over the past six months, when she'd bought it, but still hadn't been sure. Couldn't bring herself to do it.

Now, she was certain. But how would she tell her family she'd failed?

Grief plunged into her heart and sank it like a ship in Mayday. The knot in her belly was heavy as an anchor. Tears blurred her vision, but she blinked them back, unable to stop herself from tracing the bold, brazen, betraying letters.

F-O-R.

S-A-L-E.

Chapter Two

Kip Stewart wadded up the rain-soaked prisoner costume, pivoted, jumped, and shot the ball of clothing into the open washing machine.

"Two points!"

Clad in nothing but his boxers, he collapsed on the couch just as his smartwatch dinged. He flicked his wrist.

TOUR REQUEST: BRICKS & STONES. NO.: 4. TIME: 6:30P.

TOUR REQUEST: DRUNKEN SAILOR PUB CRAWL. NO.: 10. TIME: 8P.

He sprang from the couch, flinging open the dryer door. Empty. Leaning over the washer—or clothes bin, as he used it—he rummaged through the stinking garments until he caught the sleeve of a white linen shirt, then the wrinkled tail of a suit jacket. With a groan, he glugged detergent into the washer and set the load to speed wash.

Food. Gotta eat fast.

His feet shuffled into the living room, into the kitchen, and—bam!—right into the bag of canned goods that had sat on the floor for a week.

"Ow!" He hopped, grabbed the loaf of bread, snatched a knife, and splatted PB&J on it for a quick snack. "Bookings are good, bookings are good."

He meant it. Between being the one-man show behind Jubilee's only tour company—the Jolly Trolley—and his regular gig as community relations specialist of Jubilee's Historic Society, his business life trekked a steady, uphill climb. If only his personal life would follow.

Speaking of which...

He snatched his phone from the charging station on the counter, tapping in Travis' digits. His friend's voicemail greeting sounded, then beeped.

"Hey, man. Two more tours just booked tonight. Not gonna be able to make it out with you and LaTisha to meet Kenna beforehand. A beer after about nine thirty might work. Sorry. If it's meant to be"—he flinched, imagining his friend's gagging response at Kip's romantic nature— "it'll go from there."

He ended the call.

Go from there. He snorted a laugh. *From there, to what?*

In his direct, very personal experience, the only place a romantic relationship would go is down the tubes. Fun for a while? Yes. Exciting? Definitely. But depending on a woman to show up, day in and out, especially through the darkest times? That's what's called 'getting your hopes up.'"

Mom dashed those when she went on a "girl's weekend" and never came back, twenty years ago.

Nah. Even if he hit it off with Kenna—and let's face

it, despite his cynicism he was more apt than she was to fall head over heels—she'd no doubt give him some line about "not being ready" or "needing to find herself" and be out the door, leaving his heart flayed open and rawer than brisket. It had happened plenty of times before.

Flopping on the couch, sandwich in hand, he stared absently at the large, waiting Christmas tree. It twinkled with colored lights and dripped with store-bought, plastic globe ornaments, a valiant effort at creating comfort and joy that still fell short.

No matter how many times he'd moved or how many different girlfriends Dad brought to Christmas dinner over the years—the number was surely longer than a popcorn-cranberry garland by now—Kip couldn't bring himself to let go of the box that sat in the attic, filled with homemade paper handprint ornaments, painted pinecones, and footprint reindeer, all from the fraction of his life when a happy family was possible.

Was it possible?

It would take an impeccable woman to make him open that box again.

****

Tabby wrapped the paint roller in plastic wrap, snatched yet another fig bar from the box—her definition of "dinner" lately—and munched, staring at the front room. She hadn't minded the scuffs that had accrued over the years, and the memories made with them, but her family would love the way Intellectual White's pristine hue brought out the divots and lines in the shiplap.

Potential buyers would love it, too.

She swallowed, surveying the remaining mess. The piano could sit catty-corner another day or two. Her neck and shoulders couldn't handle shoving the monstrous upright around a second time.

Her phone dinged from its charging station on the counter. With all the flexibility and grace of C-3PO, she tottered over to check the text message. Victoria, always one for a night out.

Tabby! Beer with Chelsea at Tygue's On Tap tonight. If Chelsea can come out of her hidey-hole, you can, too. Do I have to kidnap you?

Tabby smiled. *Can't. "Hidey-hole" is in need of great repair. Maybe I should kidnap* you *to come help!*

She sent the message fully expecting no response.

Liz would've helped me.

Her childhood best friend was always dependable. But sky-high dreams had taken Liz Marshall to White Plains, far from Tabby's reach. Even if Liz did make it home for Christmas, Tabby wouldn't dream of taking a minute of her friend's precious time with the family she rarely saw. Especially not after the deeply difficult year the Marshalls had experienced.

Her phone screen blackened and flashed the clock. Tabby grunted. Sunset was barely more than an hour away, and she still had to give Alexander his daily riding lesson. Tugging a hoodie over her paint-stained clothes, she stepped into her boots and trudged across the pasture toward the barn. Alexander kicked his stall door and brayed.

"You think I like this any more than you do?" She gave him a good scratch behind the ears and opened his stall. The donkey trotted out to the middle of the barn, and Tabby entered the tack room.

"Look, you've got two weeks to learn how to let a human ride you, and we've gotta practice." She snagged a saddle, blanket, and bridle. "Mary and Joseph are way less experienced than I am. So do me a solid and—"

The door to the tack room slammed shut.

"—don't buck me off this time."

Tabby froze. Dropped the saddle, blanket, bridle. "Alexander?"

The donkey brayed.

"Oh my God, Alexander?" She rushed to the door and pushed. Locked—the latch had fallen with the force of the door. "You ass," she breathed, "did you lock me in here on purpose?"

Hooves beat against the door in affirmation, then faded as Alexander trotted out to pasture.

A cold sweat flushed her chest and neck. Frantic, she patted her jean pockets—empty. Her phone was still charging on the counter.

Anger and panic blasted through her. Harnessing those emotions, she tightened her jaw and eyed the door. Rolled her neck from side to side. Hunkering down, she backed against the far wall. Charged the door.

BOOM!

She cried out, clutching her throbbing shoulder. The door hadn't budged.

Of course it hadn't—the latch was one thing on the property that *didn't* need replacing.

Sucking in until her lungs burned, she did the only thing she could do.

"HELP!"

****

Kip scrutinized himself in the mirror, adjusting his dark brown hair under the Victorian top hat. The coat and tails were still damp and definitely wrinkled, but hey, tourists should be looking at the charming architecture of Jubilee's historic district, not his rumpled appearance. Stuffing the pirate costume in his backpack, he slung it over his shoulder and strode out the door, locking it behind him.

The sound of a yelling female stopped him short.

"HELP!"

He tilted his head. Turned. The voice came from the direction of the farm property next door. It escalated in pitch and frequency and panic.

Tucking the top hat under his arm, he raced toward

the farmhouse, climbed the fence—and ripped the seat of his trousers.

****

Tabby swallowed. Her dry throat stung. Nervous sweat dripped down the back of her neck. She struggled out of the hoodie and hurled it at the locked door.

"This is what I get?" she shouted, voice cracking. "After everything I've done for the love of this place, this is what I get?"

Angry and exhausted and solidly alone, she slammed a fist against the door and slumped to the ground.

"Hello?" A male's baritone sounded from the barn.

She scrambled up, massaging her smarting fist. "Over here! The tack room!"

Footsteps rushed closer. The latch jingled. The door opened.

Standing close, he was taller than he appeared. Wavy chestnut locks fell over his ears, framing hazel eyes that watched her with intense concern.

"Are you all right?"

"Yes, I—" Her gaze dropped, taking in his clothing. The coat. The tails. The top hat squashed under one arm.

Relief mixed with exhaustion like Coke and Altoids. She bubbled with laughter.

"Excuse me?" The neighbor took her by her upper arms. "Are you *sure* you're not hurt?"

He led her to a bench outside the tack room.

She plunked down, giggling, shoulders shaking. "I'm fine, I—that stupid donkey locked me in—it's just—I'm so exhausted—and do you ever wear normal clothes?"

To her surprise, the stranger snickered along with her. "You see me, do you?"

"Well, I'm here working a lot, so I see who comes and goes, and"—a snort sounded from the barn's opening, signaling Alexander's return—"oh no, you don't. I'll handle you later." Frustration with the animal sobering her a bit, she turned. "I'm sorry. I'm Tabitha—Tabby—Larsen."

"Kip Stewart."

A lopsided grin broke across his face. Impish twinkling lit his eyes.

She broke their gaze, heartbeat lilting like an Irish flute. "Well, I can't thank you enough for coming over here when you"—she stood and her glance flitted up and down his person without her permission—"clearly have somewhere to go."

"A tour." Kip rose. "I own Jubilee's only tour service—not whatever lewd business you're hypothesizing about." He bit his lip and cocked his head.

"Point taken. And tonight's tour is?"

"Bricks and Stones, a walking tour showcasing the architecture of Jubilee's historic district."

"And the prisoner costume from earlier?" she blurted without thinking. Her cheeks heated. She lifted the lid on a trash can and bent over it, filling a scoop with goat feed to give herself something to do other than look at him. Peter, Polly, and Mary came running and bleating.

"'From Chain Gang to Charmed Town: Jubilee's Convict History.'"

"My ancestor was one." Tabby straightened, pride squaring her shoulders.

Recognition widened his eyes. "Ezekiel Drummond Larsen—"

"British convict sentenced to Savannah in 1740. Eloped with a reverend's daughter in 1742. Absconded with her to Jubilee around 1745—"

"And his grandson became the first mayor of Jubilee after its incorporation. A real rags-to-riches story. That his home, over there?"

"His land." She led them out of the barn and toward the house. "The original structure burned down in 1817. That one's been standing since 1818, when Jeremiah Ezekiel Drummond Larsen built it."

Tabby pursed her lips, stifling her urge to recount the story she loved to tell. Her eyes cut over to the impossible donkey. In his attempt to avoid his daily riding lesson, Alexander had certainly not been unsuccessful. Twilight dimmed, winter-weak, making everything appear to be half made of shadow. There would be no riding tonight.

"Original floors?" Kip's voice shook her from her internal grumbling.

"Live oak," she said with a wistful sigh. "Wide-planked. Scratched-up. One-of-a-kind."

"I'd love to see them."

She halted and turned to face him. His eyes sparkled despite the darkness, generous mouth ticked up in a curious smile.

Is he flirting?

She licked her lips, thoughts firing like her F-250's engine on a brittle cold day. "I, um…that would be—"

"It's okay." His hands twisted the top hat he carried. "I have a tour soon anyway. Maybe another time."

"Sure," she said, relieved. "Another time."

"Nice meeting you, Tabby. Despite the circumstances, I mean."

"Right. You too."

Her tall neighbor turned, shadowy frame striding toward the fence.

"And watch what you say about my however-many-greats-granddaddy," she called. "Especially while wearing that outfit."

Kip stopped at the fence. He pivoted slowly, somersaulted the top hat up his arm and twirled it atop his head. Holding it in place with one finger, he gave a dramatic bow and leapt the fence with a finesse that rivaled Gene Kelly's footwork.

If Gene Kelly had ripped pants.

Tabby chuckled. Her neighbor was strange, a bit silly, embarrassingly not self-conscious…and he'd come to her rescue. Maybe she could forgive his noisy Bronco.

Chapter Three

Beer steins clink-clink-clinked in cheers. Kip sipped his Scotch ale while tucked in a booth at Tygue's On Tap with Travis and LaTisha on one side, and him and Kenna on the other. While the guitarist switched songs and changed keys, their group hovered in awkward silence.

"So Kip"—LaTisha tipped her chin—"Kenna's father actually works in the archives at a college in Savannah."

"Oh." He turned to the olive-skinned brunette who sat thigh-to-thigh with him. "He must handle some interesting documents."

Kenna giggled and the gaping neckline of her silky top slipped from one shoulder. She adjusted it, watching him with large, deep brown eyes. "And don't you as well? Handle interesting *documents.*"

Kip's gaze snapped over to Travis. He cleared his throat. "Um—"

"Plenty." Travis grinned.

"But not *too* many. Not memorable ones. I mean—um."

Kenna scooted away. "Will you excuse me? Bathroom break."

As soon as her leggy figure disappeared through the crowd, LaTisha leaned far over the table. "What's wrong with you? Look at her!"

"I *am* looking."

A lot.

Kenna was everything he usually set his sights on: Fun and flirty and very-very forward. "She's hot—I mean, pretty, and uh, friendly. But—"

"Dude." Travis raised one brow.

"Hmm, our friend Kip's got some 'splainin' to do…"

"Her, um, *attributes* might not be what I'm looking for anymore."

"Man, you're the weirdest blend of romantic and cynic I've ever met," Travis said. "You've never been looking for anything but a good time. What's switched your gears?"

His mind flashed on the memory of kinky-curly wheat-brown locks, peeking out from under a stained baseball cap. The memory of her honest laughter, honest smile, honest speech. "A girl next door."

Travis slapped both hands on the table and guffawed. The ring on his left hand gleamed.

Kip blinked.

His friend sobered. "Wait. You're serious? What's so special about that one?"

"Not sure. But she seems honest."

Travis leaned back as though he'd been hit by a sudden gust of wind. "Whoa, buddy."

LaTisha shot her husband a you-know-what-this-means look. "If that word's skated to the top of your shopping list, you got a whole new thing going"—she tilted her head in the direction of the women's room—"and it ain't Kenna."

"Never thought you'd head our way, man." Travis twisted his wedding ring.

"Never thought I'd find an honest woman—"

LaTisha cleared her throat.

"—except you, LaTisha." Kip winked.

"Wow." Travis shook his head.

"Sorry to throw you off, man. I swear I can see canaries circling your head. Trust me, they're circling mine, too."

"Yeah. Never saw this coming. Good news for later, but as far as tonight goes"—Travis leaned forward and whispered as Kenna sauntered toward them—"you either gotta close the deal or close the tab."

He closed the tab.

****

Tabby threw herself into more painting, ignoring the stinging protests of her back and arm muscles. Up. Down. Up, down. Up-down-up-down-up-down—in tandem, her thoughts and roller brush zigzagged.

Another time? I can't afford to give Kip any time.

Not because he wasn't interesting (she snorted at the thought). Not because he wasn't attractive. Not because he wasn't charming, in a Lewis-Carroll-character type of way.

It had nothing to do with him. It had everything to do with the endless chore list that claimed her every minute. The mounting repair debt, mortgage debt, vet debt.

Debt which—without selling her home—would choke her to death.

Then again…selling her home would choke her, too.

Whether she stayed or left, she'd have no breath. Not in Jubilee. She couldn't handle the farmhouse alone, but she couldn't watch someone else make it home.

She had a plan, and she'd grimace and bear it: Once the ink was dry on the closing papers, she'd take a breath. Take space. Take flight.

To Iceland.

If she had to sacrifice one dream, she was determined to achieve another.

No, she couldn't, shouldn't—mustn't—indulge in a minute more with the guy next door.

Chapter Four

"How's he healing, Dr. Metter?"

Tabby twisted the hem of her T-shirt and waited as Dr. Nina Metter examined John's flecked front leg inside his stall. The Appaloosa was eager to be set out to pasture on this sunny Monday morning. His nostrils flared, but he kept still.

"No sign of swelling or infection." Dr. Metter's fingers lightly traced the deep laceration encircling the gelding's cannon just under the knee. "Blood coagulant worked great. Still giving him the antibiotics?"

"Yep."

"Good. I think he'll heal beautifully, but he should still take it easy."

"Do you think he'll be ready for dressage season at the beginning of the year?" Tabby bit her lip.

The veterinarian winced. "That wire got him good. Cut all the way to the tendon. I don't know if he'll be good for any January shows. By February he should certainly be fully functional, but the wound may still be visible. Why not take Ringo instead? Or one of your other Beatle boys?"

"Ringo's my baby, but he's not my top show horse.

John wins the most." The horse leaned into her chest, and she caressed his head. "I really need some wins."

Dr. Metter straightened and offered a sympathetic—strained?—smile. "I'll get you more of the powder coagulant and antibiotics." She exited the barn and disappeared into her truck, a large animal veterinarian's armory on wheels.

Tabby touched her forehead to John's. "You gotta heal up, 'kay? I love you. I need to take care of you. But I need money to make that happen."

To get you healed—and get you boarded at a farm after this place sells.

"Think you can prance pretty for me by January?"

The horse's gentle, loving nudge could have been a sucker-punch to her heart. She hugged John close.

Dr. Metter returned with medicines in hand. Tabby reached for them, but the vet didn't let go.

"Tabby, I—this might be the last round I can give you, if…gosh, this is difficult to say." She let out a breath, shoulders slumping. "I've been here for your animals since the beginning of Larsen Livestock. I care about them, and I care about you. But—I can't work for free. Not even for a friend."

"You're not working for free." Tabby held the medicine and the vet's experienced hands in both of hers. "You're not. I'm booking everything I can. Expenses are swamping me this time of year, and John's initial treatment bills maxed out my credit card. My brothers think I should've just sold him—as if he's some toy horse and not my family—instead of paying for treatment but I *need* prize money from dressage if I'm gonna be able to—"

"Stop," Dr. Metter spoke calmly, reaching with her free hand to pat Tabby's. "I'm so sorry. You've got a lot on your shoulders. Payment can wait. Take the medicine. Consider it a Christmas gift."

Her cheeks flushed with building tears. Not trusting herself to speak without opening the floodgates, she threw her arms around Dr. Metter.

When she closed her eyes, she saw herself holding an equity check. An equity check with enough zeroes to pay everyone back, with interest. An equity check for the sale of the farmhouse and the last ten acres of Larsen land.

"I'll pay you back in full, Dr. Metter. I promise."

Her life, her love, her Larsen legacy—her entire world for the price of an equity check.

****

Hours after Dr. Kit's departure, Tabby's throat and chest still stung with shame. A few more rooms had yet to be painted, but she couldn't bear the thought of trapping herself inside with the paint fumes and roller brush's lonely *whoosh*. The good thing about farm work was that there was plenty to do outside.

Her heart sank low, but the sun crept high. If she

tethered herself to the sun today, perhaps it would lift her spirits in its ascent toward high noon.

She toted the new screen door from her truck's bed, delighting in the placid sight of her horses in pasture and the little spurts of blathering and bleating, conversations between goat and sheep as they moseyed about the field. She soaked it all in, these moments with her furry, woolly family. It wouldn't be long before she'd have to find all of them new homes.

Leaning the door against the back patio, she returned to retrieve the box containing a new light fixture. She hopped up the steps, pulled a screwdriver from her tool belt, and set to work removing the loose, rusted light fixture, bobbing as The Beach Boys' "Wouldn't It Be Nice?" emanated from her phone.

She broke into a devilish grin, remembering how Hank hated it when she blasted her favorite oldies music.

Somehow, somewhere, I hope these songs drive Hank insane.

From his grazing spot several yards away, Alexander stared at her, stamped, and hee-hawed.

"I'll settle for annoying you, though." She pointed her screwdriver at him. "That's karma for ya, donkey."

A couple songs later, sadistic satisfaction turned into full-fledged singing. Tabby disconnected the fixture, pulled it down, and lost herself to the music in the last half of "God Only Knows."

"*Hee-haw!*"

"Hush!"—she shot a killing look at Alexander and repeated the chorus with a twist on its intended meaning— "God only knows what I'd be without *you*."

"*Hee-haw!*"

She rolled her eyes. "God only knows what I'd be without—"

"God only knows…"

She jumped at the sound of clear singing from across the yard.

Kip strode through the pasture, beaming. "Hi there."

She wanted to hate the way that smile made her skin tingle like Pop Rocks, but she didn't.

You can't be here.

"Hi."

"Need help?" He leaned against the porch rail.

I shouldn't say yes.

But she needed it. She eyed him. "Don't you need to change clothes?"

"Hm?"

"You're wearing regular ones."

He bent his head when he laughed, broad shoulders shaking under the thin cloth of his T-shirt, but he held her gaze.

She gestured to the box at her feet. "Mind holding the fixture up while I connect and secure it?"

"Hand it over."

His six-foot-something leaned over her five-foot-five, arms canopied over her head while she worked. The closeness was strange. And him, a stranger. Yet his subtle scent—cedarwood, maybe—was confusingly familiar.

She tightened the last screw. "That does it." She looked up at him to offer thanks, but he was already watching her. His face mere inches from her own made her breath stall.

"Team work." The reverberations of his voice tingled so near her ear, his eyelids half closing as his attention dropped to her lips. As though he'd touched a hot wire, he backed away. "So what is it you do, Tabby?"

"I own Larsen Livestock. My animals are rented out for all kinds of events, all throughout the year. The troublemaker you met Saturday night"—she pointed to Alexander, busy frolicking and chasing a goat—"will be in the live Nativity coming up at Jubilee Community Church. And I participate in dressage shows.

"So even *you* will don the occasional top hat."

She pointed her screwdriver at him. "Not the same."

"Tsk, tsk. Anyway, how long have you been managing all this?"

"My whole life, in a way." She turned to the dented screen door and began loosening screws. "But it's been all mine for the past five years."

"That's commitment, right there."

Tabby couldn't pinpoint the tone in his voice. Pride?

Admiration? Whatever it was, it made her uncomfortable. She focused on the final screw, then popped the door out of its frame, leaving a gaping entry into the living room where she'd forgotten to close the wooden door.

"Wow, look at those floors!"

Tabby stopped mid-reach for the wooden door's handle. "They're something, aren't they?"

"Incredible. Do you mind if I...?" He gestured through the doorway.

"If you don't mind the disaster inside. I'm getting ready for my family's arrival for the holidays."

Kip walked in and knelt, running his hands over the planks, all but oblivious to the mess surrounding them. "Look at these. And your ancestors built it all by hand. Watch out, you're unleashing the history *and* woodworking geek in me.

"Woodworking?"

"Self-taught, in both subjects." He straightened. "No money to study either one, but my Dad and I fixed up rental houses together for several years after my mom left. I'd love to have my own shop, but I don't have the space right now."

Tabby opened her mouth to offer condolences, but Kip spoke first.

"A lot of trouble you're going through just for your family to visit. Wouldn't some lights and a tree be enough?"

She shrugged. "I promised them certain things would be done."

He needs to leave.

"If it gets down to the wire and you need help, you've got an extra pair of hands next door."

"Gosh, where have you been all this time?"

"Not paying close enough attention, apparently."

He watched her too intently. She broke eye contact, adjusting the bill of her baseball cap. "Well, if I knew I had such a handy neighbor, I'd have introduced myself a long time ago and paid you in cookies."

"Cookies?" He cocked his head.

"It's all I'm good for in the kitchen."

He gestured to the home and land around them. "You've got plenty on your plate."

"True. Just not dinner."

"Your ass says otherwise."

Tabby jolted. "Excuse me?"

He gave a curt tilt of his chin in the direction of the back door. "Your donkey. He'll apparently take dinner into his own hands. Er. Whatever."

Tabby turned. "Oh. My. God."

Alexander stood by the back patio, nudging and gnawing on the shiny screen door, ears catawampus with confusion as though he'd expected it to taste better.

"Donkey! No!" She dashed outside, arms flailing.

Alexander skittered, bit down harder, and cantered

away—dragging the screen door with him.

"Drop. It!" Tabby chased him, growling through clenched teeth like the mother of a rebellious toddler. "Drop-it-drop-it-drop-it!"

His front hoof caught in the screen, tearing it. He released the door. It smashed to the ground, and he gave it a thorough trampling with all four hooves. Standing on the bent white metal, he brayed.

Two birthday parties paid for that screen door.

She tightened her jaw until she felt the tension of her bones throbbing in her temples.

Two Saturday mornings of work, trampled in the dirt.

Alexander's tail lifted. He urinated.

She'd never tasted donkey meat, but there was no time like the present.

Kip's footsteps padded on the grass beside her. "Did you, um"—he cleared his throat—"did you keep your receipt?"

Chapter Five

Kip leaned over the counter in Travis and LaTisha's half bath, tugging the bandana around his head so it slanted over one eyebrow, just right. The rugged, black leather tricorne hat fit perfectly over it all, revealing just a strip of the red cloth and its dangling tails underneath.

"Knock, knock."

LaTisha leaned against the door frame, hand-on-hip, eyes narrowed in assessment. "You'll do."

"He's still going to recognize his honorary Uncle Kip." He dusted the lapels of his waistcoat.

"What am I supposed to do, call Johnny Depp's publicist? It's a birthday party. Darien's five." One shoulder lifted in a never-you-mind shrug. "You'll do."

"Happy to be of mediocre service. Where are all the kiddos?"

LaTisha moved into the hall and headed toward the spacious living room, and Kip followed. "The first arrivals are with Travis in the backyard, helping our other entertainment set up."

"Other entertainment?" Kip halted in front of the long couch that sat underneath a wall of windows covered in plantation blinds. "Isn't Blackbeard the Pirate enough? I'm hurt."

"Darien's been begging for a *dog*"—LaTisha's large brown eyes rolled toward high heaven—"and it's the one thing on his birthday list he's *not* getting. We figured we could at least let him enjoy a petting zoo."

"A petting zoo-pirate party? That's a…blend."

"He's five." Kip's longtime friend flashed her widest, most devious smile and yanked the pull cord.

Sunlight flooded. Kip squinted one eye, then popped both wide open. "No."

"Oh, yes."

The white Ford F-250—LARSEN LIVESTOCK printed in red on the side—was parked in the backyard, trailer attached.

He hadn't seen her since Monday. Five days ago. Awash with guilt that he'd distracted her and given the donkey the opportunity to pull his stunt, he'd offered and offered and offered to buy her another screen door, but she'd refused.

"*LaTisha…*" He said her name in a cautionary sing-song.

"She's entirely different from the other girls you've dated."

"And by that you mean…?"

"Reality TV-star looks. Reality TV-star brains. I've always hated reality TV."

Kip sighed. "Me too."

LaTisha erupted in an openmouthed belly laugh. "Well, I'm glad you're changing the channel. So I had to do my recon on her. I like her."

He looked out the window and lost his train of thought. Tabby stood talking to Travis. Her jawline met the slope of a long neck. No baseball cap today. Wild light-brown ringlets fell to mid shoulder blade. She planted her feet wide, cocked one hip, and crossed arms toned from years of manual labor.

"I like her too," he said, distractedly.

She is *different. Determined. Strong. Caring. Committed. And*—conviction sharpened inside him—*I have to make her mine.*

"Weird you didn't ride together, though, considering you're dating your neighbor."

"We're not dating." Even to his own ears, his voice sounded absent, unconvincing.

"Well, why don't you fix that?" LaTisha swiveled on high heels and sashayed toward the French doors leading out onto the back patio.

"This is meddling mother-in-law behavior you're exhibiting," Kip called after her. "When he's of marrying age, I'll warn Darien—whoa!"

A tiny pirate stepped from behind one of the thick window curtains, glaring under his eye patch and oversized tricorne hat. "Hi."

Kip made a one-eighty into full-pirate mode, bending

to look into the boy's eyes. "Arrr, and who be this matey, if not the fearsome Captain Darien of the Three Rivers? I thought you might be takin' a caulk."

"Huh?"

"A nap." Kip tweaked the hat on the boy's head.

"No caulk for me, Uncle Kip. It's my birthday! I'm five."

"So I heard, aye."

He shook his head. "I'm five."

"All right, then. No pirate-speak. Good hiding place, that curtain."

"I'm extra sneaky now. I'm five."

The back door creaked behind them.

"Mmm, yes, I remember turning five myself. I was so sneaky, I was next to invisible." Kip straightened to see Tabby behind the boy. He started. "Hi! Surprised to see you here."

Darien craned to look. "Why? She's not invisible. She's not five. Colton!" The boy ran like an uncrated greyhound out the open back door toward the newest partygoer.

"On that exclamatory note…" Kip put his hands in his pockets. "I didn't know you knew the Houghtons. They're longtime friends of mine."

"I didn't know them. They attend Jubilee Community Church. Reverend Angie is a friend of mine from high school. She gives me a lot of referrals. I figured the church sent them to me."

"I guess they did. Will you please let me replace your screen door?"

"Stop worrying, Kip!" She grabbed his shoulders, giving him a playful shake, and he tried to ignore the pleasant firmness of her hands on his biceps. "I promise you, Alexander would've just destroyed something else."

He couldn't help but look at one of her hands, still placed on his arm.

She jerked it away as though he were the coils of a hot electric stove.

"Dinner, then," he said, with calm finality.

"What?"

"If I can't buy you a new door, I'll buy you dinner. Tonight."

"That's kind, but I can't spare an hour." Syrup-brown eyes searched his. "Honest. My family will be here in barely more than a week."

He shook his head. "I'll help you. I'll bring you dinner and help you with whatever it is you're working on."

He couldn't read her gaze but thought he saw the faint flicker of a wrestling match in their glint. The skin around her eyes tightened. A pit grew in his belly. He almost released an audible sigh when the tautness disappeared and her mouth ticked in a half-smile.

"That's very kind. Thank you."

He straightened, ready to square his shoulders with pride worthy of the pirate costume he wore. But her hesitance held him in check.

Why is this such a difficult choice for her?

Chapter Six

Tabby pulled the last long strand of painter's tape down from the living room's crown molding. Her arms felt hollow as straw—and not only from all the work she'd done since the birthday party that morning.

A date. I accepted a date.

Crumpling the sticky wad of tape in her hands, she looked at the clock. Eight. He'd arrive any minute. She had to make sure he knew: Her apparently down-home life was nothing short of up-in-the-air.

"Brrrrrrrring!"

The eruption from her cell phone made her jump. Sprinting from living room to the eat-in kitchen, she pulled the phone from its charger and answered.

"Hi Cashel."

"Tabs."

The younger of her older brothers used her childhood nickname, yet his voice sounded anything but warm. Sticking the wad of tape to the kitchen counter, she twisted the side door handle and walked around to sit on the front porch steps, hoping the clear night sky and chilly evening air might calm the jitters inside of her.

"Can't wait to see you next week," she tried.

"Yeah, me neither. Look—this isn't easy for you to

hear, or me to say, but I hope there'll be a check in my stocking this Christmas."

Tabby swallowed.

"The kind of check that makes me believe you're up to all this."

She rapped her knuckles on her knees.

"The kind that gets you up to date on payments."

An orb spider spun a web in the eaves of the porch. She stared at it, using it as a focus object as she tamped down the sadness rising in her throat. Spin, pull, spin, pull. Spin, pull, spin, pull.

"Tabitha?"

"I'm here. I have a plan."

"Heard that before, sis."

"I do. Please understand, I would never have got behind on payments if I'd had another choice. If it had only been house expenses and my payments for the portion of its worth to you and Hank, I might've been able to swing it better. But John was injured, and you know how expensive vet bills get—"

"So sell the damned horse!"

"He's the best show horse I have! He and I have earned big winnings before"—she gripped her knees until her fingernails nearly dug through the worn denim of her jeans—"winnings that can help me get majorly close to current with you guys."

"'Majorly close to current.'" He laughed low.

"Maybe you shoulda looked into law school, Tabs."

For a moment, they both halted. Finally, Cash spoke again. "I'm glad you wanted to stick by our home. It took major guts to take the job on by yourself, and we all benefit from your hard work, but—damn it, Tabitha—it's not like no one ran the numbers for you before you made the commitment. You knew what was owed—"

"Cash, please trust me. Your stocking might not have a check in it, but I promise—I have a plan. You and Hank will get all the money you're owed."

Eight days until Hank's arrival. Rooms painted, but porch rafters need replacing and painting...

She shook her head, resisting the impulse to tally the rest of her list. Shadowy movement in her peripheral vision startled her. "Cash, I gotta go." She ended the call.

"Hi." Kip lifted two plastic bags in greeting.

"Hey." She stood. "How much of that did you hear?"

He floundered.

"It's okay." Embarrassment heated her neck and cheeks. "I owe my brothers money. I'll say it flat-out. My parents were going to sell the place and split the money three ways for us, but Hank and Cashel wanted money and I wanted—well, I wanted the place. Can't have it free and clear, so I pay two-thirds of the home and property's worth to them." She pressed the heels of her hands against her eyes. "In theory, anyway. It's proven to be more than I can handle."

Kip's warm fingers encircled one of her wrists. "Hey"—he gently pulled her hand from one eye—"let me help you then."

Oh, if you only knew.

She forced a smile. "You're kind. Come in?"

"I have tacos. From that little shack in Stiltsboro."

"Let me rephrase. Get. In. Here."

Kip set the bag of takeout on the counter. Reaching into the other one, he produced two top hats stacked inside each other. He separated them and placed one on her head, a devilish sparkle firing in his hazel eyes. "Thought you could use a dose of whimsy."

She threw back her head and laughed. He lunged forward, both arms outstretched on either side of her to catch the hat. He did—then froze in that almost-embrace.

Everything in her stilled. She watched his throat muscles move as he swallowed. He straightened, replaced the hat on her head, stepped away.

"Tonight, sure," she said. "But don't get used to it."

The next two hours consisted of painting accented by taco breaks—the most complete meal she'd eaten in days. Kip was efficient, accurate, a riveting conversationalist. He spoke of history with the authority of a doctoral student but with the passion of an actor. He asked her questions and gave his full attention to her answers. They finished the last of the painting earlier than she'd expected, and slouched with bent knees at the base of a dry wall, sipping

Belgian ale and munching on the last of the crunchy fare. She couldn't help but grin every time she saw his top hat and caught the brim of her own in her peripheral vision.

Strangest sane guy I've ever met.

"So *no one* in your *entire* family cared what happened to this place?" he asked.

"They care," she said between sips of beer, "they love our home, but Dad and Mom were ready for a change when they retired, and my brothers have never wanted to be tied down. They got the adventurous gene strong. Somehow it skipped me."

"Oh, no. No, no." His knee toppled tiredly toward hers and he jerked it upright again.

"What do you mean, 'no, no, no'?"

"The adventurous gene didn't skip you. Just depends on how you define an adventure."

"Ha! I'm about ready to redefine it."

"What do you mean?"

Said too much. Can't say it until the family knows first.

Tabby twirled the bottle cap. "Only that it's been a lot for me by myself. Doesn't feel adventurous right now."

"That sucks. But the best adventures have some treacherous parts. At least, all the books I read as a kid did. Just think of it that way."

Tabby sniffed a laugh and stood. "Maybe this is an adventure, but I'm not the heroine of an adventure story."

"Perspective is everything."

She smiled, fully appreciating his optimism and encouragement.

My perspective of this "adventure" is that the author wrote me into a trap requiring nothing short of a deux ex machina.

"Last on the docket tonight is getting the Christmas tree down from the attic," she said. "Interested in *that* adventure?"

Kip rose. "Of course."

Moments later, Tabby led the way through the dark attic, hunched over at the waist, shining the thin beam of her flashlight here and there, checking rodent traps. "It always creeped me out up here as a kid, yet it's always been my favorite place in the house."

"I get it," he said.

"You do?" She stopped in the middle and turned, prepared to see a sarcastic smirk on his face, but his expression was earnest.

"Yeah!" He sat on his heels and looked around with such eagerness she thought he shared the same vertebrae as an owl. "Downstairs is old. Beautiful. Original. But this, up here"—he reached up and rubbed a hand down one of the attic's smooth, round beams—"it's damned near frozen in time."

Pride and love swelled in Tabby's chest. She met him by the beam, running her own hands over it. "Tree trunks," she said. "Jeremiah Larsen chopped them down by hand, stripped them of bark, and they've held this place up through all kinds of weather for two hundred years. And—"

"These hand-hewn square nails!"

He placed his thumb on one; she, on another, relishing the coldness of old iron. Their eyes met. His looked dark in the dimness of her little flashlight, yet she could still perceive some glint in his eyes.

A kindling.

"I know why you chose this place instead of money, Tabby. A pile of cash as high as—"

Her lips were on his before she could think. His hands on her waist kept them both upright. Kip kissed her softly, slowly, meaningfully. One of her hands traveled up from where she gripped his shirt to cup his stubbled cheek—

Iceland. Iceland.

The word blared in her mind like a tornado's warning siren.

Stop this. Stop this. Stop this.

As abruptly as she'd set upon him, she pulled away. "I'm sorry—"

"Don't be."

"—I shouldn't have done that without asking you—"

But the pendulum had already swung one way, couldn't help but swing back, and Kip had her in his arms again. He held her close and tight and fierce, and kicked the flashlight away. It spun fast, urgent, flashing on the sides of the attic like the warning beams of an ambulance.

Danger. Danger. Danger. Danger.

Chapter Seven

Bang! Bang! Bang-ba-bang-ang!

Tabby's hammering interrupted and overlapped Kip's.

Porch rafters—done.

"Nice work," Kip rasped as he climbed down from his ladder. "A couple good coats of paint, and the porch is done."

He threaded the hammer's handle through his belt loop, and she threaded her arms around his waist, raising her mouth to his. "I can't"—but he stopped her after every word with a kiss—"thank—you—enough."

"Stop." He held his lips to hers. "Or I'll pull off your baseball cap and reveal your hat hair to all of Jubilee."

She chuckled and leaned her head on his chest. Saturday's impulsive kisses became Sunday's hesitant hand-holding, became Monday's long embrace and Tuesday's careful joining of lips. Kip had only left if he'd had a tour or shift at the Historic Society. All other hours, he was by her side, helping and joking and—whether he realized it or not—rescuing.

"I can't stop," she argued. "If it weren't for you, I'd never have slept while trying to get all of this done before my family's arrival. And now, with three days until the live Nativity and a full *five* before they get here, I'm almost done except for decorating. I don't even know what I'll do with all this extra time."

"You don't?" He tipped her chin with the crook of his forefinger, kissing her again.

"You've nearly saved my Christmas."

"*Nearly?*" He pulled back and mock-shoved her away. "This rivals Rudolph guiding Santa's sleigh on a cloudy Christmas Eve, if I say so myself."

Tabby laughed, but her emotions warred. In the passing days, she'd wrestled with how to tell him the truth of her situation. The sign that would stand like a traitor in her yard come January first. Not to mention the one-way, business-class ticket that would take her a snowball's throw from the North Pole.

She didn't want to lead him on. She didn't want to lie. She didn't want to lose him. He'd been a help, a blessing, a darned-near Christmas miracle.

But he hadn't saved her Christmas.

The only things that would save it would be a check to cover all her debts and a stocking stuffed with self-respect.

And how to tell Kip any of this? The question clogged the words in her throat any time she tried. She couldn't make him any promises. Couldn't offer him any money. Couldn't even offer him the truth. Not before she told her family.

What *could* she do, for someone so kind and generous and supportive?

It had to be something special. Something she'd never done for anyone else.

****

Wednesday's winter evening air hovered between temperate and chilly.

Such is Christmas in Jubilee.

Tabby tightened her grip on Alexander's reins but refused to let the rest of her body give him any indication of her nervousness. The donkey had improved a bit through daily practice, but a night ride through Fancy Bluff Creek's tidal estuaries was a big, final test.

Yards behind, Kip rode atop her faithful favorite, Ringo.

A moonlit ride among the tidewater and marshes. Her absolute favorite pastime, and she'd only ever enjoyed it alone. Would Kip share in another of her deep joys? Unable to stifle her curiosity, she glanced over her shoulder. His wide, unabashed smile rivaled the glow of the full moon.

"Doing okay back there? Ringo treating you good?"

"Fantastic." Kip leaned and stroked the gelding's shoulder. "He looks majestic under the night sky. As do you."

Her shoulders rose to her ears and she turned, tugging

the reins a bit to navigate Alexander through a patch of marshland dotted with puddles. "I know most people like going to Stiltsboro—Jubilee's own 'little Venice' on Fancy Bluff Creek. I like it, too, but my favorite times are out here, in the quiet. Me and my horse—"

Alexander brayed. Tabby cringed.

"Er, donkey," corrected Kip. "No worries, mate, she meant no offense."

"Just wishful thinking."

"You don't plan to keep him?"

"I *can't* keep him. Do you want him? Consider him your payment for all your help."

"Ha! And what a Christmas gift that would be."

"Just a little longer, and you'll see your Christmas gift."

They meandered among reedy grasses and jutting miniature peninsulas, their journey punctuated by the musical *plonk* of hooves in water, of the last whispering sounds of species that lingered in wintertide. Far to her left, the lights of Stiltsboro twinkled with nightlife. Far to her right, the shadowy backsides of some of Jubilee's oldest homes. Finally, ahead, she glimpsed it.

"There." She pointed at the wide, squat silhouette.

"Um, is this trespassing?"

"If it is, I've been doing it for years. Honestly, I don't think anyone even explores this area—much less knows this is here."

"What's here?"

She led them closer. When she reached the circular, brick foundation, she stopped and dismounted, running her hands over the pocked, eroded grey brick. "It used to be a gazebo."

Kip executed a clunky dismount and walked to her side. He knelt, running his hands over it. "Grey brick?"

"Dredged from our own Fancy Bluff Creek. Turned by hand. Here's a fingerprint"—her fingers felt the thumb-sized indentation, reading it as though it were her own personal Braille—"all these generations since…"

"The man who turned these to dry out in the hot sun left his signature."

Tabby's fingers slowed. Her eyes met Kip's. "I love thinking about that."

His smile warmed. "How'd you find out about this place?"

"My parents."

And my grandfather proposed to my grandmother here.

She wanted to share it with him, that special story of love cemented forever like grey brick with limestone mortar. But she couldn't. It was too intimate. Too promising. And she couldn't promise him anything.

Standing, she returned to Alexander and opened the saddlebag, retrieving the flask of eggnog and the batch of fresh-baked gingerbread cookies. A family recipe passed down from the early eighteen-hundreds. She sat next to Kip and opened the bag for him.

"I told you I'd pay you in cookies."

He laughed. "Cookies and a secret treasure of Jubilee's history." He planted a soft kiss just behind her earlobe. "And an incredible woman. Perfect."

She tucked her head onto his shoulder, hiding the tumult that must have shone in her eyes, even in the darkness.

He'll feel so used. I never meant to use him—yet I couldn't do it without him.

'It' began with the farmhouse. She couldn't have finished all that work without him. And yet, the 'it'— without her consciousness or consent—had grown to encompass so, so much more than the house.

I couldn't do it without him.

Her hand found his. She squeezed, pulsing the tiniest current of hope into her fingers.

What if I could do it with *him?*

Maybe, just maybe, he would want to go with her when she traveled to Iceland. Or maybe he would wait for her until she got back.

A big ask. They'd only just met. She needed more time to think. To tell him the truth—to see if he'd go with her. Surrendering her ancestral home might sear less if Kip stayed by her side.

"Merry Christmas," she whispered.

Chapter Eight

Lights, camera...

From the meadow that connected to the church parking lot, Tabby awaited her cue beside the church members costumed as Mary and Joseph. She twisted the hem of her blazer jacket with one hand and stroked Alexander's stick-straight mane with the other. In a matter of minutes, the floodlights would bathe Jubilee Community Church's live Nativity in the glow of blessed deliverance. Baby Jesus, the infant Savior of humankind, with Blessed Mary, the Virgin Mother standing behind.

And Alexander, to drive Tabby out of her mind.

Stop worrying. He did perfectly well during the marshland ride and during dress rehearsal. Certainly he can manage standing.

Footsteps on crunchy winter grass made her turn.

"Tabby?" Reverend Angie's voice took on a nervous twinge.

"Yes?" she answered. "Are we in the wrong place?"

"No, no, you're perfect. Joseph will lead Mary on Alexander's back once the narration begins. I know we paid you for the donkey, but one of our shepherds suddenly fell ill. Would you mind..."

In her imagination, Kip roared in laughter.

"Just putting this on"—Reverend Angie held out a folded pile of tan clothing—"and standing in?"

Her heart raced. Stand in front of people? In a *costume*? "Um…"

"All you need to do is stand there and look at baby Jesus. And say these two lines." She held out one page from the script, already highlighted.

Heart racing, Tabby looked at her high school friend. Stress lined her eyes. Her irises shined with pleading. Sympathy overcame stage fright, and Tabby sent a silent prayer of thanks that Kip was leading a tour and wouldn't be there to tease her about succumbing to "whimsy." She took the clothing. "If Alexander can stand still, so can I." She eyed the man playing Joseph. "Are you okay if I stand behind the crèche and leave you with Alexander?"

He gave a thumbs up.

Moments later, Tabby stood in the stable, twisting the shepherd's clothing that puddled around her feet. Joseph led Alexander and Mary across the meadow, past whispering audiences sitting on picnic blankets and folding chairs. He bobbed his snout as if in greeting as he walked to the first verse of "O Little Town of Bethlehem." She hoped none of the audience could see that she was the only person staring at the coming Christ Child with eyes full of terror instead of adoration.

Good donkey. Tabby swallowed and took a steadying

breath. *Good, good donkey.*

She let the air out through her nose when Mary arrived. She almost allowed herself to relax a bit as the children's choir sang "Away in a Manger."

Joseph approached the innkeeper, maintaining a confident hold on Alexander's reins. The donkey stood calmly by.

The tiniest bit of pride rose in her chest like bread in the oven. "Good donkey," she whispered. "You did a good—"

CRACK!

Everyone jumped. Sparks lit the night sky. Alexander brayed and did a nervous jig. Mary squeaked but held tight. Tabby watched Joseph pull the reins taut.

"Steady, Alexander," she whispered. She began to edge closer to the donkey, but fumbled and nearly stumbled over the excess fabric of her robe.

Fireworks?! That was not *in the rehearsal.*

He stepped on the toe of her boot. She bit back a squeal. His ears flicked.

CRACK! CR-CRA-CRACK-CRACK-ACK!

Alexander jerked his head and yanked the reins from Joseph's grasp. The three wise men collectively reached for him but only spooked him further. He bucked. Mary yelped and fell to the ground.

Tabby lunged forward, but he bucked again. "No—!"

But the donkey couldn't be stopped. He jumped over

the manger. Swerved toward the children's choir. The little ones screamed and scrambled. Alexander galloped into the dark meadow as red embers fell from the sky.

Tabby gathered her robe and charged after him.

****

Humiliated twice over, Tabby rushed Alexander to her truck and loaded him onto the trailer without bothering to pull off the shepherd's robe. She clambered into the front seat, stabbed the key into the ignition and wrenched it.

The engine sputtered like a startled click beetle.

"No."

Nothing. Of all the items on her to-do list she had checked off, the one thing she hadn't was getting her truck into the shop.

She tried again. "Don't do this to me now…"

Nothing.

Panic dripped in a cold sweat down her neck. She glanced out the window. Plenty of the crowd still remained. She could ask one of them for help—but she didn't dare show her face after the fiasco her donkey had caused.

Pulling her cell phone from under the driver's seat, she called the only person she could barely tolerate seeing.

****

Kip released the truck's hood. *Slam!*

"Electrical problem."

"What?" She stared at him with wide, horrified eyes that peeked out from underneath the headpiece that must've been made-to-order for Yao Ming. He bit the insides of his cheeks to keep from grinning.

Not the time to tease her, Kip.

"I'm sorry. Other stuff, I can do. But electrical problems are out of my range." He pulled the prisoner's cap off his head and scratched. "I've got the Drunken Sailor Pub Crawl coming up—if we hook the trailer up to my Bronco, I can take you guys home and get back here quick enough. The tour starts at Tygue's, just several blocks from the church."

Tabby blinked, digesting the information. Her facial muscles relaxed a bit. "Yeah, that might work."

Minutes later, the trailer was unhooked, and—with the F-250 in neutral—they pushed the truck out of the way to make room for the Bronco. Kip hopped into the driver's seat, humming "What Do You Do with a Drunken Sailor?" and turned the keys.

The Bronco sputtered like a stallion with a noseful of trough water.

"No," Kip groaned.

"You're kidding."

"You're *surprised?* It's a '96." He banged his forehead on the steering wheel in frustration. "Probably a dead battery. I don't have time to fix this before the tour. What can we do?"

Hooves stamped. The trailer rocked.

"Hee-haw!"

****

Tabby hunched on top of Alexander, as though slouching would obscure the sight of a shepherd and prisoner riding a donkey through Jubilee's historic district. "I can't believe this is happening."

"Write a Psalm about it, David," teased Kip.

"Sing a song about it, Sam Cooke."

"Nice oldies reference, for someone who predates modern music altogether."

She groaned. "I'm taking this thing off."

"Can't. You're sitting on it. Why'd you keep it on in the first place?"

"I'm not thinking straight, okay?"

Kip chuckled. "Look at us. A dystopian version of the ride to Bethlehem."

"Stop." But she grinned.

"Tygue's On Tap is a block over. Wanna hop—"

Tabby halted Alexander and slipped off, throwing the shepherd's robe over her head and wadding it into a wrinkled ball. "I should've just given this back to Angie or left it in the stable, but all I could think about was getting out of there."

"Stuff it under your shirt and you can be pregnant Mary with convict Joseph."

She rolled her eyes. "Helpful suggestion, thanks."

When Kip hopped down, she squeezed his arm. "Really, thanks for coming out to help me."

"Anytime." He winked. "How do you think Alexander will handle eleven drunk tourists?"

"Hopefully better than he handled three wise men."

****

Two hours later, with the tour concluded, Tabby's feet throbbed. She waited in the Bronco while Kip got a jump from one of the more sober of his tour-goers, and they drove the Bronco and trailer back to the farmhouse, stabled Alexander, and collapsed onto the living room couch.

Kip leaned back, splaying both black-and-white striped arms along the top of the sofa, staring at the twinkling Christmas tree. The living room was *Southern Living*-December-issue pretty, with thick, baubled garlands draping over the fireplace mantel, wreaths hanging by red ribbon in every window, and rustic-looking plaques dotting the walls, offering effusive wishes of JOY, PEACE, COMFORT to all who entered.

"Travis said he can come by tomorrow morning. We'll get your truck to the shop so you can keep working around here."

Tabby snuggled into the crook of his arm and released a sigh. "Thank you. *So* much."

"Wasn't that a colorful evening to kick-off a bland Christmas?"

She turned. "Bland?" In the back of her mind, a latent wondering had hovered. How was Kip able to give so much of his time? To be there so often? Her to-do list constantly distracted, and she'd never asked. "What are your Christmas plans?"

"Nothing's nailed down, but they generally involve my dad passed out on the couch while I indulge his latest girlfriend in mind-numbing conversation."

"I'm sorry."

"Don't be. That's the beauty of growing up, though, isn't it? Eventually we get to craft our own Christmas."

Tabby traced the curlicues on the throw blanket in her lap. "You're welcome to join my family for Christmas dinner. You, and yours."

Presumptuous, to extend such an invitation before she'd told her family—or him—the truth. Presumptuous…or hopeful.

"Thanks, Tabby. I'll let you know." He squeezed her hand and turned his attention back to the Christmas tree. "You forgot the angel on top. I remember bringing it down from the attic. Where's it at?" He stood.

"Front room, maybe?" She stifled a yawn. "On top of the piano—or maybe beside it. Near it, somewhere."

Kip went to get it. Tabby fought her drooping eyelids—but they popped wide open when he returned, carrying something much bigger than the Christmas tree topper. And much less angelic.

Confusion and pain flickered on his face. He held up the incriminating sign. "For sale?"

"I was trying to figure out how to tell you." Tabby got to her feet and went to him, but he took a step back.

"So all this time…I've been helping you not to get ready for Christmas, but to list and stage your house?"

"Both"—she shook her head—"but I never asked for your help. You offered it—repeatedly."

"And you couldn't have mentioned any of this earlier?" He shoved the sign toward her, like a dog owner with a chewed-up leather loafer.

"I have to tell my *family* first, Kip! And it's *kind* of the type of information that's best told in person."

"Merry Christmas to them. Won't they be excited to learn their family farmhouse—"

"My brothers will be paid in full once it sells." Tabby sputtered a sarcastic laugh, but the pain of the truth hit her like a blow to the head. She wiped her hand across her eyes. "You have eyes. You can see how difficult this was—is—whatever—for me to manage myself. You heard me on the phone with my brother. You know it's a huge financial burden. You think I *like* this?" She swept her hand down into a fist at her side. "I hate it!"

"Do you think I go around flirting with women and fixing up their houses, Tabby?" Kip flung the sign to the floor. "I can't remember the last time I gave a woman as much as I've given you. And now, after all this—after *you* kissed *me*—I find out you're abandoning ship."

"Shouldn't you be in the pirate costume when you say that?" she muttered.

"I'm not joking. Do you know what you've done to me?"

"I know I've fallen for you. But I couldn't tell you—a close-to-perfect stranger—before I told my own family." Tears spilled. "And everything after Christmas is a complete mystery to me. I couldn't promise you anything"—she wrung her hands on every syllable—"I have nothing to give."

Kip's lips curled in hurt and disgust. "And where will you go?"

"I don't know." She sniffed. "Iceland, until I figure it out."

"*Iceland?*"

She nodded.

"How long?"

She shrugged.

"I can't. I just—I'm sorry, Tabby." He spun and strode toward the door. Yanked it open.

"Kip—"

Slam!

Tabby slumped to the floor. Buried her face in her hands. "I was going to ask you to go with me."

Chapter Nine

Kip flopped onto his couch in front of his measly Christmas tree and stared, unblinking. He wanted his limbs to tense with indignation. He willed his chest to heat in anger. But numbness pulsed in his mind, and his body wouldn't move.

That was the worst of it all: He felt completely dead inside, as though his body—hardwired from childhood for abandonment—had expected this outcome all along, this outcome that his mind didn't want to acknowledge.

You idiot, you let yourself expect more. Believe in more. Want more. Idiot, idiot, idiot!

All the women he'd dated had plenty of tally marks against them. Sure, they were superficial. Yeah, they were irresponsible. But they were what-you-see-is-what-you-get. They didn't commit. Didn't expect much from him, didn't give more than a good time.

Didn't lie.

Maybe he needed fate to smack him in the face, remind him of reality.

Maybe Kip the Idealist needs to be boxed up with all that crap from childhood Christmases past.

The lights of the Christmas tree blurred and coalesced

together in a blob in rhythm with his slow-blinks and growing exhaustion. By the time he awoke, the sun blazed through the living room windows, and his phone vibrated in his pocket.

"Hello?"

"Rough night, Kipper?" Dad's voice didn't sound much more perky than his own. "Wanted to let you know Melinda and I'll bring subs for dinner tomorrow, if that's cool with you."

"Tomorrow?"

"Tomorrow's Christmas Eve…"

"Oh. Yeah. Sub sandwiches. Fine."

There was a long pause on the other line. "You okay? You're not one to overdo it with the drink. That's one thing you didn't inherit from your old Dad, glad to say."

"I'm fine." Kip sat up on the couch, leaned over his knees and cupped his head in his free hand. "A friend's truck died last night. Long night. Gotta go fix it this morning."

As if on cue, the doorbell rang. Kip rose, opened it, and waved Travis inside.

"That ain't the voice of a guy with a broke-down truck. That's the voice of a guy with a broke-down heart."

Kip pursed his lips. "I don't wanna go there, Dad."

"Who's that?" asked Travis.

Kip put the call on speaker and let his Dad's voice emanate.

"I'm sorry, son. Is it really a surprise though? Take it from me—don't ask for much, you'll never be disappointed again. And we always have each other, eh?"

"Yeah. Hey, Travis is here. Thanks for the talk Dad. Subs are great for tomorrow."

Click.

Travis stared, eyebrows raised. "That's your Dad's sage advice?"

"Only a penny per thought."

"What's up?"

"Tabby's a no-go."

"What? She won't date you?"

"She's not who I thought she was. You ready to go?"

Kip started for the door, but shorter, faster Travis dodged in front of him. "Nope. Hold up. Say again."

"I thought she was honest. She's not. I should've known." He reached for the door handle, but Travis batted his hand away. "Dude—"

"Nah. I talked to that girl for a good hour at my son's birthday party. Tabby's got more honesty in her ponytail holder than any of the bimbos you've dated *combined*. Did you even give her a chance to explain, or were you so triggered by your past that you heard nothing more than a teacher out of Peanuts, 'wom-wom-wom-wom'?"

"Can you drop it?"

"I don't think I can, man. Tisha and I have watched you for too long—George Carlin could've done a skit on you."

"Huh?"

"'Inside every cynical person is a disappointed idealist.' That's you. Disappointed once, selling yourself short ever since. Not this time, my friend. Relationships take work—and you are just as ready to bolt as your mother was."

Anger fired in Kip. He shoved Travis into the hallway before his mind registered what he'd done.

"There we go." Travis staggered back but grinned. Striding toward his friend, he returned the shove. "Now we get to the real issue. You're not afraid of a woman bolting on you—you're afraid that *you're* the one who can't be depended on"—he shoved with one hand—"can't be trusted"—shoved with the other—"just like mommy."

Kip bellowed and pushed Travis with such force he fell over the arm of the couch. "Leave me be! I didn't invite you over to kick me while I'm down."

"Uh-uh." His friend scrambled to his feet, totally unfazed. "You think you're down now? Give yourself another decade of this crap, and *then* you'll be down. I'm kickin' you because I want you to stand the hell up." He marched toward Kip and gave him a friendly punch in the shoulder. He opened the front door, still talking as he walked toward his truck. "Now remind me where we're going again? To take your lying, good-for-nothing girlfriend's truck to the shop?"

Kip followed behind, silent.

Travis looked over his shoulder. "Yeah, you're not done with her yet. And I'm not done with you."

Chapter Ten

With her truck incapacitated, Tabby was trapped at home until Christmas Eve. Nowhere to go except the stables. Nothing to do except cook, clean, care for animals—and watch for signs of life next door.

She caught glimpses of him coming and going, but he never so much as looked toward her property. A corkscrew lodged in her heart. Every hour with no word from Kip, it twisted, twisted, twisted…

All her attention and effort went to the animals. To her astonishment, Alexander was sensitive to her emotions, following her around the yard, nudging her in the back. She'd even indulged him in another ride since the live Nativity, and he'd performed remarkably well. This afternoon, he and Ringo took turns nosing her shoulder while she laid fresh pine straw around the bases of trees. More sweet times like this, and she might even be able to forgive the little ass.

An engine purred. Gravel crunched under tires. Tabby glanced up to see the white Prius rental roll into the carport. At least Hank and Yvette would provide distraction.

She jogged up to meet them. The trunk automatically

popped open, and Tabby began unloading bags while her oldest brother and his long-term girlfriend climbed out. Her stomach flipped with realization—by midnight, her entire family would be assembled. By morning, she'd have to tell them.

Nervous energy fizzed and bubbled out in a string of questions. "How was your flight? I'm sorry I couldn't get you both—thanks for understanding. How's New York?"

Hank wrapped her in a hug with one muscled arm and clamped the other over her mouth. "Good. Of course. And great—my latest play was a big hit. Yvette performed the lead role." Hank removed his hand from Tabby's face.

She gawked appropriately. "That's great, Yvette! And Hank. Such good news."

Yvette, with waist-length blonde hair and straight-cut runway-model bangs, flashed a wide smile—then teetered in her stiletto boots on the gravel driveway.

"Five years visiting and you still haven't learned." Tabby wrapped Yvette in a hug. "Need some work boots?"

"Will they go with my outfit?"

"Not a bit. Let's get your bags inside."

Yvette walked ahead—carrying only her large Marc Jacobs purse—but Hank hung back. "The place looks amazing, Tabs. I know it's a lot of work and I haven't helped like I told you I would, but...it really means a lot to be able to come home every holiday."

Tabby swallowed past the lump in her throat. No

matter what she did, she'd be a disappointment to everyone—even herself.

Hank shifted. "Has the money gotten lost in the mail? The Postal Service is less and less dependable these days." He broached the subject with heaps more gentleness than Cashel had during their phone conversation, yet still, she wanted to shrink from him.

"It hasn't gotten lost." The words came out snippier than she intended. She walked ahead, lugging Yvette's two suitcases.

"New York is expensive"—now Hank's tone darkened—"I'm not trying to breathe down your neck, but—"

"I'm doing all I can. I have a plan."

"Ease up," Hank snapped. "We'll talk about it later."

"Yeah." Tabby sobered. "We will."

****

"The night before Christmas, and all through the farmhouse…"

Tabby lay awake, fingering the hem of her bed's quilt. Cashel and Lila from Los Angeles brought Mom and Dad from the Savannah airport, fresh from Rome, and the entire jet-lagged crew crashed in bed after bleary-eyed, obligatory hi-hellos.

"Not a creature was stirring…"

A lump of sadness lodged in her throat, clogging Mr. Moore's words that her mother recited every Christmas

Eve. Carols by the piano, cookies and milk while cuddled on the couch. Traditions long gone with the drudgery of growing up, but she could call them to mind anytime. After all, the memories were held within these walls.

She wiped a tear. Tomorrow, she'd tell them. After breakfast and presents, after one last round of carols by the piano. She'd give them all—give herself—one last Christmas morning untainted.

The rugged square cut out of her bedroom ceiling caught her eye. The second, crude attic entrance hovered over the six-foot ladder she'd left in her room since painting.

Fingers and toes tingled to climb. Scuttling across the cold oak floors, Tabby pulled her pocketknife from the belt of the pants she'd tossed on the floor, fanned out the ladder and climbed up. Pushed aside the cutout.

One. Last. Moment.

The attic smelled of timber, the air musky with time. Through the small attic window that overlooked the back of the property, moonlight filtered in, casting silvery slivers that crosshatched lines of shiplap walls, curved over roundness of knotted pine beams.

"Frozen in time," Kip had called it.

Kip.

She might have grown to love him, too, if she could have kept him. Her last visit to the attic—with his lips on hers—flashed, but she shoved it away. She couldn't bear the thought of Kip. Not tonight.

In the thin light, she crawled toward it, that trunk of pine different from the rest for the particular human scar it bore. One of the countless precious details she'd soon say goodbye to, forever. For all her life, she'd remember it— the exact location of the attic beam, the crude, boxy letters, their crooked orientation. That treasure carved in slivered cellulose. She ran her fingers over it, let her heart break open, let her tears run.

J. E. D. LARSEN. 1818.

The knife handle was cold and strong in her trembling hand. Doing such a thing was unthinkable before—not to do it was unthinkable now.

If I can't take a piece of you with me, I'll leave a piece of me with you.

With every careful gouge, love and memory and loss washed over her until she finally finished and her imprint sat under her ancestor's.

T. E. LARSEN. 2018.

Hands cupping the beam on either side of the carvings, Tabby hung her head and released the cries she'd stifled for so long. When her tears ran dry and her breathing calmed, she looked up, out the window, at the one heavenly beacon blazing brighter than the rest. On this, the most miraculous of nights, she dared to whisper her only Christmas desire. Her wish upon a star.

God, I bit off more than I could chew. I was silent

when I should've shared the truth. Oh, but God! If there is any way in Heaven I can keep my home, please...please let me keep it.

Her fingers traced the letters—old and new—and imagined them carved on her heart, forever.

Please, please...let me keep my home.

Chapter Eleven

The kitchen saw more bustle Christmas morning than it did the entire year. Tabby marveled as Mom—jetlagged though she was—hopped-to and got bacon sizzling, eggs frying, and French toast toasting. They ate breakfast still wrapped in their bathrobes, opened presents, and moved to the front room for caroling. Cashel twisted the tuning keys on his guitar, and Tabby's gut twisted along with it as her moment closed in.

Give us five songs and we'll be done. I'll have to tell them.

She'd hidden the FOR SALE sign in her bedroom closet—no repeats of the debacle with Kip.

"What should we sing first," mused Hank. ""Jingle Bells"?"

Tabby sat at the piano and popped her knuckles. "Only the rendition that doesn't include, 'Jingle bells, Tabby smells.' I know you thought the lyrics were clever but they weren't."

"I'm a Big Apple playwright now, I've gotten clever-er."

"But clearly no brighter-er."

He gave her a playful smack on the back and cleared

his throat before singing to the tune of "Good King Wenceslas" "Jolly sister Tabitha, freckled, short and smelly—"

"I've been meaning to say, Tabitha"—Mom rolled her eyes at Hank—"the house looks like a dream."

Tabby swallowed and lightly played the keys to distract herself. "Thank you, Mom. Lost a lot of sleep over it."

Dad placed a comforting hand on her shoulder. "How about we start with "Little Saint Nick"?"

"God, no!" Hank groaned.

"Oh, and there's the man I get my love for the oldies from." Tabby grinned and flipped through the songbook. When she got to the song, an envelope fluttered down, landing beside her on the piano bench. Her eyes traveled up to meet her father's.

"One last Christmas gift for you." He winked.

She opened the envelope, peeked inside, and shut it fast. "Dad."

"Just a little allowance."

"Allowance!" Cashel moaned.

Dad held up a hand. "For the farmhouse—nothing else. I know it was your choice to stay here, Tabs, and none of ours. But we gain a lot from your love of the place—we get to come home whenever we like. Seems fair to help out a bit."

Tabby shuttered her eyes, trying to stay her welling

tears. "Thank you."

Too much crying. Can't take anymore.

The amount was good—it would've definitely helped with expenses, if it had come sooner. But the monthly stipend wouldn't cover the debt she owed her brothers. Wouldn't change the fact that she couldn't keep up with the workload.

Wouldn't answer her prayer.

She met her father's gaze. He smiled under bushy eyebrows, thankfulness reverberating from him like a note played with the sustaining pedal.

She'd told herself that her family wouldn't care if she sold the place—but she'd lied.

They cared a great deal. No matter how far they moved, they always knew someone held down the fort.

They always knew they could come home.

How to tell them the truth?

Better do it now.

The envelope shook in her grasp. She took a deep breath. "Dad, Mom. Hank, Cashel. A lot has happened. I need to tell you—"

"Tabitha, do you have a boyfriend?" Lila spun on her knees until she leaned over the back of the couch, looking out the window.

Kip took the steps to the side entrance in twos. Tabby's pulse felt like it went into suspended animation.

"Oh my gosh"—Mom's hands went to her heart—"is

that the Alexander you were telling me about?"

"Alexander is an *ass*, Mom—"

"Shush, that's awful!"

"—a *literal* donkey." Tabby leaped to her feet and moved toward the kitchen door. "That's Kip, my neighbor." She opened the door a crack. "Hi."

"I know it's Christmas, but I, uh, I have to talk to you." He stared at her with an intensity that could bore holes into metal.

Tabby glanced over her shoulder. Mom, Lila, and Yvette waved her away while the men in her family gaped, clueless. "Oka—"

He took her by the hand and jogged, pulling her along, all the way down the driveway until they stood at the halfway point between her mailbox and his.

"I'm sorry, Tabby." Kip took both of her hands in his. "I'll say it forever and never say it enough. I'm sorry."

"*I'm* the one who should've—"

"No. My head's spinning with all I've got to say. Look—from the moment I met you, I've *seen* you. You! I watched in amazement as you showed up, day in and day out, committing to something you loved no matter how much it required of you." His hands fluttered over her forearms, shoulders, finally resting to cup her face. "I couldn't understand why you wanted to quit, because I've *never tried* to commit to something so hard, Tabby. I've never seen anything like it. Never met another woman like you. You *show up*, no matter how hard it gets. And I know you'd show up until your legs won't even let you stand anymore—I know walking away isn't what you want. And God"—he leaned to rest his forehead against hers—"if there's one thing I know now more than anything else, it's that you don't need to walk away. You need someone to walk beside you."

Tabby pulled back. "What?"

"I got you a gift. You don't have to accept it, though, if you don't want it."

He took her hand, threaded his fingers through hers, and she could swear she felt them trembling. He led her to the mailbox. To a sign planted in his yard.

FOR SALE.

Tabby pulled her hands from his grasp. They shook like winter leaves as she brought them to cover her mouth. Her breathing came ragged and squeaky.

Kip blinked, half-smiled. "Are you laughing or are you crying?"

All she could manage was a frenzied nod. Kip gathered her into his arms, pressing his mouth against her ear.

"Never stop showing up, Tabby. If you'll have me, I'll never stop showing up for you."

THE END

Leah's Recipe

Clara Else Larsen's Molasses Gingerbread Cookies
Abt. 1801

3 1/2 cups flour
1 Tablespoons cinnamon
1 Tablespoons ginger
3 Tablespoons candied orange peel, diced
1/3 cup sugar
2/3 cup molasses
1 egg, beaten well
1 1/4 cups ~~Sour Milk~~ milk + 1 tbsp lemon juice
1/2 teaspoon ~~pearl ash~~ baking soda

Preheat oven to 325 F.

Mix flour with cinnamon, ginger, and candied orange peel in a large bowl.

Separately, whisk the egg with the molasses.

In another bowl, mix the ~~pearl ash~~ baking soda with the ~~sour milk~~ milk/lemon juice. Stir the milk mixture into the molasses and egg mixture, then add wet ingredients to dry ingredients.

Knead the dough and roll out until about half an inch thick. Cut into desired shapes.

(Continued on next page)

Bake for 25 minutes.

Enjoy as-is, or with this **simple orange glaze:**

1 1/4 cups confectioners' sugar
3 Tablespoons orange juice
1/2 teaspoon vanilla extract

Leah Noel Sims

When her two toddlers curl into bed for the night (and the German Shepherd is finished begging for leftovers), Leah Noel Sims journeys into her imagination, weaving stories about characters that can't help but ask questions—only to discover realities they never thought possible. Outside of writing, Leah plays ditties on her flute (and her children no longer complain about it) and gobbles up ghost stories more eagerly than she gobbles actual food.

Connect with Leah at her website:

https://www.leahnoelsims.com

THANK YOU for purchasing this book. If you enjoyed the book, please leave a review at the online outlet where you purchased it and consider Goodreads, too. Authors depend on loyal readers to spread the word about good books and reviews are a very important way to do that.

Also, if you enjoyed the stories, please check out the authors' other titles. Links to their websites are include on their biography page for your convenience.

We hope you enjoyed your visit to Jubilee. Life is a celebration there, and we will be bringing more titles in the series releasing in 2019. You won't want to miss what's going on there!